ACTS OF CONTRITION

ALSO BY JENNIFER HANDFORD

Daughters for a Time

ACTS OF CONTRITION

JENNIFER HANDFORD

Published by Lake Union Publishing, Seattle

www.apub.com

ISBN-13: 9781477809501
ISBN-10: 1477809503

Cover design by Anna Curtis

Library of Congress Control Number: 2013910125

Printed in the United States of America

For my loving husband, Kevin

PART ONE

CHAPTER ONE
Ordinary Time

I AWAKE BEFORE THE ALARM sounds. It's early—five thirty early—the dreamy time of predawn when the golden light softens what's real, blunts the sharp edges of daily life. It's in these quiet moments when my perspective is the most forgiving, Zen-like. *There are many paths that lead to happiness,* this enlightened outlook reminds me, knocking out of the way my judgmental point of view that admonishes me for making wrong turns. For a few breaths—inhale, exhale, inhale—I'm free from my blundering.

Then the alarm blares.

I roll onto my side and reach over my husband, Tom, to hit snooze. Still enjoying the gauzy calm, I kiss the top of his arm, give his scruffy head a rub, and put my face in front of his. "Time to wake up, sleepyhead."

"Argh," he groans. "Too early."

"I know," I agree.

"Where are the critters?" Tom asks, referring to our twin four-year-old boys who burrow their way into our bed each morning.

3

"Still asleep. Hilarious, right?" It's hilarious because the boys are crack-of-dawn early risers. But today happens to be the first day of preschool for Domenic and Danny, and neither of them is as excited about it as I am. I adore the boys, and while I routinely stare in wonder at the pint-sized cuties, identical with their skin as fair as alabaster and hair as glossy as black licorice, I'm still beyond eager for school to start, checking off each day on the calendar for the past month with a thick, indelible Sharpie. If the morning goes according to plan, in exactly four hours, I'll be sans children for the first time in nine years, sipping the frothy goodness of a venti vanilla latte and savoring the sweet, warm dough of an apple fritter. I'll be cloistered in my car, listening to the raunchy DJ on DC101 talk about something unacceptable, like underpants or threesomes or sex toys. The escapism will be pure bliss.

But first I need to mobilize the sleeping beast husband and four children.

"Come on, babe!" I nudge Tom. "You have a plane to catch and I've got children—all of the children—to get to school."

"Big day," he says, offering a small smile and rolling onto his back, hooking my head into a gentle half nelson.

I settle into the crook of his shoulder and latch my arm over his chest. "Seriously, honey, you *need* to get up. I've got to get the girls to the bus stop and the boys to preschool, and I really don't have time to help you get out the door this morning. You're on your own."

"Just give me a minute."

Tom reaches for the remote and turns on the news. Traffic and weather, and then, in the next instant, even though I'm still pressed up against him, we're no longer snuggling. It's more like a judge has just issued a heavy thud of his gavel, delivering a guilty verdict, sentencing me to life.

On the screen is a photo of my ex-boyfriend. The crawler below it reads: VIRGINIA ATTORNEY GENERAL LANDON JAMES DECLARES INTENTION TO RUN FOR SENATE SEAT IN VIRGINIA.

Landon James, the darkest of the many wrong paths I've taken.

The golden hue of the room brightens to white. The soft edges render into right angles. My life: husband, kids, house, and an unforgiving past.

Even though I haven't seen Landon in person in nearly a decade, he still occasionally tromps through my life, leaving designer footprints. I met Landon a lifetime ago, though I remember our first meeting as clearly as I can recall the scent of my children's skin. I was only nineteen when we first met, twenty-three when we were reintroduced, twenty-nine when I finally got sober from his brand of loving me and then pushing me away. The fact that he took things from me and never gave them back—a decade of my life, a piece of my heart, and the end of the thread that could unravel my entire life—is never buried far enough in my thoughts.

Tom slides his arm from around me and is already on the way to the shower before I can call to him. "Tom?"

"Nothing like seeing Boy Wonder first thing in the morning," Tom grumbles before he turns on the water.

"On an empty stomach, too," I call over the shower's noise, using the technique I've now perfected: siding with my husband *no matter what*. Years ago there was one argument—the nadir of Tom's and my mud wrestling over Landon—where this lesson was drilled home. Tom commented—innocently enough—on Landon's swagger ("Guy's got an ego the size of Texas") and ostentatious polish (the perfectly styled hair, the tailored suits, the gleaming cuff links). Stupidly, I jumped to Landon's defense. He really wasn't like that, I said; underneath the ego he was actually a decent guy, a pretty *normal* guy, who came from humble beginnings, who had been through a lot of hurt. Tom huffed away in disgust, said he couldn't believe I'd defend him after he'd strung me along for so long, couldn't believe I excused Landon's every trespass.

That taught me a valuable lesson: Never defend the man who wasn't my husband.

When Tom steps out of the shower, I slide past him with a bland smile (knowing better than to chance a touch) and hop in for a five-minute scrub down: a quick wash of the hair, a lathering of soap, and a few swipes of the razor over the lower half of my legs. As I work some conditioner into my shoulder-length brown bob, I exhale in a long, slow stream, quietly so that Tom—at his sink, just feet away—doesn't hear. *Play it cool, Mary. Act as though seeing Landon meant nothing to you.* Early on with Tom, I made big mistakes: I told him how deep it went with Landon, how strangely addicted to each other we were.

Even now, seeing Landon heats my chest and speeds my breath. I push it down and bottle it because the feeling is irrational, and Irrational Me makes Logical Me sick, because Logical Me has everything she's ever wanted.

With a towel wrapped around me, I glance over at Tom to assess his mood, but his expression is washed clean of clues. I lean over and kiss his cheek. "I love you," I say, and even to my ears I sound guilty, like I'm trying too hard, like it's obvious what we're both thinking.

I duck into the bedroom to retrieve clothes to wear. Tom has casual Friday at his engineering firm. I have casual Friday every day. The suits and pumps I once wore to a swanky Connecticut Avenue law firm have long been donated to St. Vincent de Paul and replaced by jeans and chinos, T-shirts and sweaters, a classic wardrobe from the Old Navy moms department.

By six o'clock I'm downstairs, out on the deck, feeding our golden retriever, Daisy. Drawing in the cool morning air restores me to myself, settles me down, brings me back to normalcy: husband, kids, house. Inside, I start packing the lunch boxes and preparing breakfast.

Sally stumbles down the stairs a few minutes later. At age nine she's my oldest, and an amber-haired beauty. Tall and bold, with broad shoulders and mile-long legs, she resembles the Greek goddesses she's been obsessed with since studying them last year. If Sally were truly a Greek goddess, she'd be one of the tough ones, like Artemis, a hunter strapped with a bow and a quiver full of arrows. *You want a piece of me?* I can imagine her saying, staring down a three-headed monster twice her size.

"Tired," she moans. "Hungry." Sally's always hungry. She eats more than Tom and me, hands down. But she's active, and at least for now her metabolism is besting her appetite.

"Waffles? Eggs?" I say, coming around to give her a kiss. When she slips off the stool to hug me, the top of her head reaches my mouth. She's growing tall and I'm short, a combination that will soon leave us lopsided.

"Both," she answers. "And hot cocoa, please."

This morning she is wearing green flannel pajama bottoms and a tight tank top revealing an inch or two of tanned belly. The straps from her training bra tangle with her tank top. People mistake her for older, easily twelve years old. Her body has grown and matured faster than her peers', which nearly kills me, but I've done a good job of keeping my cool, like it's no big deal to talk about cup sizes and getting her period. *Yeah, whatever,* that's me. The cool mom who is accessible. *Talk to me,* my easy disposition says, *I'm here.* It's not that I wasn't aware that she would someday grow up. It's just happened so fast. Smacked me in the face like a snowball I hadn't seen coming.

She bellies up to the counter, lowers her face to her hands, and sets down her Nancy Drew. Sally is a voracious reader and doesn't go anywhere without a book, even downstairs to breakfast.

Sally arrived earlier than we had planned, approximately eight months after we were married. And while my daily-Mass parents weren't born yesterday and pretty much knew I had spent most nights at Tom's prior to the wedding, we all did our part to pretend Sally was a honeymoon baby. I wasn't the first Catholic bride in history to walk down the aisle wearing white, and pregnant.

Following Sally's birth, I fell into a deep depression. My sisters and my mother thought I was suffering from postpartum blues and I was only too glad to grab onto that as the reason. Tom felt guilty he was at work so much, putting in ten-hour days, traveling, but I was grateful he wasn't around to see me heaving and sobbing out tears I couldn't explain. Each day before he came home, it was all I could do to bathe, put on some makeup, and try to hold myself together for a few hours. Put a happy face on the hysterical new mommy.

"Why are you so sad?" Tom would ask, because it was so obvious how much I loved Sally.

"I'm not sad," I would cry.

"Then what?" Tom would ask patiently.

"Being a mother, having a daughter, becoming a family . . . It's huge," I'd blurt, gasping for air. "Her *life* is in my hands. What if I do it wrong? What if I've already done it wrong?"

After I slide Sally's two fried eggs onto her two waffles and add a scoop of Ovaltine to her mug of milk, my eight-year-old, Emily—with her dimpled cheeks and giant chocolate eyes—floats her way down the stairs, our modern-day Mary Poppins. I meet her at the bottom, placing my hands under her arms and hoisting her up. It's a promise I've made to both the girls: no matter how big they get, I'll still be able to lift them.

"What about when we're thirty years old?" Sally asked one day. "Will you still be able to lift us then?"

"Of course," I assured her. "I'll work out. I'll still be able to lift you. We'll just look very silly."

I nuzzle my nose into the crook of Emily's neck. She exudes sweetness from her pores, like rose water, because she appreciates beautiful things: music, art, dance. Her latest thing is to declare everything either "gorgeous" or "dreadful." The middle ground is too boring to notice.

Emily wraps her legs around me, pulls back to see my face, and plants a juicy kiss on my lips. "Good morning, pretty Mommy," she says in her best Cockney accent. Her theater group is rehearsing for *Oliver!*

I return her kiss and issue a sigh of relief, grateful that I haven't fallen into the dreadful category.

"Morning, Em," I say, kissing her freckled nose. "Breakfast?"

"Do we have any fruit and yogurt?" My budding actress is already concerned with her calorie intake.

By seven thirty, Tom has already done an hour's worth of computer work and is now rushing down the stairs, his small suitcase in one hand, his briefcase in the other. Tom was a boxer in college and has the been-crushed-more-than-once, off-center nose to prove it. He's stocky and strong and can still lift the girls effortlessly, flying them through the air like winged fairies. He has the brownest eyes and a beautiful wave to his amber hair. Most people assume Sally takes after Tom because of their matching hair. I think Sally resembles Tom because of their special bond, their mutual admiration of each other.

"Do you have everything?" I say, standing before him like an MP. "A change of clothes, underwear, socks, belt, shoes? Did you bring your exercise clothes, your tennis shoes? Do you have your money, your credit card, your driver's license, your cell phone?"

"Mary," Tom says, leaning in, kissing my mouth. "I have it all. I only make this trip to Chicago about twenty times a year."

"I know, I know," I say, rubbing his arm. "You're right." Tom is an engineer for a software company whose major customers are the government and the defense industry. Every couple of weeks he makes a trip to Chicago to update the status of their latest projects at his company's corporate headquarters.

The girls wrap their arms and legs around Tom like protesters coiled around a redwood. "We'll miss you," Sally says, kissing Tom.

Emily sings from *Oliver!*, snuggling into him.

"We love you," Sally says, and the depth of emotion in her voice nearly chokes me.

"That's nice, Sal," Tom says. "And maybe someday your love will grow up and be as big as my love for you, but for now, your love is a puny little weakling."

Sally smiles. My most competitive child loves playing her special game with her father: whose love is bigger. "My love could kick your love's butt." She steps back and assumes a boxer's stance, just as her father has shown her, left foot forward, dukes up.

"Your love dreams of kicking my love's butt," Tom says, throwing little punches in the air for Sal to block. Then he pulls her into a hug and she melts, because her love for her father is a landslide, the kind that sometimes buries her, leaving her breathless.

When I issue a little squeal, Sally looks up, points at me, and smiles her know-it-all smile. "We made Mommy cry," she says to Tom.

"Our love is so big it always makes Mom cry," Tom says.

It's true, seeing Tom love our children puts my heart in a vise. Sometimes it's just too much—seeing my bounty. It makes me remember how fortunate I am; how much is at stake; the risk in having a cup so full. Sometimes I'll see families—less *happy*, for lack of a better word: divorced, disobedient kids, financial troubles—and I'll think: their hearts are actually on firmer ground, *those people.* They've already fallen from the top rung we're clinging to. Looking up the ladder might not be as glamorous, but wouldn't there be a safety in the steadiness of it, rather than fighting to keep balance at the top?

After a few more minutes of proclamations and declarations of the best and biggest love, I walk Tom to the car. He'll fly out of Reagan, the closest airport to our home in Woodville, Virginia, a sleepy suburb only twenty miles outside the beltway.

"So what are you going to do with your three hours of freedom?" Tom asks.

"Think. Breathe," I say. "Go to the bathroom without a kid climbing onto my lap. Maybe take a walk. After that luxury, I'll get down to the usual business of paying bills, cleaning house, and managing the kids' schedules."

"All that sounds good," he says, kissing me once more, then sliding into the driver's seat. "Don't get sucked into watching the news all morning . . ."

He stops. Intentionally or not, sometimes Tom can't help jabbing me in the side where Landon James is concerned. In this instance, he's testing me to see if I'd be tempted to sit around all day watching the news, mooning over my ex. Remarks like these used to crush me, not because he was being unreasonable but because he had every right to be wary. My past, my reappearing ex-boyfriend, the phone calls—the reported ones and the ones he rightly suspected I didn't report—were more than a man should have to bear. The guilt I carried from dragging my past into his future nearly killed me. I'd cry, we'd talk—but of course we couldn't talk it all the way through. We'd just have to decide not to talk about it anymore, walk up to the wall and stare at it, then at last turn away.

One day Tom made a biting comment and, rather than letting it leave marks, I sloughed it off. It worked—we slid, laughing, past the moment—and I'd since made a habit of it. I had come to grasp the nuances of marital subterfuge, though it made me a little sick to do so. Minimizing my husband's concerns is more like a cheap trick than mere artifice, but it's better than engaging in a conversation that might show my cards.

"I was thinking of taping it," I joke, leaning down and sticking my face goofily in front of his. "So I can watch it over and over."

Tom smiles stiffly, attempts a conciliatory chuckle, but the light behind his eyes has dimmed.

"Seriously," I say, kissing his mouth, then looking him straight in the eyes. "I have no interest in watching the news."

He smiles a bit. It's forced, but he's trying.

"I love you, okay?" I say. "I really, really love you."

"No mistakes," he says, our family's safety motto.

"No mistakes," I repeat, though the fact that it's a little late for no mistakes is not buried far from the surface for me.

After I watch Tom drive away, I go back into the kitchen and check on the girls. As I pour and sip another cup of coffee, I study Sally in her "so Sally position," slumped over the counter drinking cocoa through a straw with her eyes plastered on her Nancy Drew, her plate of waffles and eggs scraped clean. Then I look at Emily, sitting up straight, holding her cup with her pinky perched high.

I am the youngest of four girls, and when I look at my daughters, their relationship reminds me most of my connection with my sister Teresa—less primal, more situational. Sally and Emily love each other because they're sisters, but if they weren't, they might not choose each other as friends. That's how Teresa and I were, and still are now. I've always felt Teresa's lifelong compulsion to try to crack my moral code springs from her desire to assert her superiority over me. I see some of that in Sally's know-it-all attitude toward Emily.

My relationship with my sister Angie is different. Only separated by two years, we're both highly emotional, excessively demonstrative with our love, chronic touchers. When her high school boyfriend cheated on her and broke her heart, I cried alongside her. When my mother asked *me* what was wrong, I wailed, "It just hurts so bad." I was a surrogate for her pain.

And then there's my big sister Martina, who's ten years older than me, and whose children are grown. It's undeniable that my life could have taken a path similar to Martina's if circumstances had been different. That I made it through college, law school, and a few years of a career wasn't so much because I was a modern woman who wanted to make something of myself; it was more because I was holding out for a guy who didn't love me enough to marry me. The diplomas on my wall are thanks to his indifference to me. Certificates for hanging in for too long.

Tom has one brother, Patrick. Four years his junior, Patrick struggles to stay sober and employed, a frequent guest at the Virginia Beach Alcoholic Rehabilitation Center. He and his wife, Kathy, have a five-year-old daughter, Mia. Kathy puts up with his shenanigans until she reaches the breaking point, then packs a suitcase and heads to her mother's house.

Yet Patrick and Tom are close, a bond I don't always understand and one I don't always support as strongly as I should. Partially because there is no love lost between Patrick and me. He's never been too subtle in hiding his opinion that I'm not good enough for his big brother. The morning of our wedding, I overheard him say to Tom, "You barely know her. She's got a lot of baggage. It's not too late to bail. I've got a twelve-pack in the trunk." I locked myself in the bathroom and cried into a wad of toilet paper with my eyes wide open, for fear my mascara would run, prompting questions that would have to be answered. The room spun and the corset of my dress dug into my ribs as I tried to rationalize my impending walk down the aisle.

It was true, Tom and I had been dating for only six months, and I had just gotten out of a six-year relationship with a guy I had pined over for a decade—a guy who, I'd proven all too clearly to myself, still had his hook buried deep in some disgustingly helpless part of me. I knew I wasn't everything Tom deserved, but still, I wanted my marriage to him, wanted the children I had been craving for so long, wanted the fairy-tale life I'd dreamed of. And I wanted to slam the door on Landon James for good. I *had* to do that, even if it meant deceiving my new husband.

Dear God, I prayed that day, *I promise to come clean, I promise to tell Tom everything, and more than anything, I promise to be the best wife and mother in the world.* That was the deal I made that day—that I'd be so good, it would overwhelm all bad. I would confess my sins, do my penance, and amend my life. My acts of contrition would be transformative.

And I clung to Tom's reaction to his brother's warning about me. "She's the one," he said, completely unruffled. "Trust me, she's the one."

Ever since then, my relationship with Patrick has been fragile. There have been times when I have tried hard to make him like me, and other times when I was partially glad to see him fall. His failures served as evidence in my corner that maybe he wasn't the greatest judge of character. In case Tom ever recalled his brother's concerns about me, Patrick's stumbling would give him pause before giving them too much weight.

By seven forty-five, Tom's gone and I've awakened the twins, Domenic and Danny—both named after their great-grandfathers. They're still half asleep and in their jammies when I strap them into the double stroller and corral the girls out the door.

"Sal, you got your backpack, your lunch box, your sweater?" I list. "Em—how 'bout you? Your binder, your composition book, lunch box?"

Both acknowledge that they have their stuff.

"Teeth brushed?"

"Yep," Sally says.

"Me, too," Emily says.

I reach for a wipe from the package on the washer and swipe it across Emily's face.

"Then why is there milk still on your lip?"

"Honest, I brushed my teeth," she says, baring her teeth for me to inspect. "Swear to God."

"Don't swear to God," I remind her.

I push the button to open the garage door, and we begin the walk to the end of the road where the bus picks up. The other moms, who are my friends and neighbors, whistle and catcall at me like it's my wedding night.

"Congrats!" my friend Susan says with a wide smile, patting me on my back. "You made it."

Another friend, Sarah, wants to know what I'm going to do now that I'm a lady of leisure.

"Don't jinx it." I shake my finger at her. "It's not a done deal yet. I've still got to get these guys to school."

"Do something fun!" Susan says. "I don't want to hear that you went grocery shopping."

"Grocery shopping without kids doesn't sound so bad," I say, imagining a leisurely stroll through the aisles of Wegmans, sampling Gouda and French bread along the way.

While we wait, I pull a brush from my pocket and run it through Sally's hair amid her cries that I'm killing her. "Brushing your own hair is always an option," I remind her. She's reading her myth book, a tattered hardback she's read a million times. One time I overheard Sally telling Emily, "Mom is like a Greek tragedy, the way she fusses and worries over us, very Persephone and Demeter."

Emily shrugged. "I think it's cool that she loves us so much."

Sally harrumphed. "I'm not complaining about being loved. Sometimes I just wish she would chill out."

When the bus comes, I pull Emily over near Sally and kiss each of them, covering their faces. I touch my palm to their cheeks, place my mouth on the crowns of their heads, and kiss them again.

"Enough, Mom," Sally says.

I step back, not wanting to be so Greek tragic. "Safety first," I say.

"Never last," they chime.

"Love you, girls."

"Love you, too," they sing.

"Stick together," I say.

"We will."

"Make good choices!" I holler after them, but they've had their fill of my bus-stop affirmations. I'm the affirmation queen. I dose them out each morning with their vitamins, scratch them on notes in their lunch boxes, pack them in the kisses I cover them with each night. My promises manifest in words, notes, and flesh. *If no one else, you always have me.* I open my mouth and then stop. It's time to let them go, to trust that they won't be swallowed into a chasm in the earth.

The boys and I wave furiously at them as the bus pulls away. Like that, 50 percent of my kids are on their way to school. I kick the lock off the stroller, holler, "See ya, ladies!" to my friends, and head home at breakneck speed. I'm in the final stretch.

CHAPTER TWO

Transgressions

TOM

I'M NOT EVEN INSIDE THE beltway and I'm already stuck in traffic. It'll free up after I get beyond the merge. DC traffic is the worst. Maybe not LA bad, but bad enough. A twenty-mile drive could easily take an hour. Longer, on any given day.

I was thinking of taping it, plays over and over in my head—not just Mary's words, but the tone of her voice and the dopey look on her face, like *I* was being paranoid. Like she would be completely okay if the tables were turned, if my ex-girlfriend were on every television.

Sometimes I think about my ex, Cassandra. She's a nice daydream when I need a break from the Mary-and-Landon nonsense ricocheting in my mind. Cassandra was a knockout by all standards: a dancer with stick-straight posture, a tight little ass, and perky breasts. She and I met at an office party. She came with another guy but left with me. I don't deny I felt like a million bucks that night, her arms wrapped around my waist. We went back to my place, and I learned that everything guys said about going to bed with dancers wasn't just wishful thinking. She was still there in the morning, her willowy limbs crisscrossed over mine.

We went on to date for almost three years and I have to admit she wasn't a bad girlfriend. She used to say she was the "nesting" type. She'd cook me dinner, we'd watch movies, she even knitted me a chunky Irish sweater for Christmas one year. She was loyal, too, leaving me notes written on scraps of paper. Lots of *x*'s and *o*'s and a smack of her red lips. As hot as she was, she sometimes worried I would leave.

She might have been needy, but she didn't care for anyone else who was. She never volunteered to do a damn thing; in fact, she'd make up excuses to get out of anything that didn't benefit her directly. I'd catch her in little white lies. One day I overheard her telling our neighbor she *wished* she could help him out with jumper cables, but she didn't have any. She had them, all right. I had packed them in her car just the month before, after her battery died. When I asked her about it, she said it seemed like a hassle and she was on her way out the door for a pedicure.

One night we were in DC, on Pennsylvania Avenue, walking back from dinner out. We passed a homeless guy sprawled across a grate, warming himself against the winter cold. "God, that sucks," I said to Cassandra after we walked by. "It sucks that he has to be there." I was speaking philosophically, politically, from a humanity standpoint. Without knowing this man who was on the ropes, I wanted more for him, wanted his existence to be something other than seeking refuge on a warm grate.

"No kidding," Cassandra said, wrinkling her tiny nose. "Go to a shelter and take a shower."

It bothered the hell out of me that she wasn't compassionate. I'm far from a bleeding heart and am the first to say that a man needs to fend for himself in this world and not ask for handouts, but at least I could sympathize. I guess I could thank my brother and father for that, each of whom could have easily ended up sprawled across a grate, homeless, following one too many rendezvous with whiskey.

Mary and Cassandra couldn't be more different. One time Cassandra and I were watching television and our show finished and a paid program for St. Jude Children's Research Hospital came on. A toddler named Cailey was being profiled, a cutie with giant blue eyes, a can-do attitude, and a perfectly shiny scalp. Cassandra grabbed the remote, said something like, "Add that to my list of eighty reasons why I don't want kids," and turned the channel. I remember watching her walk away: her giraffe legs and sashaying hips, her blond hair fanning down her back. That was when I realized it would never work with her. I wanted a family. I wanted to be a dad. And I wanted a woman who cared whether Cailey lived to see her next birthday.

Then came Mary. The first time I met her was at a softball game. I was filling in for a guy on her law firm's team. My buddy Joe was an associate at the same firm and had called and asked me to come. Mare says we met on the field, which is true, but I actually saw her about a half hour before the game started. She was walking down Connecticut Avenue. I was walking behind her, though at the time I didn't have a clue we were going to the same game. I remember watching her, thinking she was cute. Short as hell, like five foot four, if she was lucky. A curtain of shiny brown hair, swinging side to side. And she was wearing athletic shorts and an oversize T-shirt. She looked like she was barely twenty years old, but God, she was cute. I remember thinking how Cassandra wouldn't be caught dead in a T-shirt and how her athletic clothes were always clingy spandex that framed her perfect curves.

There was an old lady who was struggling to hold her grocery bags. Why she thought she could carry so many bags was beyond me, but she had them lined all the way up her spindly arms. Mary went right up to her and asked if she could carry her bags. I trailed behind as she walked two blocks down D Street and into the lady's building. I waited for about five minutes to see if she came out. Finally she did, holding a stack of cookies the old lady must have given her. Mary proceeded to chomp her way through the entire stack as she walked briskly in the same direction as me. *A girl who eats,* I thought, as if it were the most interesting observation. I was so used to Cassandra and her cardboard protein bars and six-packs of cottage cheese—Cassandra who would cook for me but never eat anything herself. Hell, Cassandra wouldn't even eat fruit. Too many carbs. All I could think was that I wanted to take this short girl eating cookies out to dinner. Carmine's, maybe, to share a gigantic bowl of pasta and a basket of bread.

When she and I walked to the same softball field, my heart flipped. The older guys greeted her like she was their daughter and the women welcomed her with hugs. She was loved. People wanted to be around her. *I want to marry that girl,* I thought at that moment. I found my buddy Joe, and asked him about her. He said she was great. He thought maybe she was just newly single.

What I saw that day in Mary is truly who she is: open, loving, giving, accessible. She made our house a home. She taught us to be a family who loves deeply, who puts each other first. She loves our kids with excess and abundance, like Santa's bag, with all of the gifts magically multiplying. Scrapbooks, photo albums, artwork covering our shelves, paintings plastered on the refrigerator, a hallway covered in school pictures. She's the mom who serves herself last because she wants each of us to have the best of everything. *Take mine,* she says, sliding her helping of dinner onto Sally's plate, leaving herself with bread heels and overcooked ends of the roast. *I like it this way,* she says, and the thing is, she does like it that way: her family having the best.

Mary and I were only together for a month when that same St. Jude commercial came on. Mary was dressed in a suit for work. She was a new associate at the time and putting in a sixty-hour workweek was typical. She was running late, her arms clutching a stack of files, trying to find two matching shoes—following a screwup a few days earlier when she went through her day wearing one blue pump and one black one—when she saw the commercial. She sat down, rested the files on her lap, and leaned forward. She sat there for maybe a half an hour and blubbered as she watched the sick kids fighting for their lives. Afterward her face looked like it had been stung, so swollen and red. I helped her gather her mountain of Kleenex, and when she hugged me tight she just kept saying, "We've got to help. We've got to help." That was eleven years ago and we're still making monthly contributions to St. Jude. Mare says our children are healthy and we'll support St. Jude for the rest of our lives just to thank God for our blessings.

So why am I daydreaming about careless Cassandra instead of Mary? Why does Mary, the sweetest, most compassionate person I know, sometimes leave me unsettled, as though I've witnessed a crime I'd never be able to report? Because Mare dated that dickhead for six years before she and I met, and at times it's like the bastard never left. Mary doesn't lie. Ever. But she lied about Landon. He called and she didn't tell me. I found out later. Mary and I are as close as a married couple can be, but whenever Landon James is involved, somehow I end up feeling like someone has moved the goalposts. I dated Cassandra, a real knockout, and she never once made me feel as insecure as Mary has.

CHAPTER THREE
Moral Inventory

"OKAY, BOYS, LET'S DO THIS!" I clap my hands together and set the twins up at the counter. I never meant to raise my kids according to gender stereotypes, but it just happened. I find myself all of the time calling the boys "sports fan" and "buddy" and "champ." We are always hitting the ball out of the park or scoring goals or touchdowns.

I place bowls of apple oatmeal in front of them with small glasses of milk. I lean over the counter to get their attention.

"Boys, do you know what today is?" I ask. My voice is as enthusiastic as an infomercial.

They look at me blandly.

"It's the first day of preschool!" I gasp, my hands flying in the air. "Can you believe it? You're going to school! Just like Sally and Emily! You're big! Are you excited?"

"I don't want to go to school," Dom says.

"I want to stay with you," Danny says.

"That's great, guys!" I say, finding the Vince Lombardi in me. "But you're going to school, and you're going to love it! It's going to be the best! Come on, now. Eat up your oatmeal so we can go check it out."

Each swirls his spoon through the gruel. Danny, my child who barely eats, looks at me with worried eyes.

"Four bites," I say. "Because you're four years old, right?" I hold up their lunch boxes. "Look! You're all packed. Dom, remember, you picked out Spider-Man, and Danny, you picked out the one with all the dinosaurs! Look, T. rex! I even packed you two Oreos!" I slap my hand over my mouth like it is truly scandalous to give them two whole Oreos apiece.

The boys shrug and begin to discuss dinosaurs.

"T. rexes are the best," Danny says, anchoring his elbows along his sides, waving his menacing little T. rex arms.

"Yeah, but brachiosaurs have really long necks," Dom says, sticking out his neck so far his mouth stretches and he looks like a skeleton.

It still amuses me to hear my four-year-olds say pterodactyl and triceratops. I'm a girl who has been surrounded by girls her entire life: first sisters, then daughters. The boy stuff still has a way of shocking me. Dinosaurs, trucks and tractors, peeing contests.

By eight fifteen the boys have eaten a respectable amount of oatmeal and drunk their milk in exchange for mini-marshmallows, and we are upstairs preparing to get dressed.

"Let's go potty!" I yell, and start in the direction of the bathroom. Instinctively, the boys start to waddle, splaying their feet, their hands out to the side, quacking. When we began potty training, I had pretended I was the mommy duck and they fell in line behind me. Once something sticks with kids, there's no getting rid of it.

My oldest sister, Martina, once told me, "Don't think that what you're doing with them now won't be the same exact thing you're doing with them ten years from now." She was talking about bad habits, like letting the kids sleep in our bed or leave the table without cleaning their plates. But I know the stickiness rule applies to other things, too, like the way Tom and I profess our love to our children each day with a ferocity that leaves no question as to how we feel about our treasured gifts. If something sticks, I hope it's that, a film that covers each of them like a security blanket, an assurance that leaves them with a resounding echo in their ears, "I'm loved."

Danny goes right away, quacking all the while.

"Good job, baby duck!" I cheer. "Mommy duck is so proud!"

Dom's hovering in the doorway.

"Come on, Dom. Your turn. Quack."

"I don't have to go," he says, holding his hands across his pants, as clear as a NO TRESPASSING sign.

Dom is *just* barely potty trained, and the preschool had made it clear, in no uncertain terms, that the children must be! No Pull-Ups. If they kick him out of preschool on his first day, I will seriously need to check myself into a mental hospital.

"Come on, buddy! You can do it!" If he can just go now, he'll be fine for the three hours of preschool.

"No," he says, tightening the grip across his crotch.

I kneel down and look into his eyes. "What's it going to take, champ?" I say, lowering my voice, sounding awfully like a used-car salesman. "We need to get this done."

"I don't want to go," he says.

"M&M's," I say.

He shakes his head.

"Marshmallows."

He shakes his head.

"Chocolate chips," I say.

"I want six," he says.

"Four."

"Five."

"Fine," I say, "you little tyrant," and breathe a gigantic sigh of relief at the satisfying sound of trickling wee-wee.

I know from the girls that no good can come from lingering in the classroom. It is always best to drop off the kids and go. So after I get Dom and Danny situated in their preschool room, unpack the backpacks and lunch boxes into cubbies, and hang sweatshirts on the hooks, I slip out of the room as stealthily as a secret agent, while the boys are building a wall out of brick-sized cardboard blocks.

Once in the minivan, I breathe a gigantic sigh of relief and think maybe I'm hearing a chorus of angels, but then I realize that the Laurie Berkner CD is blaring through the boys' headphones, which are plugged into the van's sound system. I head straight to Starbucks, get the latte and apple fritter I've been fantasizing about, and then cross the road and park in front of the nail salon. With the fritter on its way to my thighs, I take the rest of my latte and head inside. I pick out my nail polish (Tasmanian Devil Red) and the latest *People* magazine and head back to the comfy massage chairs, exhaling and sinking into the soft leather glove. The technician starts the massage rollers and I close my eyes.

"Relax, miss," she says.

"I'm trying," I say, and take a deep breath, willing my shoulders to drop. "Believe me, I'm trying." I hasten to tell her that I've been here before—literally and figuratively—and though I wasn't usually superstitious, I had every reason to be wary.

Four years ago I attempted to scale this version of Everest only to be kicked down to base camp, landing flat on my butt. The day I dropped off the girls at school for the first time was the day I found out I was pregnant with twins.

As the technician massages my feet, and the automatic rollers knead my back, I am finally in the zone, finding that pure relaxation I so seldom enjoy. I exhale deeply and take stock. Four kids, a great husband, a nice home in a good suburb with reputable schools. Mom and Dad just down the road. All three of my sisters still in the DC/Virginia/Maryland area. A few bucks stashed away for the kids' college and our retirement. Our eleventh anniversary just around the corner. A celebratory trip to Ireland has been mentioned. Life is good, I'm thinking, as the technician lifts my foot and begins scrubbing at my heel.

I take another deep breath. Sure, there were sacrifices. I had practiced law for only three years when I gave it up to marry Tom and to have kids. But it was worth it. It's what I had always wanted. The only ladder I ever wanted to climb was the one that ended around the same dinner table every night. Now the payday was upon me. After ten years filled with three pregnancies and full-time child rearing, I was finally having my day. A few hours to myself. In no time Danny and Dom would be in school full-time like Sally and Em, then my days would really be my own. Maybe I'd go back to work. Maybe I'd just volunteer, leaving plenty of time for Tom and the kids.

After Sally and Emily were born, Tom and I considered the possibility of another baby. Definitely, we both agreed. And seeing that we'd conceived Emily on our first try only months after Sally was born, we were certain we could get pregnant whenever we wanted. But month after month my period arrived like clockwork. I chalked up those frustrating first months to pure exhaustion. After all, I was caring for two babies day in and day out. Then a year passed and still no pink line. Then another year.

After a battery of tests at the gynecologist's office, I was ruled to have secondary infertility.

"Stress can be a huge factor," the doctor said. "Are you under an unreasonable amount of stress?" He directed the question to me because Tom had already been checked out, receiving a silver star sticker for his sperm's high count and speedy motility.

I nodded but didn't speak. I didn't wish to elaborate on the fact that the decade before I met Tom was a snowball gathering speed, and if it crashed into me, I'd be flattened. Enough stress to level a town.

"There's stress," Tom answered for me. "A boatload of stress." The doctor nodded sympathetically. Who knew what he thought Tom was referring to—the stress of caring for two young girls, maybe—but I knew we were talking about Landon. Or, mostly, furiously *not* talking about him. After several years of absolutely no contact, my ex-boyfriend had resurfaced.

The girls were little—Sally was three, Emily two. We were at Gymboree class when my cell buzzed. While the girls played under the balloon of a parachute being flown in the air by a circle of eager parents, I slipped around the corner and took the call. Landon was headed overseas for work and had a small life insurance policy that his grandmother had taken out on him when he was a child. It wasn't much, but he wanted to name me as the beneficiary, just in case his plane went down over the Atlantic.

That's crazy, I said to him, name someone else. But he insisted and later that day called me again when I was at home. Rattled— I was alone with the girls, but still—I gave him the information he needed, and jotted down a few chicken-scratch notes about the policy on a scrap of paper I stashed away in the back of my drawer. Months later, Tom was rummaging through my desk,

looking for stamps, when he came across it. Though I was terri-
fied, there was a strange relief in being caught, a relief in knowing Tom would finally understand how deep it went with
Landon. I would finally come clean, tell my husband everything,
and start anew on truthful footing. But my words lost their courage somewhere around my throat, and rather than digging up
the truth, I buried it further.

That was a rough year for us. We'd tried our best to put it behind us and go on with our plans of having more children, but
month after month, the pregnancy stick came up with a single,
lonely line. It was no wonder, really, with the stress and anxiety
that had taken up such sturdy residence right above my heart
and below my throat.

That day, as we drove away from the doctor's office, Tom gath-
ered himself and said, "It is what it is, Mare. He is what *he* is,
whatever the hell *that* is." He stopped himself, took a breath.
"The point is, there's stress in our life and it might be affecting
our fertility. We'll do our best. If nothing happens, then so be it.
We've got two beautiful girls. And they'll get twice as much attention because of this."

"Yeah," I said, feeling a surge of love for him for trying to get
past this. "Nothing wrong with being smack in the middle of
the bell curve, right?"

"It's fine, Mare. Really, we're fine."

While Tom might have been satisfied with two kids, I wanted
more. Each month I hoped. Years passed and I continued to
hope. I needed more children. I needed our family to be bigger,
our familyhood to be harder to breach. I needed our castle to be
impenetrable, and it seemed to me that there was strength in
numbers. So I continued to hope. I hoped and hoped and hoped

and hoped, right up until the time the girls were getting ready to start school.

Then, all of a sudden, the nagging worry disappeared. I was no longer anxious. The truth seemed to lose relevancy, like a photo fading over time, until my recollection of the image was dated and worn. What mattered was the state of my family, and my family was strong. Tom and I had grown as a couple. Our family was solid. All was quiet and right in our life. The want for more children might have still been there, but the need wasn't. I was at peace. And I was ready for a break. Finding out that I was pregnant the same day I dropped off my girls at school for their first time seemed not so much like a joke, not even really an irony. It seemed more like I'd been the subject of a prank.

My eyes are closed and I'm wishing that the young Vietnamese girl who is massaging my legs will never stop. She's rubbing sea salt exfoliant onto my calves, kneading her palm into my muscle, and it feels so good I can hardly stand it. I do the quick math, considering the possibility of a weekly pedicure. Forty dollars a week, about two thousand dollars a year. Money that we could send to the kids' college accounts. Okay, maybe not *every* week. Maybe once a month. Maybe I should get a part-time job first.

What should we have for dinner? Grilled chicken, maybe. There's a package in the freezer, but I'll need to remember to take it out when I get home or it'll never thaw. Mom's birthday is next month. I'll need to get her a present. Emily has rehearsal for *Oliver!* tonight. Sally has soccer practice. I wonder if the boys will take a nap when they get home. I need to make some doctors' appointments—physicals for the girls, well-baby appointments for the boys. Need to call the dentist—confirm the kids' cleanings. Pay the bills, milk and eggs at the store, dry cleaning to be picked up. My eyelids stop twitching and fluttering.

I'm finally in a state of blissful relaxation when—for the second time today—I hear the one name that still sends a tremor shooting down my spine. I look up at the television screen and, in spite of myself, I warm at the sight of Landon James. I tell myself it's like spotting a friend in a high school yearbook and marveling, *Where has the time gone?* But it's more than that, of course. Years ago he promised to love me and he didn't. Then years later he promised to let me get on with my life and he didn't. And, more years later, after I was happily married with two daughters and trying for more, he showed up in my life again with the bizarre life insurance request. After that Tom and I fought to regain balance in our relationship, to get on with our lives, and eventually we did. But there were two other times— once before Tom and I were married, and once after—that I saw Landon, too. This, my past—and the truths that are held in it— keeps me on guard every day of my life, for fear that I will be revealed as exactly what Tom's brother, Patrick, suspected me to be.

CHAPTER FOUR
Powerless

IT'S SUNDAY MORNING AND THE six of us are crammed into a pew at nine o'clock Mass at St. Andrew's Catholic Church. I'm nodding hello to our neighbor, who is sitting a few rows up, when Dom or Danny slams the kneeler down onto my foot. I grumble an expletive under my breath while my eyelashes flutter double time trying to quell the impending tears. I send an empathetic grimace to the Jesus statue, swallowing the metallic taste pooling in my mouth. My foot is throbbing, and even worse, I'm mad at myself for making such a rookie mistake. Always put the kneeler down immediately! Any Catholic parent of small children knows that.

Sally and Emily sit on the other side of Tom. Half an hour ago they were still in their pajamas. Now they're wearing shiny dresses from holidays past: Sally's in a mint-green dress from Easter that now, five months later, is pulling tight at her arms and struggling to hit knee level. Emily's wearing a taffeta Christmas skirt with a bright yellow cardigan and a polka-dot scarf wrapped around her neck. Her Ugg boots stick out from the floor-length skirt. Her outfits are crazy and would make anyone else look like a gypsy or bag lady, but Emily pulls them off, like a Manhattan hipster. Each girl has opted for a headband, our compromise for dealing with shoddy hair brushing. They know I'm relatively happy as long as the mops aren't in their faces.

I'm sandwiched between the boys, whispering commands to them every five seconds: look forward, hands together, sit up, be quiet. The priest is talking about our opportunity to repent and to return home, to leave our hopeless state, and is referring to the parable of the prodigal son. I'm covering Dom's hand with my own and putting my arm around Danny, signaling for him to pay attention, to listen to the priest. When I was younger and my senses were more keen for recognizing moral rightness and wrongness, I remember taking issue with this parable. How's that fair? I remember thinking. Where's the justice? My sister Teresa and I used to debate parables such as that one. She, arguably the most faithful of us sisters, would criticize my brand of belief.

"*Your* faith, Mare, isn't blind," she would say. "You go at it like a lawyer. Your faith is *negotiated*: 'If you do this, God, then I'll do this.'"

"Fair's fair," I'd respond, even though I knew that Teresa was right, that the real measure of faith lay in receiving home a son no matter where he had roamed.

It's time for Communion and I watch Sally and Emily stand, each with her prayer hands, head low, eyes forward. Emily made her First Holy Communion this past spring and Sally made hers the year before. For each girl we had a huge celebration, presents piled high, flowers covering the tables, a banquet of food that rivaled a wedding meal. Mom cooked for days: trays of antipasto; gnocchi, ravioli, and lasagna; filet mignon, a crowned rack of lamb; cakes, crème caramel, and cannoli as far as the eye could see.

On both occasions, my parents and sisters came, Tom's parents and brother. A photographer took portraits of the girls in their white dresses, veils, and gloves. Rosary beads cradled in their hands. The pride swells in me as I remember, and I choke back a gulp of emotion. These girls are growing up faster than I can process, and sometimes their beauty seizes me in a stranglehold.

Dom and Danny walk up with me and whine when we sit down because they want a wafer. I tell them we'll get doughnuts if they're good and then slide onto my knees and apologize for making deals during Communion, though I doubt I'm the first mother to negotiate her way out of this in similar fashion.

I signal again for the boys to pay attention, put their hands in prayer position, and sit up straight. And while I'm acting so pious and devout and obedient as a role model for my children, I'm thinking of Landon James.

Landon James, whom I'd loved with such fervor and devotion and who'd loved me back in schizophrenic waves of excess at times and treated me with icy distance many others. But now here I am, living the life I treasure with a husband and children, whom I adore, and I'm full, truly full, and more than anything, I am *grateful*. Yet Landon James still seeps into my brain like a daydream I can't shake, still holds a claim ticket on my life that I fear every day he will someday collect on.

I met Landon when I was nineteen years old. The winter before the summer I met him, I had taken a job as an office clerk in the downtown DC law firm of Becker, Fox & Zuckerman. The firm was on the eleventh floor of an impressive glass building on Connecticut Avenue. I could see the Washington Monument from one named partner's office, the Capitol from several others'. I spent my days sorting through correspondence and pleadings and memos, dashing in and out of the lawyers' offices to file important documents. When I wasn't making the rounds, I worked in the gigantic file room itself. Some days I would hide in the back of one of the aisles with a thick stack of paper, reading all the filings, from the first motion. I was fascinated by the legal process, and exhilarated by the charged, personal nature of the information I was reading. *I could be a lawyer,* I thought. Until I fall in love, get married, and have children, I definitely wouldn't mind being a lawyer with an office in a building like this with a view of the monuments.

The lawyers took a liking to me, especially the middle-aged men, some of whom were lecherous but many of whom were simply solicitous of me, and impressed that I was working full-time while chipping away at my degree. When summer rolled around, a group of handpicked summer associates descended on our offices, seeking corporate law firm experience. Most were book smart, panicked, and lacking in social skills. But one, a gorgeous guy named Landon James, stood out. He was tall and broad-shouldered and he exuded confidence like the cocky quarterback of a winning high school football team. The law firm had sent around a sheet of biographies. From that I knew he was from Colorado, held a literature degree from Loyola, had gone to law school at Notre Dame, studied at Oxford.

One day, after having seen Landon around the office and traded smiles and hellos, I leaned into the doorframe of his office, my arms filled with brown accordion files brimming with legal documents. "How's it going?" Though I was younger than he, and just a peon file clerk, this law firm was my territory and I was comfortable ducking in.

"It's going," he said, looking up, a sly grin playing across his face.

"How do you like being a slave?"

"I was hoping there would be more beer involved."

"Beer's good." I laughed. "You might want to do some work first, though. Show the old men that you know how to write a motion."

"What's your deal?" he asked.

"My *deal*?" Half flirty, half snotty.

"Yeah," he said, examining me closely. "What's a girl like you doing in a law firm like this?"

"What, you don't think it's my life's ambition to file pleadings for a bunch of midlife-crisis lawyers?"

That got a laugh from him. "Tell me how you really feel," he said, his killer smile reaching to his gorgeous blue eyes. "But seriously."

"I'm in college," I said. "But I also like money and I'm impatient, so I'm working full-time and going to school at night."

"Admirable," he said. "What's your major?"

"Criminal justice."

"What are you looking to be: a cop or a lawyer?"

"I was thinking more of a superhero," I said, my answer surprising myself, feeling a blush flood over my cheeks. "I've always wanted to be a vigilante."

"Root out injustices?"

"Only by night, of course," I said, trying to tamp down my smile, which was pulling so wide my cheeks ached. "In the daytime, I'll probably be a schoolteacher or a librarian."

"Right. Something with a bun."

"A *bun*?" I repeated, as laughter tumbled out.

"You know—a bun, glasses."

"Yes, a bun and glasses." I laughed again, hardly able to believe I was having this conversation with this guy.

"What will your actual power be?" he persisted.

"The cleverest legal mind in the history of the bar. I'll win every case just from my pure brilliance."

He beamed at me. "Maybe you'd like to have a beer with me sometime so that some of that brilliant jurisprudence will rub off on me."

"I'm not *really* a superhero, Landon James," I said. "A mere mortal."

"I'll still buy you a beer," he said, locking his blue eyes with mine.

"We'll see," I said, and walked away, keeping my head up and my stride confident until I made it back to my crappy little desk shoved into the corner of the file room. There I sat in my chair and put my face on my desk, inhaling the smell of wood and musty papers, and half giggled and half cried at my moxie. I had just met the most amazing man of my life and I had batted banter back and forth with him like I was a comedian. Maybe I did have superpowers: super *flirting* powers.

Weeks passed and Landon and I continued to see each other in the hallway, exchange hellos over coffee in the break room, and engage in our brand of witty repartee. Finally, a month into his stay, we both pressed the up button on the elevator at the same time.

"When are we going to grab that beer, Mary Russo?" he said, sending my heart into a tumble.

"Here's the thing, Landon James. I'm only nineteen," I said, a blush heating my cheeks.

"Maybe we could order you a Shirley Temple."

"Nice," I said. "I usually get served, but I'm just warning you. I don't want you to be embarrassed."

"I'm capable of handling a much bigger scandal than that," he said. "So, tonight?"

That night we met at the bar at Old Ebbitt Grill off Pennsylvania. Landon was already bellied up to the brass rail by the time I got there, two frosty ales in front of him.

"I took the liberty," he said, walking with our beers toward two empty barstools.

"Thank you," I said, taking a long, cool sip, feeling the beer slide down my throat and warm my chest.

"How long have you lived in DC?" Landon asked.

"Less than a year," I said. "But I grew up nearby, in Arlington."

"I love it here," he said.

"Really?"

"Oh, yeah. The monuments, the Mall, the Supreme Court. It's amazing."

"Have you ever been here before?"

"When I was in high school I came here with my Boy Scout troop."

"Boy Scouts? I think maybe you were lost," I said. "The mountains are thataway."

"I didn't say we were camping," he said, nudging my arm. "We came to see the archives. The Declaration of Independence."

"So you were a Boy Scout, huh?"

He took a half step back, feigning offense. "You don't think I'm Boy Scout material?"

"I haven't decided yet," I said, and took another long drink of beer, enjoying it while it was cold just in case the bartender didn't serve me another one.

"Altar boy, too," he said. "In case that's important to a good Catholic girl like you."

"What makes you think I'm a good Catholic girl?"

"It's written all over you," he said, clinking his glass against mine.

I narrowed my eyes at him, lifting my hand to the gold cross hanging around my neck.

"Let me guess," he said. "Mary Katherine? Mary Regina? Mary Margaret?"

"Margaret," I admitted.

"Mary Margaret," he repeated. "MM."

"You think you're so smart," I said. "But you have no idea. Any more than I know if you're a nice Catholic boy."

"Oh, I'm not," he said. "And not even Catholic anymore."

"A *recovering* Catholic, are you?"

"Recovering implies that I've sought treatment for my affliction."

"Wow, you're bad. Equating Catholicism to an affliction, huh?"

"Suffice it to say, I've *opted out*."

"What about the Scouts? Did they offend your fine senses, too?"

"Let's put it this way," he said. "You can count on me to always be prepared."

"If I need someone to build a fire from rocks and sticks, you're the first person I'll ask."

"What about you?" he asked. "Any Scouting in your past?"

"Of course. I was a Girl Scout for years."

"Then you can answer a burning question of mine: What *really* went on at Girl Scout camp?"

"Oh, the usual," I assured him. "We snuck out of our cabins, skinny-dipped in the lake, brushed and braided each other's hair."

"I knew it," Landon said, his arm brushing against mine.

"You're giving away all of your fetishes," I said. "First librarians shucking off their glasses and letting down their buns, now Girl Scouts frolicking in the moonlight."

"What can I say, I have an active imagination."

I shrugged. "Pretty standard stuff, I have to say."

He shrugged back and grinned. "Gotta love the classics."

After taking another drink, I eyed him. "Tell me this," I said. "What did the Catholic Church do to you?"

"Oh, you know. All the standing and sitting and kneeling and genuflecting. Who can keep up?"

"I'm serious," I said. "I want to know."

Landon grinned and downed the bottom half of his beer in one swig. "That's hardly first-date material," he said, leaning in close enough for me to smell the soap on his skin.

"We're not really on a date. Just drinks," I said, clinking my pint against his. "So you can tell me."

Landon looked at me and our eyes locked. He was the first to look away, his power smile dropping. "All right," he said. "I went to high school with a kid named Andy. He was smart and nice. Very shy, but I liked him. He had a dark sense of humor for anyone who bothered to talk to him. One day I go to school and find out that Andy hanged himself the night before. His parents found his body swinging from the banister when they woke up in the morning. The next day I'm at church for some youth meeting thing, and all of the Catholic kids start talking about Andy, and how he's not going to go to heaven because he killed himself and how that's a mortal sin. I remember so clearly thinking, *That's messed up. Why is a kid like Andy, who clearly was in some sort of pain, being denied access to heaven? Of all the people who needed salvation . . .* That was it for me. That was the day I decided it was all a bunch of bullshit."

"I'm so sorry," I said. "That sounds horrible."

"It was a long time ago," Landon said. "I still think about him, though."

We stared at our beers for a moment, and then I said, "So if not Catholicism, Landon James, what do you believe in?"

Landon signaled to the bartender for two more beers. "Pure, unadulterated pleasure and pain. That's what life boils down to."

"You're full of it," I said. "There's got to be more to you than that."

"There's not," he said.

"So you live your life in search of pleasure? In the avoidance of pain?"

"Don't you?"

"No," I said. "In fact, I'm probably more like the opposite: I seek pain and avoid pleasure. Why else would I choose to work full-time and go to school at night? And I hardly ever do anything fun, and if I do, I feel guilty."

"Catholic down to your bones," he said. "My grandmother would love you. But you've got it all wrong, MM." He swiveled toward me so that our knees rested against each other's. He placed his hands on my knees and pushed them up my thighs until the tiny space between us could be filled with a shot glass of my remaining confidence. With his mouth only an inch from mine, I gasped slightly, and when I did, he smiled—that gigantically gorgeous smile—and then leaned in until his lips brushed mine. I pulled back, and inhaled slowly.

"You are seriously cute," he said, and I blushed because at the moment, that was exactly what I felt like: cute. Not beautiful, not sophisticated, about a thousand miles out of Landon James's league, but for whatever reason, he was having a good time—an amusing time—hanging out with nineteen-year-old Mary Margaret, Catholic to her bones, file-clerk peon.

"You are seriously hot," I replied, shocking myself by upping the ante. Maybe I could be more than cute. "Pleasure and pain?" I said, and this time I placed my hands on his thighs and knocked him off balance.

"Getting a little toasty in here," he said.

"I like toasty," I said.

"Serious question," he said, stroking his finger over my hand. "Do you still have your Girl Scout uniform?"

"Why?" I asked. "Do you want to try it on?"

"If you try it on, I'll try it on," he said, and kissed me again, this time laying his palm on my cheek.

Later that night, Landon walked me home to my brownstone on Capitol Hill. At the top of the steps to the door to my apartment, I turned to him and said, "We should probably call it a night." As worked up as I was, I knew better than to blow a good thing by inviting him in. Three older sisters had taught me that.

"We'll have to save the Girl Scout uniform for another night," he said.

"I'll make sure to have film in my camera."

"I'll pass on the photos." He laughed. "You should, too. You might be up for the Supreme Court someday. You wouldn't want an embarrassing photo ruining your career."

"Wow, you've got grander plans for me than I do."

"I think a lot about what the future might hold, it's true," he said in a decidedly softer tone. Cocky, pleasure-and-pain Landon seemed to have a gentler side.

He kissed me again, wrapped his arms around my waist, and gently slid his hand up my blouse and onto my back. "Seriously cute," he said again, kissing me once more. We stood there, grinning stupidly at each other, and then finally he turned and started his walk in the direction of the three Senate buildings.

|||

For the next three weeks, Landon and I merged into one person; we inhabited the same space, we held nothing back. We ate lunch together, we met for drinks, we sat on the steps of the Lincoln Memorial, our view stretching across the Mall. On nights when I had school, he would wait for me afterward, with a few bottles of Sam Adams and a bag of burgers and fries. He'd carry my backpack home as we discussed con law theory, and then we'd sit on the steps of my brownstone, eating and drinking. Some nights he would help me at the law library, locate cases and decipher the decisions. And we kissed, and touched, and kissed some more, and drove each other wildly crazy.

A few times, we went fishing. Landon was an avid fly fisherman but guarded that activity as his solitary pleasure. When I asked if I could come, he cocked his head and said, "You don't want to fish."

"I do, seriously," I said, even though, truly, I *didn't* want to fish, but I did want to be with him. And so he took me along, let me enter into his private world that he had shared with no one else. As we sat on the bank of the Shenandoah River, our legs warmed from the glittery rocks, he showed me his collection of flies.

"Where'd you learn to tie them?" I asked.

"My dad," he said. "The best thing he did for me."

"What's he like?" I asked.

"He's not like anything," Landon said. "He left early on."

"Why?"

"Who knows," Landon said. "He used to say that living an honest life was like the river. You might start in one place and end up somewhere entirely different."

"Poetic," I said.

"Bullshit," Landon said. "He's a deadbeat. That's all."

"And your mother?"

"She's a train wreck. Because of him, of course. When he walked out, my mother checked out. I kind of bombed it in the parents' department."

"How old were you?" I asked.

"Eight."

"That's when he left?"

"Uh-huh," Landon said. "I was down by the creek behind our house. It was summer and I was bored. I was skipping rocks. He squatted down beside me and said, 'Son, people leave all the time. Better to learn it now. Always best not to get too attached. Fact of life: people leave.'"

"What'd you say to that?" I asked.

"I said okay. He had never steered me wrong before. He taught me to tie these flies and to cast my rod, so I figured he knew what he was saying."

"Then what?"

"A year later he drove his point home when he packed his bags and left. He never came back. He never called."

"I'm so sorry," I said.

"Sometimes I think about that conversation down by the creek. He must have known he had one foot out the door."

"Your poor mom."

"She fizzled to nothing. Spent her days in the kitchen—coffee cup in hand, same terry-cloth robe over the same ratty nightgown. Hair pulled back into a greasy ponytail. Dead eyes staring out the window at the tire swing. Some days she'd look out the other window, the one with the road leading up to our house. I always wondered about that. Were those her good days or her bad days? The ones when she thought he might come back?"

"I'm sorry you went through that," I said, pressing in next to him, resting my cheek on his shoulder.

"I'm not whining about it, but in a lot of ways, I don't think you can really overcome a childhood that messed up," he said. "The damage is done."

"I don't believe that," I said. "There's always room for forgiveness, for redemption." That day I fell a mile deeper for him. My assumptions—that Landon came from a wealthy, upper-crust family—were enormously wrong. He wasn't just gorgeous, smart, and sexy. He was also in need of saving.

"Maybe," he said, and at that moment I really believed that we had started something. He told me he was falling hard. I reciprocated, and told him I could get used to this: us spending every weekend together, me with a fishing vest of my own.

A few days later, the reality that Landon had opened a door he hadn't intended to open must've hit him in the face like ice water. He more than just eased off and assumed a cooler stance; he canceled our plans, stopped showing up at my school, and avoided passing my desk. He and the other summer associates were due to go home in a few weeks, and the partners had them heavily scheduled with cocktail parties and baseball games and other events meant to sweeten the pot in order to entice the soon-to-be lawyers to choose Becker, Fox & Zuckerman. We talked a few times in the hallway, on the way up and down the elevator, but it seemed Landon had decided that spending every weekend with Mary Russo was too big of a risk to his heart. Whatever that said about me, my craving for him grew with every step he took away from me.

CHAPTER FIVE
Unmanageable

WE HAVE DINNER AT MY parents' house every Sunday night. Regina and Robert Russo live in the same Arlington split-level I lived in as a kid. The house sits at the end of a cul-de-sac, is brown clapboard with yellow shutters, and is shaded by a gigantic oak tree. The three bedrooms and two baths now seem more like a dollhouse with miniature furniture, but somehow the six of us lived comfortably there. Somehow we all found ample space kneeling around my parents' bed each night to say the Rosary. Somehow we always went to bed with full bellies in a heated house with love in our hearts.

Hand-me-down shoes, sharing a bedroom, and stretching one pound of ground beef into a meal for six made up our roots, dug us deeper into our family soil, braided our branches around one another. None of us ever complained about hardship because it never seemed that way to us. Dad brought home a modest government salary, Mom stayed home and cared for us, and we had everything we needed. We were public school kids who walked home together, played outside until dark, and ate dinner around the same table every night. Summers were spent at the community pool, vacations were trips to visit relatives. Nothing fancy, but there was a lot of fun, a lot of laughter.

Growing up, everyone in our neighborhood was in the same boat: trying to make ends meet while juggling kids and a mortgage. Birthday parties were simple: backyard games and a homemade cake. When I was older, I was allowed to have a friend spend the night. These days my kids are invited to birthday parties at gyms and bounce houses and bowling alleys and petting zoos. It's an excess that's easy to fall into. We all want to give our children so much. But then I think of my birthday parties, the flour-sack races, pin the tail on the donkey, Mom's beaming pride as she'd round the corner with candles flickering on her birthday cake masterpiece, and I think, *What can be better than that?* There was a deep richness in the simplicity of it all.

Once when I was in high school, I asked my mom, "We're middle class, right?"

She scrunched her face and considered the question. "Lower middle class, I'd say," she said. "If you're talking in terms of economics." She knew I was—my free enterprise book was sprawled across the counter. "But you can't label what we have. Not truly what we have," Mom said.

The house I share with Tom and the kids is a step up in terms of space and style from my parents' house, but still, there's something primal about driving up to the house I called home, a gravitational pull that summons me when I get within a half-mile radius of 29 Terrace Circle. I never tire of approaching the three steps that lead me home. My shoulders always drop a half inch as I step through the front door and inhale the smells that accompany my history. If my world exploded tomorrow, if I were in need of refuge, at least I would have this home.

My four kids barrel into the house as if it's their own, yelling hellos to Nana and Pop. My mom has carved out special nooks and crannies for each of them, places they know they're allowed to go, things they're allowed to touch. Sally loves to flip through the photo albums, as if secrets are hidden in each one, and it's her job to see beyond the obvious. She especially loves the pictures of me and my sisters when we were young. She has just finished reading *Little Women*, and she is certain I was the Jo in the bunch. I'm honored that she regards me that way—brave and principled—but I definitely wasn't the Jo; that would have been Martina or Teresa. Sally would be disheartened to know how unsure of myself I am most of the time.

Emily has been granted access to my mother's hatbox, which overflows with costume jewelry. In no time, my daughter is swimming in heavy strands of pearls and dangly clip-ons. The fact that my mother *has* a hatbox teeming with jewelry kills me. My no-nonsense mother wears the same three pieces of jewelry every day: a tight pearl ball in each ear, her wedding ring, which has nearly burrowed under her skin, and a thin gold crucifix around her neck. So where'd she get all of the costume jewelry? She picks it up here and there, flea markets and garage sales, just for Emily. Mom doesn't part easily with a dime, so it touches me every time I see that the hatbox has a new addition. It tickles me that Emily's nana is so different from the mother who made me beg for three years before getting my ears pierced.

The twins head to the coat closet, where they sit under the drape of garments, playing with the Old MacDonald's Farm and Lincoln Logs from my childhood. The toys are in mint condition. The four of us girls veered more toward Barbies than building cabins. Another non-Jo fact about me that Sally would be disappointed to learn.

Once inside the front door, there's no room for indecision. Two steps up brings me to the dining room and kitchen, where I'll find my mom. Two steps down brings me to the dark-paneled den, where I can reliably find my father. I choose to go up to the kitchen first to see my mother, who is standing guard over the stove like a sentry, a Diet Pepsi in one hand, a cigarette in the other. When she sees we're here, she smashes her cigarette into the tray and flicks on the little air purifier that sits on the table. With the cigarette extinguished, the kitchen now fills with the aroma of sauce.

"Hi, Ma," I say, kissing her cheek. She smells of rosemary and Virginia Slims, and though it baffles me that she and my father still smoke in this day and age, I love it because it's always been her. She swears that she's cutting down, only two cigarettes at night, one in the morning. The State Farm office where she has been office manager for twenty-five years has gone "smoke free," so she's given up daytime smoking completely.

"How's my girl?" she says. Mom wears black slacks, the pleated polyester kind that have the elastic waist around the back. On top she wears a blouse—polyester, too. Mom runs the risk of being highly flammable. Once she gets home from work she covers up in an apron, which she'll wear until dinner is finished and the dishes are done. Her hair falls in long brown waves, and for as long as I can remember she has twisted the length of it into a bun at the base of her neck. A few rogue curls spiral around her face, springing in every direction. Though my sisters and I cringe at her ancient wardrobe and the fact that she still smokes cigarettes, Mom is Sophia Loren beautiful.

"Sauce smells good," I say. "How'd you make it?" I ask every time. She never tells.

"No recipe," Mom says. "Just a little of this, a little of that."

"I'm your daughter," I say, faking heartbreak. "How could you not tell your own flesh and blood?"

"It comes out a little different every time," she says with a shrug. "It's no secret."

The thing is, it *never* comes out different. It's always exactly the same, fresh and earthy with spicy notes of oregano. When I was little, I used to eat Mom's sauce straight out of a bowl, like soup. The only thing that changes is whether there's hot and sweet sausage swimming through it or Mom's meatballs. Always a fresh loaf of soft Italian bread from the bakery. Always thick pats of butter. And always the imposter of a salad: torn pieces of iceberg lettuce drenched in two parts oil, one part vinegar, heavily salted and peppered.

Tonight we're celebrating Emily's ninth birthday. For the next six days, Emily gets to claim being "the same age" as Sally, until her sister turns ten on the third day of November. I see Mom's made her famous double-layer chocolate cake. It's decorated with sprinkles that shimmer like diamonds. Perfect for Emily, our little diva.

Though Mom cooks every night, she's as thin as a rail. A healthy regimen of Diet Pepsi and cigarettes will do that. Her real pleasure is from watching her family eat. She and my dad are addicted to Diet Pepsi, though they drink a pot of decaf with dinner every night. Mom sits with her coffee, a small bowl of pasta that she'll only pick at, and watches everyone else eat. She scans our plates, passes bowls, and throws in the occasional "Are you sick? Not hungry?" for anyone who pauses or begs off seconds or thirds. Mom reserves her fondest affection for the person who eats the most and, since we all want her love, we stuff ourselves to win her prize and leave uncomfortably full every Sunday night.

"Go say hello to your father," Mom says, and kisses me again. I head back down the two short levels of steps. Dad's pushed back in his recliner, each foot pointing outward, his arm behind his head. His vices are the same as Mom's: Diet Pepsi and cigarettes, both purchased in bulk at Costco. I see that I'm not the first to get to him. Sally's on the arm of his recliner, her arm slung around Pop, his around her. They're sitting cheek to cheek, watching the highlights from the baseball game. Dad's a man of few words, but he's accessible.

"Hey, Pop," I say, leaning over to give him a kiss on his cheek. I slide one over to Sally, too.

"How's my angel?" he asks, chucking my chin with his hand.

"Great! Good," I say. "What do you have Tom doing in the basement?" I can hear him rumbling around down there.

"Just looking through some of my old tools," Dad says. "What am I going to do with three ratchet sets?"

Dad is always talking like he's going to keel over and die at any moment. You'd think he'd lay off the cigarettes, sausage, and bacon. He's always sticking Post-it Notes on miscellaneous items: For Mary. For Tom. For Teresa. *Whomever.* It makes him feel better knowing that his prized possessions will be in good hands.

He stares at the television. He looks at me like he wants to say something but then doesn't.

"What's up, Dad?"

He looks at Sally, who is engrossed in the sports reel, and then arches his eyebrows over his horn-rimmed glasses and says, "Sal, honey. Why don't you go check on your father?"

"Okay, Pop," Sally says, sliding out of the recliner and clomping down the stairs.

Dad takes a breath. Rubs his eyes. "I've been seeing a bit of news coverage on that Landon character," Dad says.

"I know, I know," I say, waving it away. "It's been nice and quiet these last few years with him as attorney general. Not a lot of news coverage anyway."

"And now he wants the Senate," Dad says.

"Lofty goals," I say. "But who knows, maybe he'll make it." I pray to God that he does make it. So long as Landon is in the public eye he'll stay out of my life. It's in his times of defeat when he wallows and grasps at what might have been.

"Why not?" Dad says. "He doesn't have a bad message."

"True, but a lot could happen in a year," I say. "We'll just have to wait and see."

"What's Tommy say?"

"He hates seeing him. Wishes he didn't exist."

"Talk to him," Dad says. "You know it's not easy on him, seeing your ex-boyfriend, your ex-fiancé, whatever, plastered across the television."

"I know," I say. "It sucks that we can't ever get away from him completely."

"As long as he's a public figure—a politician, of all things—I don't think you ever will."

At dinner we stuff ourselves on spaghetti and meatballs, until we're slouched back in our chairs with our buttons popped on our pants. Mom pours coffee and asks Sally to dim the lights and bring in the cake. We do our most dramatic, operatic, over-the-top singing of "Happy Birthday" to Emily, a girl who appreciates grand style. She claps and takes a bow and throws kisses to us all. Then we shove down more food, each of us polishing off our generous slices of Mom's chocolate layer cake with fudge frosting. Tom asks for seconds, sealing his status as the best son-in-law *ever*.

When we get home from my parents' house, Tom and I start the nightly turndown service: While he feeds Daisy and throws her a tennis ball in the backyard, I usher the girls in and out of the shower and bathe the boys in the tub. Once the boys are in their jammies, Tom reads them a stack of books. I start another load of laundry, empty the dishwasher, and fill my hands and arms with a million small items that have somehow popped out of drawers and cupboards and trunks throughout the day.

It's ten thirty by the time I fall into bed against a stack of three pillows with my book in hand. Tom's on the computer in the corner of our bedroom. When a text message issues its burbling-water sound, I look up and see that my cell phone is on the desk.

"Toss me my phone, babe," I say. Tom lobs it onto the bed.

I assume it's from my sister Angie. She and I text each other frequently. But it's not Angie. It's Landon James. I drop the phone instinctively as if it's hot, look at Tom, and steady my breath. The walls pull in, the room seems smaller, the air thicker. My heart thumps in my chest. Despite Tom's worries, Landon hasn't contacted me in years—not since the life insurance phone call seven or eight years ago—so the fact that he's texting me now is as alarming as an intruder in my house. I pick up the phone again. Read the message again.

We need to talk, the message reads.

"Who wrote?" Tom asks.

"One of the moms from preschool," I lie. "I forgot that I'm supposed to send in cupcakes tomorrow." Meanwhile I type *Why?* and hit send.

"You want me to run to the store?" Tom asks. "Or can you stop in the morning?"

Can I call you? he writes.

NO! I text.

"Mary?" Tom asks. "The store?"

"I'll go," I say, trying to rearrange my face into something that feels normal, but my skin feels tight and tingly, like I've been shot with Novocain. "I think one of the kids has an allergy. I'd better check the ingredients." I'm disgusted by how easily the lies flow, like I do it all the time.

I stare at my phone. Wait.

Call me then, Landon writes.

"Sound good?" Tom asks.

"What?"

"I asked you if you wanted to watch a *Seinfeld* rerun when you got back."

"Yes!" I say, shooting my arm in the air like a cheerleader. "Definitely! A *Seinfeld*!"

Behind the wheel, I wait until I'm around the corner and then dial Landon.

"Landon?" I say, like I can't believe it's him. It's been forever, so long that it's almost incomprehensible to make sense of my past life squeezing like this into my current life.

"It's been a while," he says, and the sound of his voice ignites nostalgia in me like the flick of an arsonist's match. Not lust—I no longer crave Landon—but familiarity, like our shared past is still connected by live wires.

"Why are you calling me?" I say in almost a whisper, because talking to my ex is the equivalent of cheating, and I already have enough judgment bearing down on me.

"I'm running for Senate."

"I saw that."

"There is a potential problem."

"What kind of problem?"

"Listen, Mary, don't freak out, but there's a photo," he says.

"A photo?"

"Of us."

"From when? Doing what? And why's it matter?" I flip on my turn signal, pull into the shopping center, and into a parking spot.

"It's when we met in DC at the Mayflower."

"As in ten years ago?"

"I haven't seen you since."

"I had Sally with me that day."

"The photo is of just you and me. You can't tell that you're holding a baby carrier."

"So they have a picture of you and me in the lobby of the Mayflower," I say. "So what?" As though flippancy on my part will make this matter less.

"I'm leaning into you," he says. "I'm kissing your cheek."

"Oh, God." My heart plummets to the pit of my stomach like on the antigravity ride I took the girls on last summer at Kings Dominion. I remember Landon's harmless kiss. "We weren't in the lobby then."

"No, we were leaving the hotel room. That's the problem."

That day is etched in my memory. *Is there somewhere private we can talk?* I had asked, and then followed Landon up to his tenth-floor room.

"But we were just *talking*. There's got to be some way to prove that we were just talking."

"That's beside the point," Landon says. "What matters is how it looks."

"I don't get it," I say. "Why was someone taking a photo of you? You weren't even the attorney general then."

"They weren't after me," he says. "The photographer was a snoop PI hired by the wife of one of my firm's partners. She suspected him of running around and using the room at the Mayflower to meet his 'friend.' We just got caught in the crossfire."

For a moment neither of us says anything. Then I ask, "Have I been identified in the photo as your ex-girlfriend? Or whatever it was that I was to you."

"If it's any consolation, you can't entirely see your face. Your head is down and your hair is everywhere."

I reach up and grab a handful of said hair. A wave of relief floods over me. "So maybe it'll be okay."

"Let's hope. I don't know what this guy intends to do with the photo."

"Can't you make a deal—buy it from him?"

"If I make him an offer, he'll know it's worth something. It's better to give him the impression that it's worthless."

"Can *you* tell that it's me?"

"I can, of course. There's a slice of your profile that you can see, plus if you know what you look like, you'd be able to tell."

"So my husband will know?"

"I don't know," he says.

"God!" I say, squeezing the steering wheel. "How will you explain who I am, why we were together?"

"I don't know. I'll just say you were an old friend and we happened to run into each other. I'll explain that you were holding a baby carrier. That I invited you up to my room so that you could nurse. Yeah, that's it. That'll make me sound very pro-women, pro-nursing."

"That's all that matters to you, isn't it!" I seethe. "What about me? What am I going to tell Tom?"

"Tell him the same story I'm going to tell. That you happened to run into me."

"In the lobby of the Mayflower? He'll want to know what I was doing downtown. I had just had a baby. It's not like I was working then."

"I don't know, Mary! Make up some goddamned story. Say you met a girlfriend for lunch to show off your new baby and you happened to run into me."

"You can't let this hurt me, Landon."

"I've got my eye on a US Senate seat. You think I want a scandal on my hands?"

There is a pause across the phone lines. I listen to Landon breathe. I lift my chin to slide the impending tears back into place, exhale slowly.

"The last thing in the world I want is to hurt you, Mary," Landon says in a tone I heard only occasionally throughout our relationship, a tone that soothed me, like crawling into his arms after days of not hearing from him. "God knows I've hurt you enough."

I look down and watch two fat teardrops fall onto my thighs.

"What am I supposed to do?" I ask because I have no clue.

"Just go about your normal life," Landon says. "There's a chance this photo will never see the light of day."

In the grocery store I walk through the fluorescent-lit aisles in an equally fluorescent daze, buying two dozen cupcakes I don't need. At home I check on the kids and then crawl into bed with Tom. I curl into my husband, and instead of paying attention to our *Seinfeld* rerun, I pray for forgiveness for my decade of sins, and try to breathe through lungs that are too small for this crisis.

That day at the Mayflower, the day the photo was taken, I went into DC to meet Landon.

We settled into two overstuffed floral chairs in the lobby.

"I can't believe you called," he said, struggling to cross his long legs in the too-soft chair.

"I wouldn't have, obviously," I answered, rocking Sally's carrier with my foot, a mom skill I had already acquired in three short weeks. "If it wasn't important."

"How are things?" he asked. "How's marriage? Motherhood? You look great."

I looked fat, actually, having gained fifty pounds with Sally, and still holding on to a good thirty of them.

"It's great," I said. "Tom is a great guy and I can already tell that he's going to be the best father."

"That's good, really good," Landon said. "I'm happy."

"Great, good," I repeated. It seemed that our combined vocabulary had been reduced to *good* and *great*. "Is there somewhere more private where we could talk? Maybe down a dark hallway, the ice room, the laundry facilities?"

Landon gave me a look like he didn't know if I was joking or not. "There's a room," he said, haltingly. "I mean, my firm keeps a room here. For clients. We could go up there."

"That'd be great."

Sally had started to fuss. I unbuckled her and lifted her out of her carrier, reached down to grab for the handle.

"I can take that," Landon said, reaching for the handle. "Or her, if you'd like."

"I'll hold on to her," I said. "Thanks."

I held Sally against my chest, put my mouth on her velvety forehead, and inhaled her powdery scent as I followed him up to the tenth-floor room. Inside I went to the window, pulled the heavy fabric and then the sheer lining, looked across Connecticut Avenue, and strained to see the tip of the Washington Monument.

After we talked, I strapped Sally back into her carrier and stood in the hallway while Landon closed the door behind us.

As I revisit the scene, snuggled against my innocent husband in our marital bed, my fevered brain recalls him for me: the guy with an ice bucket at the end of the hall, loitering at the vending machine. The photographer. As Landon leaned in and kissed my cheek, neither of us would have seen him snatch our secret in his shutter.

CHAPTER SIX
Defects of Character

IT'S EARLY SATURDAY MORNING, AND the six of us are already in the kitchen, our central gathering post. Today is Sally's tenth birthday, but none of us is too concerned with it at the moment. We've hugged her and squeezed her and covered her face with kisses, branding her with wishes for the best birthday ever. But right now we're focused on her soccer game at nine o'clock, and the fact that I have forgotten that we're the "snack family," the ones responsible for bringing halftime and after-game goodies. Sally's sending me plaintive messages. "You *never* forget these things. How could you have *forgotten*?" she wants to know, in her most accusatory tone. Easy, I want to tell her. Riddled as I am with anxiety over the photo that might clobber me—clobber us all—surely forgetting to stop for Gatorade and Doritos packs could be overlooked, couldn't it?

I rummage through the cupboard and find a box of Thin Mints from last year's Girl Scout Cookie drive, a few apples in the crisper, and some powdered lemonade. Sally seems satisfied.

It's chaotic and loud and we're all knocking into each other. I close my eyes and take a deep breath, reminding myself to relax so that the mayhem doesn't overwhelm me. Because aside from the craziness and the fact that there isn't a square inch of clean space on the counter and I'll have an hour of serious cleaning to do later, all is well in my life. At this moment in time, all is well.

With five minutes to spare we make it to the soccer field and Sally barrels out of the van and runs off to her team. Tom unpacks the back while I help unbuckle the boys. A few minutes later we're settled on the sidelines and it's turned out to be a nice morning, crisp and clear with a deliciously warm blanket of sun wrapped around us. Emily has run off to play with another player's sibling and the boys are collecting acorns under a nearby tree. "We did it," I say to Tom, letting my eyes settle on him for the first time this morning. His face is rough with morning stubble, and I can't help but reach for his chin and rub at his whiskers.

Tom looks at me briefly, then stares ahead. "Boy Wonder is *everywhere.*"

My heart seizes like a fugitive finally boxed in, thinking that Tom knows about the phone call, the photo, the unnecessary cupcakes.

"What do you mean?"

"He's running for Senate, Mary. Big news. It's everywhere."

"The *primary,*" I say. "I doubt he'll get anywhere."

He shakes this off.

I glance over at Tom to gauge his mood. Tom has never met Landon but hates that I dated him for so long, hates that I chose to spend six years of my life with the type of guy who couldn't step up. No doubt wonders what it says about me that I did that. Tom's quiet and kind, and Landon's cocky and confident, and though Tom's qualities are head and shoulders above Landon's in the virtues department, I know that every man aspires to possess Landon's swagger, his ability to walk into a room and command attention.

Tom stands, reflexively, to cheer on Sally. "Come on, Cougars!" he roars. "Let's see some D!" He sits again and shakes his head. "I need to work with her more in the backyard. She's so close to nailing that corner shot."

"She loves when you work with her."

"Anyway," Tom says. "I could do without seeing his nauseating face all over the television."

I thought—or hoped, anyway—we'd moved on. "I doubt he'll win," I say dismissively. "Who'd vote for him?"

"He got your vote for a lot of years."

"Got my vote?" I say, eyebrows raised.

"You held on for dear life."

"Oh, yeah. He was a real life preserver."

He shrugs. "You saw something in him that made you stick around."

"Agreed," I say. "It's true. I did think I saw more in him than was there."

"But it took you ten years to figure that out."

"I dated him for six years."

"You knew him for ten years. Wanted him for ten years."

"Oh, please."

I force myself to take a breath. We've had precisely this conversation twenty times or more, but it's been so long since the last time, I let myself think we were done with it.

"So I was a little slow," I say. "A little dense."

"He must have been a smooth operator," Tom says.

"A smooth operator," I say in a funny voice, mocking his choice phrasing, attempting my strategy of making light of it. "Listen to you."

I met Tom only three months after I had broken up with Landon for good. I was playing softball for my law firm's team on the fields not far from the White House. Our team was short players that evening so one of my colleagues, a lawyer named Joe, asked his friend to fill in, a good-looking guy who happened to be Tom. I noticed him immediately as I warmed up, stretched my calves, windmilled my arms to loosen them. He looked like he could crush a softball in his fist, but when he smiled, everything about him changed. His whole face brightened, radiating warmth, sending laugh lines fanning from the corners of his eyes.

By the time the first inning was up, Tom had asked me my name, offered me a water bottle, and helped me widen my batting stance. He said that he had seen me earlier, walking to the field. I hadn't noticed him. As he stood behind me with his arms shadowing mine, I remember thinking, *I feel heat.* My heart was thumping and my palms were sweaty and I was flush with gratitude that I was capable of responding to another man, that Landon James wasn't my only hope. Maybe fate had taken me on a ten-year detour to get here.

By the end of the game, Tom had offered me a ride home, a ride that I accepted, but not before we stopped for a two-hour dinner and dessert. By the time he walked me to my door, a soothing calm had infiltrated every grain of my being. I would be okay. I would get over Landon. Tom called the next day and we saw each other every day after that. By the end of the first week, there was already an unspoken recognition that we were now a couple.

In those early weeks and months of dating, Tom and I poured out our every secret, talked of exes, skeletons in our closets. There was an urgency in getting to know each other, as if we were running against the clock. We'd found each other when we were thirty years old, not twenty. To make up for lost time, we skipped the stage of dating where we shared parts of our history in small doses—a sprinkling here, a scattering there. Why waste time dipping toes in the water when clearly a cannonball approach was so much more effective?

So in our early days and months together, we lingered in restaurant bars, slumped in the vinyl booths of all-night diners, and told each other every detail of our lives. Tom told me of his brother and his struggle with alcohol, his father and his indiscretions, his mother's stoic response to it all. And I told Tom about my family and Landon—but from the start, it was Landon he was most interested in. He would urge me on, frowning, as he dug deeper. Without giving a thought to the repercussions, I told Tom everything: how super intense Landon was—for a while he'd be all in, and then he'd cool off, leave me hanging for weeks, wondering what went wrong. How it was a rush for him to be so into me, and such a huge withdrawal when he stood back. Tom commented that I sounded like his brother, the addict, and I admitted to him that I couldn't argue with that. Then I committed an even greater sin: I told Tom about the things we did, the places we went, how we watched every episode of *The West Wing*, how we'd meet for late dinners at Old Ebbitt Grill, how we'd linger over brunch, reading the papers. What I took as interest in my emotional history was really Tom on a reconnaissance mission, gathering damning bits and details about my relationship.

I still believe Tom's motives were honest and that he truly was trying to learn about me, but the information festered in him, jabbing at him like a thorn in his side and then, later, like a dagger. Telling Tom too much about Landon was a mistake I learned too late. Much became taboo: political TV dramas, late dinners, lazy brunches. My past had preemptively tainted my future. Once the information was told—that my relationship with Landon was at once needy and passionate, and then distant and cold—there was no retracting it.

Now, from time to time, Tom holds it against me, as if our marriage—a steady, reliable ship—is lacking in comparison to the tumultuous force majeure that was Landon and my relationship.

I squint into the sun to find Sally on the soccer field. "I'm sorry you have to see him," I say, for lack of anything better.

"Please don't apologize, Mare," he says without looking at me. "It makes it sound like you're complicit, like you have a part in this. I'm not looking for you to be sorry about anything. I'm just saying, you know?"

"I know," I say, leaning in close to him, "but I *am* sorry, sorry that I brought baggage to our marriage. You could have married someone else, someone who hadn't dated Landon James for six years, who hadn't known him for a decade."

"So what?" Tom says. "That was before we met. You have nothing to be sorry about after we met, right?"

Tom has a genius for reeling me into a trap like this, a claw clamped onto my foot so that I can't move, a place where I have no choice but to lie more.

"I feel bad," I say, "because it doesn't end with him. My relationship with him ended, *obviously*, but he's still around. That's what I feel guilty about." I dodge and skirt, avoid answering Tom's question directly. "What else can I do but apologize?"

Sally's teammate passes her the ball. She dribbles it to the outside, her brows knit in concentration, fists clenched tight. A few more steps and then she shoots, sending the ball sailing over the goalie's head, wedging it into the corner of the net. Sally falls to her knees in victory. Tom stands and roars. "Yeah!! *That's* the way!"

I watch as Tom and Sally exchange a look, common nods of their heads. Their backyard practice has paid off. When the crowd calms down and the game resumes, Tom's in an entirely different mood. Sally's goal was the perfect distraction, the perfect head fake. Tom's ecstatic, and doesn't give a damn about Landon James. I know we're back on the same side.

|||

After soccer we head to Cracker Barrel. Tom's parents are in town for the day, up from their condo in Virginia Beach, and since it is Sal's birthday, they wanted to meet for breakfast. When we arrive, Colleen and Sean Morrissey are rocking comfortably in the wooden chairs that fill the spacious deck, sipping coffee and reading the newspaper. The kids run to them, fall into their laps with hugs and kisses, competing with stories to get their attention.

Tom's mother, Colleen, is lovely. She's supportive and generous and always has a kind word of encouragement for me. Whether she's praising my parenting or laundry skills, she gushes compliments at me as though my proficiency is groundbreaking, as if she herself has never raised kids or gotten a chocolate stain out of a white blouse.

Colleen wears her hair in a perfectly highlighted flip, her acrylic nails are always painted and glossy, her jewelry is a flawless complement to her country-club ensemble. Colleen's on Facebook, she texts on her iPhone, she takes spinning classes and does Pilates, she works a master Sudoku puzzle in pen. At the age of forty-five, she earned an online bachelor's degree in philosophy. Five years ago she joined the pink-ribbon crusade when she got and beat breast cancer inside of a year.

And for reasons unknown to me, she's remained devoted to her husband of forty-five years, a man who drinks too much and, according to Tom, has stepped out on Colleen more than once. To look at Sean, it seems unfathomable. To look at him, *to know him,* he seems like the quintessential family man. He's the guy who carries a photo of each of his five grandchildren in his wallet. He's the guy who pulls out his brag stack of photos for just about anyone to see. He's the guy who will call occasionally, just to say "I love you" and "I'm proud of you." Without reserve, he cried at Tom's and my wedding, the births of our children. He refers to me as his daughter, as if the "in-law" part is just a pesky appendage that serves no use.

Sean is decent-looking, with the same amber waves as Tom, though his face has turned ruddy from too much whiskey and his midsection is a tight medicine ball. He's funny and affectionate and hangs on your every word, shaking his head back and forth in amusement, scattering heavy doses of "Oh my!" and "Who would have thought!" and "Isn't that the best!"

In the beginning, I almost didn't believe Tom. "Are you sure?" I'd implore. "Are you sure he really had affairs?" Even though I was a firsthand deceiver, it was still hard to believe that betrayal could be so perfectly disguised within such an affectionate man.

Sean struggles to keep his whiskey consumption under control and, in twisted measure, he claims success compared to his father, a guy who took his first swallow every morning with breakfast. Similarly, Sean's father claimed success compared to his father, Tom's great-grandfather, who was the real-life version of the archetypal drunken Irishman, stumbling out of Dublin bars after drinking away his entire week's wages. The spiral of alcoholic DNA stopped swirling with Tom, not necessarily because he wasn't susceptible but because he stayed away from the hard stuff just in case. For as long as I've known my husband, he's never once had a drink of whiskey. The occasional beer, a glass of nice red wine with dinner, that's fine, but Tom knows better than to lean too far over his family's Irish cliff, for fear of falling to his death.

With an abundance of grace, Colleen has tolerated and endured Sean's drinking and infidelities. This baffles me because Colleen doesn't seem the type to put up with crap from anyone. This is a woman who, in the midst of chemo treatments for her breast cancer years ago, asked the doctor to up the doses just in case the cancer had any idea of coming back. She wanted to send a strong message. I've never come close to being able to reconcile the incongruence, to puzzle the two pieces together: how Sean could be loving and loyal, and at the same time unfaithful. How Colleen could forgive the unforgivable.

"It had to have killed your mother," I once said to Tom. "She must have felt so betrayed. Her entire life a lie."

"I'm sure," Tom agreed.

"Did he ever *explain* himself?" Always wanting to dig deeper, fascinated by the nuances of moral judgment.

"He said that it had nothing to do with Mom, that he loved Mom more than ever, that the affairs were separate."

"I just can't grasp it."

"There's more to the story," Tom said. "*Technically,* the times when Dad stepped out, he and Mom were separated."

"You're kidding me." Sean and Colleen were a package deal to me; I couldn't fathom the two of them apart.

"Yeah," Tom said. "There were a few times when Mom had had enough. Dad was drinking too much. It led to a bunch of crap. She basically threw him out. He'd binge, meet up with his 'lady friend,' and eventually crawl back to Mom."

For a long moment I just sat back, blinking at him as I assimilated this new information. "That does change things—the fact that they were technically separated." Even then—in a situation that had nothing to do with me—I set my bargaining wheels spinning, rationalizing the lines of morality, testing the outer edge before the slippery slope turned into a landslide.

Now it was Tom's turn to blink at me. "I don't believe being separated excused him from anything," he said. "Marriage is marriage."

"Yes, but there is a start and a finish, and in their case, some 'pauses' in between."

"Nope," Tom said. "The commitment is the bond. That should never be broken."

"Then why aren't you harder on him?"

"Because he couldn't help himself—because of the drink."

I would come to learn that the booze was a perpetual Get Out of Jail Free card for Tom's father and Tom's brother, Patrick, a disease over which they were powerless.

|||

Domenic and Danny are rocking on chairs next to their grandparents and the girls are browsing in the gift shop when our name is called. We sit at one of the larger tables, order coffee and juice, hot cocoa for the kids. Once we put in our orders, and the kids go and sit by the fireplace to play the golf tee/pegboard game, we settle in for a conversation. The starting point is always the same. Never a gentle step onto solid ground. Something more akin to jumping off a cliff.

"How's Patrick?" Tom asks, broaching everyone's greatest worry, his baby brother's magnetic pull toward the pub and the bottle.

"He's good!" Sean says, always happier to skirt difficult topics, always happier to talk about the kids and their activities. "That little Mia, she's a pip!" he says of Patrick's five-year-old daughter. Patrick and his family live only a few miles from where Sean and Colleen live in Virginia Beach.

Tom and I both look at Colleen, the one who is likely to have more information.

"He's sober, as far as I know," Colleen says. "But I have a bad feeling."

"Why?" Tom asks, leaning in.

"He wasn't feeling well the other day so he stayed home and of course, you know Patrick, he didn't call his boss to tell him that he'd be a no-show. His boss was furious. He had to let Patrick go."

"Does he have something else lined up?" Tom asks.

"He's trying," Colleen says. "But mainly he's back to talking about baseball, how he should have gone to college, how everything could have been different."

In high school Patrick was the star pitcher of the baseball team, an unassuming guy who could throw a fastball with bullet precision, leaving the batter shaking his head and feeling like a dope. He was recruited by a handful of colleges, and then, just as he was making up his mind between them, he was taken by the Arizona Diamondbacks with their last pick in the draft. Against everyone's advice, he declined full-ride scholarships and tried to make it as a pro. And he appeared to be on his way, moving up in just a matter of months from Class A to Triple-A, with his agent talking about a possible late-season call-up to the big league team's bull pen, when he blew out his shoulder. Instead of the pros, he ended up with career-ending surgery, months of physical therapy, and a deep depression. That was his first bender. It landed him first in the gutter, and then in rehab.

"Do you think he's going to drink?" Tom asks his mother. I see my husband start to agitate, watch his knee bob up and down, his fingers tap on the table.

"By now I recognize the spiral," she says, shrugging. "It's always the same: he loses a job, starts to feel sorry for himself, falls into a depression about how it could have been different. You know, then we find him passed out in a ditch. What are you going to do?" Colleen looks away and takes a deep breath. We all know her stance. Though it kills her, she believes in tough love. Sean is the opposite, he's more the enabler. And Tom wants to be the savior, the one who swoops in on a magic carpet, the one who rescues everyone from the pain.

Sean puts an arm around his wife, comforts her. I wonder how she can take it. Comfort from a man who is partially to blame for his son's affliction. Doesn't she ever want to shout: *Maybe if you didn't hit the bottle so hard our son wouldn't be in this spot!*

"It's not too late for him!" Tom says. "He's only thirty-five years old. He can still go back to school. He can coach. Is he going to his meetings?"

"He tells me he is," Colleen says. "I know they're offered every night in the church hall right next to his house."

"He has to keep up with the meetings," Tom says. "He doesn't stand a chance if he's not working the steps, leaning on his sponsor. You know what? I'm going to get involved, call his sponsor. Maybe Patrick'll come up and stay with us for a while. I can give him some work to do around the house. Maybe some neighbors need some work done. Nobody's as good with a hammer as Patrick."

Tom's face is turning red and his eyes are welling up, so for his sake I'm careful to conceal my irritation at the thought of Patrick unpacking his problems under our roof. Tom can't stand to think of his baby brother floundering, veering into the path of destruction. Tom needs to stick his hand in it somehow, *control* the situation, pull his brother out of the GD gutter. Tom told me that when he boxed in college it all came down to instincts, knowing when to step out of harm's way. He ignores this instinct when it comes to his brother, and Patrick doesn't have a shred of it, a guy who seems helpless to do anything but lead with his chin.

"Oh, honey," Colleen says. "Your brother knows you're here. He knows we're all here. We can't do it for him. You know that. He needs to face this on his own. All we can do is offer him our love and support."

"Have you talked to Kathy?" I ask.

Colleen gives a little shrug. "As much as she wants to be talked to."

Kathy, Patrick's wife, is patient and good but has always kept her distance from the rest of us, almost like she wants to minimize the collateral damage should she and Patrick fail. I've taken the opposite strategy: diving headlong into Tom's family, like paying a premium on a life-insurance policy.

"How can I just sit idly by and let him self-destruct?" Tom wants to know. "How can there not be *more* for us to do? He's my brother. It's not right that I get to have this great life, with a job and a house and a family, and he gets to be cursed by the Morrissey plague."

An unwelcome thought gnaws at my consciousness: that life has a way of evening out, that the tables may someday turn, with Patrick thriving and Tom and me festering in a ditch.

"Pick up the phone, son," Sean says. "I'm sure he would like it if you just called him and talked to him."

The food comes and we corral the kids back to the table. It's a frenzy to get them situated with butter, syrup, and jam. We help the boys cut their pancakes, get an extra plate for Emily so that her French toast isn't touching her scrambled eggs. Sally polishes off her meal before most of us have started, pulls out a *Little House* from her bag, and starts reading.

I squeeze Tom's leg under the table. I know he's hurting. He takes Patrick's failures so personally, as if he could have done something to change his brother's path. But I know that there is guilt in being successful, in having what his brother doesn't. Tom looks at me, fakes a smile, and offers me a bite of his pecan pancakes.

CHAPTER SEVEN
Admitting Wrongs

TOM

IF YOU'VE NEVER BEEN KNOCKED out, it would be nearly impossible to imagine what it's like to be bouncing on your toes one second and then flat on your back the next. You regain your sight before your hearing, so as your eyes flutter open, you see the ref's fingers flipping out in a counting motion before you hear the numbers coming from his mouth: *seven, eight, nine.*

I never set out to box. A recruiter saw me working out on the bags one day in the college gym and convinced me to give it a try. I had the right body type and, most of all, my reach was good, my arms a good inch longer than most others'. The workouts were tough and it didn't take long before I was in awesome shape, but I never got too into the actual fights. Being knocked out made me feel like I'd somehow been tricked, and knocking the other guy out just made me feel like a creep. I'm not much of a fighter, I guess.

Which isn't to say I don't have a temper. My Irish blood boils easily. I often worry that Sally inherited that gene from me, the way she gets worked up sometimes, so competitive and confrontational. Today I found my fingers clenched in fists twice: once when talking to Mary about that asshole Landon James, pretty boy running for the Senate. And again when I heard about my brother falling off the wagon. Poor Patrick, a magnet for bad luck.

I never minded that Mary had boyfriends before me. Hell, I had girlfriends, too; I get that we were already thirty years old by the time we met. But she was stuck on that loser for six years. I mean, hell, she must have really wanted him to stick around for that long. And she still gets jittery when we talk about him, like she can't control the octave of her voice. It bugs me that after all these years he still gets under her skin.

And Patrick, my baby brother cursed with the Morrissey taste for whiskey. He can't help how he is, any more than if he were a diabetic. Bad luck follows him. When he was in high school he pitched five no-hitters in a row, all while batting .440. The scouts were wining and dining him—not just the Diamondbacks but the Tigers, the Phillies. They'd take him to Outback Steakhouse: *Give this kid your biggest and best filet, a lobster tail, and throw in a Bloomin' Onion, why don't you?* They were schmoozing the hell out of him. Mom told him to be smart: go to college. Take the scholarship money. Dad was Dad, caught up in it all, telling him, "Son, when are you ever gonna have an opportunity like this again? God's smiling on you, son. Take a chance on the big leagues." That left me, the levelheaded older brother who always had the right answers. Patrick looked up to me like I could see his future and knew just how to steer him. He would have done whatever I said. I started out in Mom's camp, told him to think of his future, to go to college. That the chances were slim to none that he'd be called up from the minors.

But then there was the night in June when he was pitching against his American Legion squad's bitterest rivals. Legion games don't usually draw many fans, but this one did—partly because of the rivalry, but mainly because of Patrick. Word was out: the Diamondbacks had drafted him. I was sitting on the metal bleachers, breathing in the aroma of cigarettes, hot dogs, and popcorn. Patrick had a perfect game going and the crowd started chanting his name, "Patrick, Patrick, Patrick," until finally there was just a combined roar, a crescendo of unified spirit, cheering on my brother. The stadium lights, the smells, the sounds. The electricity—I really felt it, like someone was running a current through the bleachers under me.

As each inning passed and I watched my baby brother pitch flawlessly, I started to reconsider my position. His skill and poise were years beyond high school. That's when I got it: He wasn't just a good *high school* pitcher, he was an *awesome* pitcher, period. He already had four legitimate pitches and a fastball in the mid-90s. He didn't just show promise, he issued guarantees. That's when I changed my mind. I pulled him aside later that night. I told him that he oughta take a chance. That he was good. *Really good.* That he ought to go with the scouts, go to the minors, take the risk. He was so excited because, of course, I was telling him exactly what he wanted to hear. He wanted my blessing to take a chance and here I was, giving it to him.

By month's end he was playing for the Diamondbacks' Class-A affiliate in South Bend. Three weeks after that he was in Double-A Knoxville, his ERA at 2.40, his strikeout total climbing. The D-backs were gearing up for a postseason run, and when the rosters expanded in September they were certain to add bull-pen help. Knoxville worked Patrick hard, showing him off—and then his shoulder blew.

The stars in my brother's eyes went dark.

He saw what was behind the curtain—promises balanced on shaky ground—and the disillusionment was nothing short of devastating. We talked about college even though the scholarship offers were gone, but he had no interest. The one thing he wanted in life was gone.

His failure—the loss that led him to the bottle—was my fault. He should have gone to college. He might have had a future.

CHAPTER EIGHT

Shortcomings

TOM'S PREOCCUPIED FOR THE REST of the day. At night, after I put the boys in their room, I hear Tom call Patrick on the telephone. I hear Tom's gentle voice. "I know, it's hard. I know you can do it. Are you going to your meetings? Do you want to come stay with us? I know, it's hard . . ."

I walk into Sally's room, my birthday girl, my ten-year-old. "Double digits," I say to her. It blows my mind to think that she's ten. My once chunky, silky-smooth bundle of adoration has grown into a long-legged beauty with her head held high. Only years away from boyfriends and driving and college. I sit on her bed, lean into her, kiss her face. I mash my cheek against hers, hold her tight, stroke her hair. "What a day," I say. "Nailing a goal on your ten-year-old birthday."

"It felt *so* good, Mom," she says. "I wish I could make a goal like that every day."

"I don't think it would feel so special if you did it every day," I say. "It's the scarcity of things that makes them so amazing."

"You act like *we're* scarce," Sal says. "But we're here every day."

"Kids are different," I say. "A mother's love for her children, it's like . . ." I struggle to finish my sentence because the words I feel are bigger than the letters that could comprise them. "It's precious. Like it *is* scarce. You're right."

"You're silly," Sally says.

"I know," I say, and stop myself from telling her what it's like to be a mom: walking along a cliff of worry, breathing even though you're holding your breath.

"Happy birthday, ten-year-old," I say. "You really are my special gift, Sal. God really was smiling on me and Daddy the night you were born."

"Tell me the story," she says, snuggling her body around her pillows.

I can tell from the tone of her voice that she's asking for my sake, not hers. Sal knows how much I love traditions, stories. She's indulging me tonight. She's outgrown my nostalgia, but she knows that I haven't.

"I thought you'd never come out," I say. "I'd been at the hospital for an entire day and a half, when all of a sudden I started to feel different, like there was all of this weight pressing down on me. I told Daddy, 'I think it's time,' and Nana and Pop, and Grandma and Grandpa, and all of your aunts, filed out of the room, hollering, 'Good luck! We love you!' Then you started to come out, and when Daddy saw your little face he started to cry like I've never seen him cry before. 'She's beautiful!' he yelled, and then the nurse held up a little mirror for me to see you. I propped myself up on my elbows and saw your little head and the mat of copper hair swirled against your scalp and I thought, 'Oh my, she's got her daddy's hair,' and it was the happiest sight I had ever seen in my whole life because I wanted you to look like your daddy. I wanted you to be a daddy's girl because I knew how much Dad would love being your daddy. As much as I loved you and wanted you, I had already carried you for nine months. It only seemed fair that Daddy should get something, too. Then you slithered your way out of me—"

"Ooooh, yuck!" Sally squeals.

"The nurses got you cleaned up, put you on my chest, and when I looked at your face for the first time I thought that I'd never catch my breath again."

"Because I was so adorable."

"You were adorable," I agree, "but you didn't look like I expected. I thought you would look like Dad, because I had seen your hair first, but you didn't, really. You were your own person from the start. And I guess it was just the awesomeness of it, of you being *you,* not me, not Dad. It hit me so hard in my chest that this whole being-a-mother business was a lot more than I thought. And when that thought settled, I just stared at you, and Sally, I'm *serious,* there were no words to describe what it was like to hold you that first time. I just remember thinking, there is no WAY that there is another mother out there who loves her daughter as much as I love my new daughter. That's how I felt. Like my love was the fiercest, the biggest, best love in the world. I felt sorry for every other kid in the world, like 'Oh, poor things,' because there was no way that their mothers loved them like I loved you."

"Until you saw Dad's love," Sally says, filling in the words for me, having memorized this story throughout her life.

"That's right," I say. "Until I saw how Daddy loved you. He cradled you and rocked you, and the grandmas and the aunts had to beg him for a turn to hold you. That first night I was so tired, I fell fast asleep. When I woke up I saw Dad on the sofa holding you, tears streaming down his face, singing some song he made up."

"'Sally, my girl, best in the world,'" Sally sings.

"Yep." I nod my head. "That's how it went."

I kiss Sal and tuck her blankets tightly around her, and walk out of her room singing, "'Sally, my girl, best in the world.'"

|||

Once in bed, I open my book and stare at the pages, but think of Landon James. There were four years in between the time I met Landon for my first and second time. Following his stint as a summer associate, he went back to Chicago to finish his last year of law school. That year, in a weak moment, I wrote him a letter, asking him what he had been up to, telling him how I had left the law firm and was finishing school. It was juvenile on my part to think that a rising star like Landon would have an interest in an undergrad office clerk like me. He never responded to my letter and years passed by, but still I never forgot him. All I needed to do was to close my eyes and imagine our first night at Old Ebbitt Grill, and like that, I could feel his hands pushing up my thighs, the brush of his lips against mine, his fingers finding flesh under my blouse as he kissed me good night. I could see perfectly well how his face changed when he'd told me about his friend who had committed suicide, and more than anything, I could call up the determination in his voice as he spoke of the future.

I was twenty-three years old and in law school when I had lunch with David Kaye, an old lawyer buddy of mine from my days at Becker, Fox & Zuckerman.

"Looking good, Russo," David said. "A little stressed, a little sleep-deprived. Exactly how a first-year law student should look."

"Not like you," I said. "Living the life of Riley. Is that how it is once you're a partner? Easy street." I signaled to David's wardrobe: worn khakis and a rumpled, untucked polo.

"Hey, I did some work today," he said. "I just didn't have any client meetings."

"You did some work? What does that mean, you bossed around a bunch of overworked associates?"

David laughed, then changed the subject to my love life. "Seeing anyone?"

"Like I have time to date," I said, reaching for the basket of warm rolls and thinking about a disastrous date I'd gone on just a few weeks ago with a slick litigator who talked about himself for two hours straight.

"How sad," David joked. "No time for love."

"I barely have time to study and eat." My mind flipped to my refrigerator, which maybe held a Tupperware container of left-over ziti from Mom and a lone Sam Adams. I considered pocketing a few of the rolls and squares of butter for later.

"In that case, never mind," he said, reaching for a roll himself.

"In what case?"

"I had someone I thought I might introduce you to," he said. "But if you're too busy . . ."

"I didn't say I was too busy," I said. "Who's the guy?"

"A nice guy," David said. "New to town, just took a position with Myers & Jones."

"How do you know him?"

"Met him years ago, when he was a summer associate at Becker."

"How many years ago?" I asked. "Do I know him?"

He thought for a minute. "It was probably four years ago," he said. "Were you still at the firm then?"

"I was," I said, and because he was talking about "the summer of Landon," I had to carefully steady my breath so as not to hyperventilate.

"Then maybe you know him."

"What's his *name*?" I said, tapping my finger on the table.

"Landon."

"Landon . . . seriously?"

"Landon James."

I nodded, attempted to take a bite of roll, but the dough seemed to expand in my throat.

"Seeing that your face just turned a lovely shade of plum, I'll take it that you do know Landon James."

"I met him," I said. "We spent some time together. Four years is a long time ago. I barely remember him."

"So what do you think? Should I set it up?"

"Set it up, don't set it up," I said. "Whatever."

"If you're not sure . . . ," David said, appraising me carefully.

"Set it up," I said. "Just set it up, okay?"

A week later, I was scheduled to meet Landon James for drinks. The same Landon James who had taken me fishing, who had leaned into me and stared into my eyes and said that he was falling hard. The same Landon James who drove me to the top of a scenic mountain, and then kicked me off the cliff.

I spent an hour the night before planning what I would wear, trying to achieve a just-came-from-school appearance while still looking attractive. The last thing I wanted was for Landon to think that I primped for hours getting ready for him. It was humiliating enough to recall that I had written him a letter like a lovesick schoolgirl. I called my sister Angela, the most fashionable of the four of us sisters, for advice, and she suggested my black pencil skirt with high-heeled leather boots and a clingy cardigan.

"Just in case I want to turn a trick later in the night?" I joked, smiling through the phone lines at my sister, who had a special fondness for tight, black leather.

I spotted Landon and David sitting at an outdoor table on the patio of Morton's, a popular lawyer hangout. I hung back, taking him in. He looked the same: bold, towering, Superman. His broad shoulders in his expensive suit, his floppy yet perfectly behaved hair, his killer smile that brought me to my knees. *Turn around,* my mind blared. *Leave while you can.* Somehow I knew that seeing Landon again would be no different than taking a hit of heroin. I'd want more. He'd be stingy with it. The pain of withdrawal would be bugs crawling under my skin.

Yet I fluffed my hair, sucked in my stomach, puffed out my chest, and sashayed over, sliding in next to David.

"Mary!" David cheered. "Great to see you. This is Landon James."

I held out my hand, and as he and I shook, the junk hit my bloodstream like the strike of a match. I would like him too much, I would fall too hard, I would lay out my heart, and whether or not Landon would protect it was anyone's guess.

"Well, well, Mary Margaret Russo," Landon said. "Are you old enough to order a beer now?"

"Way past the age of majority," I said, feeling myself blush.

"Are you sure?" Smiling the smile I'd been seeing in my mind for four years. "Because I could order for you."

"Feel free," I said. "I like being waited on."

Landon and I locked eyes, and my cheeks pulled into an uncontrollable smile. He was even more gorgeous than I remembered: brown, wavy hair, steel-blue eyes, perfectly square jaw. I was sorry I hadn't taken Angela's advice of downing a shot of tequila on my way in.

"Seems like we're all old friends here." David was grinning. "And as much as I'd like to bear witness to this wonderful reunion, the wife and children are expecting me."

I cocked an eyebrow at David, daring him to tell me that he was truly headed home, not just next door to another bar.

For the next hour, Landon filled me in on his new position at Myers & Jones; how he'd graduated three years ago and had been working as an assistant US district attorney in the Eastern Division of Chicago, prosecuting everything from tax fraud, embezzlement, bank robbery, sale and possession of narcotics and firearms. He was now ready to put in a number of years with a high-profile corporate firm.

"It's a ten-year plan," he explained. "By the time I'm thirty-five, I'd like to have some firm footing in the Republican Party."

"You want to be a *politician*?" I asked. "How'd I miss that?"

"I've always wanted to serve," he said. "I've had a Reagan obsession my entire life."

"Serve in what capacity?" I asked, still baffled.

"If everything goes according to plan, I'll have won a Virginia state senate seat within the next few years. From there, who knows? Maybe attorney general? Maybe the governor? Maybe Congress."

"Wow, and to think that my goals are to be employed with my student loans paid off in ten years."

We talked easily for the next three hours. At some point we ordered dinner. And wine with dinner. Then after-dinner drinks. We ended up on the floor of my apartment, sitting across from each other, our knees bumping. Landon leaned into me, wrapped his arms around my back, and pulled me toward him. We kissed long, luxurious kisses.

"Are you sure you want to be a politician?" I asked, my mouth brushing against his.

"Are you sure you want to be a lawyer?" he asked, kissing me more.

"No," I said, and then burst out laughing. But it was true—being a lawyer was my fallback plan. I kept it to myself around my hard-charging female friends, but what I really wanted was to be a wife and a mom. What I really wanted was a house to call my own, bedrooms bursting with children, dinners around the same table every night. But I certainly wasn't going to tell Landon James that, or any guy, for that matter. "I'm just kidding," I said. "I really like law school, and I'm sure being a lawyer will be great."

"What now?" Landon asked, leaning in, kissing me again.

"You should go," I finally said. "I can drive you home."

"I was a Boy Scout, remember?" he said. "I'll find my way."

"Last time you tried to find your way home, you must have gotten lost. I didn't see you for four years."

"That's not going to happen again."

"How can I be so sure?" I said, leaning in and kissing him.

"Because when I want something, I go after it. And right now I want to see you in your Girl Scout uniform. And I'm not going to rest until I do."

"Maybe I'll even put my hair up in a bun," I said, gently biting his lower lip.

After he left, I lay on my back on the floor where we had just kissed and called Angie. "He's perfect," I said.

"Take a breath," she said. "No one's perfect."

"He is, Ang. Seriously, I could die."

The next day I woke up early and showered because I didn't want to miss hearing the phone when Landon called. By noon the phone still hadn't rung. By midnight I had checked for a dial tone umpteen times, and still no call. At first I honestly couldn't believe it. And then I did. Two more days passed—on campus, in class, at home—and I barely managed to cut through the thick fog of my days. "Are you okay, Mary?" friends asked. I nodded but couldn't speak. It was happening again. Landon had reeled me in and then let me go. How could it feel so right to be with him and then this? Angie called, almost on the hour. "It's better to know now, Mare, what kind of guy you're dealing with."

"Maybe something happened," I said, excusing his abominable behavior, giving him the benefit of the doubt that perhaps he was in a car crash, or suddenly struck mute.

Angie only sighed.

It wasn't until the fourth day that Landon called. "Hey, you," he said. "Wow, what a busy week. Been thinking about you, though. Are you free this Saturday night?"

The previous four days had been torturous. Physically, I suffered—nausea, fatigue, insomnia. Mentally, I shrunk—my self-worth boiled down and scorched. I had rehearsed what I would say to him a thousand times, "Go to hell!" being at the top of my list. Yet when I heard his voice, the heroin rush charged every atom of my being, and I bargained that maybe a busy week excused his behavior. I was desperate to see him again. I was desperate for another hit to take the edge off. "Sure," I said. "Why not?"

CHAPTER NINE
Deserving of Love

IT'S BEEN NEARLY A MONTH since my conversation with Landon about the photo and I've been saying a novena every night. Tom's busy at work and, while the kids are intuitive, they're also blessedly self-centered. They don't seem to notice that I'm preoccupied, clumsy, and accident-prone. They don't seem to notice that my head is dizzy with thought. They don't complain when I burn the French toast, or drop a plate, or allow them a soda for dinner instead of milk. My sister Angie is the only one who questions me. "You're acting *weird*, Mare."

So far the threatening photo of Landon and me hasn't shown up. Each day I flip the channels between Fox, CNN, and the local news. I search Landon James on my laptop for new stories. I read blogs, listen to radio commentaries. The photo hasn't surfaced. But still, I feel sick. What if. What if the photo does show up and I have to explain to Tom what I was doing in DC that day with Landon? Tom doesn't deserve to be hurt by this.

Time passes, though, and buffs my worry until it's no longer sharp. Each day it slips a little further from my thoughts. A sliver burrowed under my skin.

The rain starts to fall sometime before dinner on the night before Thanksgiving. Just as I'm spooning pot roast over egg noodles, an enormous clap of thunder sets the sky into a torrential pour. The girls run to the window to see the black clouds racing in, shrouding the last patches of struggling daylight.

"Get back from the windows," Tom says, and the girls leap onto the sofa, huddled together, loving every minute of the brewing thunderstorm, with all of the tumult of a Greek myth, Zeus throwing a tantrum. Meanwhile the boys huddle around my legs, koala bears clipped to a tree.

Tom clicks on the television and a warning for our county is flashing across the screen. DO NOT LEAVE YOUR HOUSE UNLESS ABSOLUTELY NECESSARY, it warns. The newscaster is using the terms "mini-tornado" and "microburst" to describe the impending storm. An unreasonable frustration swirls in me like the weather outside: Mother Nature is very inconveniently ruining our Thanksgiving plans. If the storm keeps up, my sisters will never make it. As if she were reading my mind, the phone rings and it's Angela.

"J. C., Mare. If you didn't want us to come, you could have just said so."

"I know," I whine. "This sucks. I was really looking forward to seeing everyone."

"I'm sure it'll be fine by tomorrow."

"Maybe," I say, not so sure. "They're talking about downed power lines and trees on the roads."

"Don't stress. We'll talk in the morning."

"Okay, I'll keep positive thoughts."

"Screw that," Angela says. "Say a Hail Mary. For the storm . . . and for whatever else is bugging you."

"I have been," I say.

"Saying Hail Marys?"

"A lot of them," I admit.

"For the storm? Or for what's bugging you?"

"The storm just started," I say, hanging up before I reveal too much. So long as it's not said, perhaps it isn't real. As much as I'd like to tell Angie about the photo, about Landon, I can't, because by now I'm certain of one thing: The truth is owed to Tom, no one else.

The rain pounds throughout the night. Tom and I lie in bed and listen to the *ting-ting-ting* on the rooftop as the wind gusts swoosh by the windows. I get up to check the boys, who are sleeping together in Danny's bed, the one that isn't near the window. Emily, too, is sleeping with Sally, whose bed is squished into a corner and draped with a canopy. Back in bed, I snuggle up to Tom, curling around his muscular arm. I bury my face into it and inhale his scent. "Want to make out?" I say, kissing his shoulder.

"I always want to make out," he says, rolling into me and wrapping his arms around my back.

"It's the flannel, isn't it?" I say. "This nightgown turns you on."

"A warm body turns me on," he says, yanking at my undies.

|||

By the time I open my eyes to see the morning light sneaking through the bottom slats of miniblinds, I already have two kids in my bed. The twins are curled into each other like two sides of a butterfly, and Tom is splayed out on his stomach with his arm covering them like a speed bump. I slip out of bed and look out the window. A beautiful sunny morning, birds are chirping, the sky is resplendent, but the aftermath from the storm looks like Armageddon blew through. There are branches scattered across the driveway, entire trees uprooted across the lawn. It looks as if a giant has come and picked up our neighborhood in its meaty hand and shaken it like a snow globe.

"Tom," I say. "Tommy, wake up. This is nuts."

Tom yawns and stretches and gets out of bed, joining me at the window. "Good God," he says. And then, "Chain saw."

"What about Thanksgiving?"

"We're going to have a great Thanksgiving," Tom says, kissing me smack on the mouth before heading to the bathroom. "But first I'm going to chop up some trees."

Down in the kitchen, I crack a dozen eggs with the phone tucked between my ear and my neck. First I call my mother.

"Ma," I say. "Have you seen it outside? It's like a bomb went off."

"Dad's already outside picking up sticks. We lost one big tree. The one on the side of the house."

"Did it hit the house?" I ask while whisking the eggs, worried that it'll cost them a bundle, money they don't have to spare.

"No, thank the Lord."

"Are you still coming over today?"

"Of course, honey. Early afternoon. Is that okay?"

"Great," I say. "Have you talked to anyone else?" I go to the refrigerator for a splash of milk and a handful of shredded cheese for the eggs.

"Not yet, you want me to?"

"I'll call them now."

"Call me back," she says.

I pour the eggs into the largest skillet and then dial Angela. Angie lives in Alexandria with her husband, Kevin, and two daughters, Shannon and Kelly, whom my girls worship. They're ages thirteen and fifteen, all one hundred fifty pounds of them—*combined*—decked out in their skinny jeans and hooded sweatshirts, glow-in-the-dark braces, and too much product in their hair. You'd never know they wore St. Mary's plaid jumpers and loafers most of the week.

"We'll be there," she says. "It's just a matter of when. Kevin is helping some of the neighbor guys. A pretty big tree came down in the middle of the cul-de-sac. Right now they're trying to wrap a chain around it so they can pull it out further. They'll be chopping it up for a while."

"Okay," I say, trying not to sound insensitive, but I want to know what time everyone will be here so I know when to put the turkey in. "When's your best guess?"

"Early afternoon?" Angie says. "Is that okay?"

"Yeah, okay," I say. "Let's plan on eating at four." I slide a double helping of scrambled eggs onto Sally's plate, a reasonable helping for Emily and Dom, and barely a tablespoon for Danny, my child who barely eats. Set reasonable expectations; can't expect him to clean his plate if there's too much food.

By the time I've poured milk for the kids, Sally has finished her plate of eggs.

"Did you even *chew*?"

Sally shrugs. "They're *eggs*. Can I go out with Dad?" she asks eagerly, wiping her mouth with her sleeve. She loves helping Tom in the yard, especially when power tools are involved.

The others are still waiting for their eggs to cool down.

"Don't you dare go near that chain saw!"

"Like I would," she says.

Next I call Teresa, who is four years older than me and has two boys, Matthew and Luke, who are a few years older than the twins. She lives in the country in Maryland, homeschools her children, and drags them to morning Mass seven days a week. Teresa is unwavering in her devotion to the church. Behind her back, Angie and I refer to her as "Salt of the earth" because she's so *good.* Teresa has x-ray eyes, as if her chosen-one status has given her a greater ability to see inside each person's truth. Once—when I was in law school and my vocabulary was plump with legal terms—I leveled her in a debate. She looked at me with her penetrating eyes and said, "You think you're so smart, Mare. You think you're clever, but really you're just sneaky."

"That's *mean,*" I insisted. "I'm not sneaky. I'm no mystery. What you see is what you get." I can still hear the defensiveness in my voice and see the smirk on my sister's face as she said, "Yeah, right," like it was so obvious to her that I had the potential to lie under oath, if the price were right.

When I talk to her this morning, she hems and haws. "I don't know, Mare. It might be better to stay put."

"Wimp! Get your ass over here." I hardly ever swear, but for some reason, when I'm talking to Teresa, the words flow right out, like I'm trying to shock her for sport.

"We have some parishioners who are homebound and I think I'd better check in on them, bring them a plate, just in case their relatives can't make it to them."

"Isn't there anyone else who can look in on them?"

"Mare," Teresa says in her disapproving tone, as if I have just suggested leaving children in a burning building. "What if it was Mom or Dad left alone on Thanksgiving? Nothing to eat. No heat."

"You're right," I grumble. "St. Teresa. You're a good person," I say, but selfishly wish Teresa could put her family first for just one day out of the year.

Next I talk to my oldest sister, Martina, who is ten years older than me and who was married and pregnant by the time I was in the fifth grade. Her two kids are grown and in college. She started young and never made it to college like Angela, Teresa, and me, but now her kids are independent while we're still raising ours. Sacrifices and trade-offs, that's how it goes. Last time I talked to her, she mentioned going back to school to get her nursing license. She'd make a great nurse. She was the one who taught me and my other sisters how to take care of our babies, how to get them latched on to nurse, how to settle the barking coughs of croup, how to aspirate snot from a screaming baby's nose.

"So, really?" I say. "You're not coming?"

"We'll see," she promises. "Let me check in with the kids and I'll get back to you." Martina's oldest, Kayla, is studying at the University of Virginia, her second oldest, Maria, is at the University of Maryland, and her baby is taking a year off, working at the National Aquarium.

Finally I sit down at the counter with the boys, a cup of coffee in hand.

"Happy Turkey Day," I say to them.

"Gobble, gobble," Dom replies.

"Hey, champs," I say. "What did the turkey say at Thanksgiving dinner?"

"What?"

"I'm stuffed!" I exclaim. "Get it—stuffed?"

"I don't get it," Danny says.

"You stuff a turkey on Thanksgiving," I say. "You put stuffing—you know, dressing—inside of it."

"Inside of it where?" Dom asks.

"In its tummy?" Danny says.

"Well . . . not really. Never mind! You guys want to help Dad pick up sticks?"

"He said he'd give us a penny a stick!"

"Sounds like a good deal," I say. "Go to the bathroom, and put on your fleeces and boots."

Once the boys are outside, I'm left with Emily, who is still at the counter flipping through a Pottery Barn catalog, commenting on what's gorgeous and what's dreadful, sipping her hot cocoa like the queen of England.

I open the refrigerator and start pulling out ingredients for the side dishes. Once I have what I need, I begin cubing the sourdough for the dressing. I chop the onions, celery, and sage, sauté in stainless steel with a chunk of butter, then deglaze with white wine. As I pour the mixture over the bread, I'm already thinking about a leftover turkey sandwich tomorrow, stuffed with dressing and cranberry sauce. Once I clear the kids' dishes, I start in on the butternut squash, mashed potatoes, green bean casserole. I'll leave the gravy for Mom. She has a magical way of scraping brown bits off the bottom of the roaster with a sprinkling of flour and a half bottle of red wine.

Once I get the turkey in, I'll focus on setting the table. I *love* setting the table, pulling out the special tablecloth passed down from my grandmother, rinsing off the china from our wedding, retrieving the good wineglasses from the hutch. And I always sprinkle the kids' turkey art projects around the table: a papier-mâché turkey here, a pilgrim made out of paper towel tubes there, a cornucopia stuffed with clay fruit.

Just as I'm heading down to the basement to get the turkey from the extra refrigerator, Sally and Tom burst through the door. Sal's crying and Tom's muttering words of assurance. Sally's hand is bleeding. Badly. Tom's holding his shirt over it, applying pressure.

"What happened?" I say, praying that five fingers are still attached.

"She cut herself on the scythe," Tom says through clenched teeth.

"The *scythe*?" I gasp, peeling the bloody T-shirt from her hand, revealing the palm, with a gash about two inches long, splayed open like a scored sausage.

"Ow!" she howls.

"Why'd you have the scythe, Sally?"

Sally looks down and then at Tom with pleading eyes.

"She was trying to help," Tom says, and at once I know what happened. Sally overstepped her boundaries. Trying to be a big shot. Trying to be older than ten years old. All of a sudden I know why Tom's ready to spit fire.

"I wanted to help Daddy," she cries.

"I asked her to pick up branches," Tom says. "Branches! Just a few minutes ago she was picking up branches."

"But then I saw a big branch that needed to be cut, and I thought I could do it myself."

"Gosh darn you, Sally," I mutter under my breath. And *thank you, God,* at the same time. "Miss Independent. Don't you think Daddy knows what he's talking about? Don't you think he has his reasons for not letting you use dangerous equipment?"

"I'm sorry," she says.

Sorry 'til next time. Sorry 'til you decide it's okay to scald crème brûlée with a blowtorch. Sorry 'til you decide it's okay to hatchet open a watermelon.

I look again at her cut, cover it back up, and press. I have a scar in the same spot from a bagel-slicing incident.

"She'll probably need a tetanus shot," Tom says.

"The emergency room on Thanksgiving. That'll be fun." I look at Tom. He's shouldering the blame, I can tell, when clearly it's not his to carry. But that's how it is when you're a parent. If an accident occurs on your watch, you always feel responsible.

"Which sounds least horrible to you?" I ask him. "Going to the emergency room, or staying here with the remaining three kids?"

"I'd definitely rather stay here," he says. "But seriously, I don't care. Whatever you say. You're the boss."

"I'll take her." I'll hold her hand and look into her eyes while the doctor sews up her palm. I'll pocket her look of betrayal as I pin her down and keep her still. That's what moms do. We sit on our kids as they scream for us to stop.

"How many do we have coming for Thanksgiving? When do we need to put the bird in?" Tom asks.

"Right now just Nana and Pop and Angela's family are coming. Looks like Teresa and Martina are backing out. And the turkey doesn't need to go in until eleven o'clock or so."

"It's only nine o'clock," Tom says. "You should be back by then. If not, just call me and tell me what to do."

"The boys have had a busy week," I say. "Don't hesitate to put them in front of the television."

"The doctor is going to want to know why a ten-year-old was handling a scythe," Tom says.

"I doubt it, honey. They're used to seeing kids who get into things they shouldn't. But if he asks, I'll just tell him that it's part of the slave-labor camp we've got going on here."

"Seriously, Mare. Make sure you tell him that I didn't let her."

I grab Tom's chin and give him a kiss. Good man. Good, responsible daddy.

"It's *okay*, honey," I say. "Everything will be back to normal in a few hours."

"Call me as soon as you hear anything." He bends down and kisses Sally. "Be brave, okay?"

"Can I bring Missy?" she asks. Missy is Sally's American Girl doll, and though she claims to have outgrown her, she still sleeps with her every night.

Two hours later we've made it through triage and we're waiting in the lobby. The edges of Sally's cut have dried and curled back, like they're running away from each other. I wonder if waiting this long is going to make the stitches worse. I don't mention this to Sally, who's reading her myth book with her arm held out to the side. Better to let the doctor explain. When I lean near her, I see that she's studying a picture of a Greek god—and he happens to be holding a scythe. Maybe a sickle. My heart flips. Is *this* where she got the idea? "Sally?"

"It's Kronos," she says. "He's the one who ate all of his children because he feared they'd overpower him. Except Zeus. Rhea kept Zeus hidden and instead gave Kronos a rock to swallow."

"Did he fall for it?" I ask, distracted by finding out about the repercussions for this wife pulling a fast one on her husband.

"Yeah," Sally says, wide-eyed. "Eventually Zeus made Kronos barf up all of his siblings and Kronos was sentenced to Tartarus for life."

"Tartarus?"

"An abyss—below the underworld."

"And the moral of this story?"

Sally exhales, stares at her cut as if it's a miniature version of the chasm to which Kronos was sentenced. "The books would say that it was about power, but I think it's more about how the gods thrashed around because they weren't sure who they were."

I nod, try to swallow, and rub my daughter's back. Her profundity has left me speechless. "And the scythe? Were you trying to be like Kronos?"

"No!" Sally says. "I was just trying to cut the branch in half."

"Okay, Sal."

"Besides, I'd never want to be like Kronos. He hurt his father, and what could be worse than that?"

When Sally's eyes meet mine I shrug and shake my head, because she's right, there could be nothing worse.

When the nurse calls us back, Sally crawls onto the table and I settle into the chair. The nurse informs us that it'll be a while longer. When she leaves, Sally slides down the table and onto my lap.

"Sorry I'm ruining Thanksgiving," she says, burrowing her head into the crook of my neck.

"Oh, honey, you made a mistake," I say, rubbing her back. "You love your daddy, you were trying to help him out, so I can't really be too mad at you. Next time, just be more careful, okay?"

With Sally in my lap I stare at the muted television bolted into the corner of the room. The news is on and a recap of the Macy's parade is playing through: Snoopy, Garfield. The same floats every year. When the reel is over, the newscaster shuffles her papers, and then a photo of Landon is displayed in the corner. Navy suit, red tie, ice-blue eyes, square jaw. Determined. Motivated. *Trust me*, he seems to be saying. *I can make a difference.*

I find the clicker and turn up the volume so I can just barely hear. The newscaster proceeds to give an update on the race. Landon is holding his own, and there is talk about the incumbent Republican senator retiring. This would be incredibly good news for Landon. The chance of another candidate popping up now is unlikely, the newscaster says. But if the incumbent doesn't retire, Landon might have a real battle.

The nurse comes back in holding a silver tray with a gloved hand. A long syringe stretches across it—the tetanus shot. Sally burrows her head into my chest while the nurse injects her. Sally yelps, then cries, then softens into my lap. I stroke her hair and whisper, "Shh, shh, it's okay."

"The doctor will be right in to stitch up her hand," she says and then leaves.

With my free hand I call my mother, though I know cell phones are prohibited in the hospital.

"Ma, real quick," I say.

"Tom's already called," she says. "How's our angel?"

"She's doing good," I report. "Can you call Tom and lead him through putting the turkey in the oven?"

"Oh, honey," she says. "We're on our way over now. We'll get everything ready. You just take care of that girl of ours."

I hang up and twist my head around to look at Sally. My heart skips when I see that her face has turned blotchy and her eyes seem buggy.

"Baby, are you okay?"

"Uh-huh," she says, sitting up. And then, "My chest. It feels kind of hard to breathe."

I dash into the hall and call for the nurse. "Hurry! Please."

The nurse rushes in, snapping the earpieces of her stethoscope into place. She listens to her heart. "Allergic reaction. I'll get the doctor."

Seconds later, a team of doctors pushes through the doors, a metal cart jangles in front of one of the nurses, stadium lights seem to appear overhead. I hear the rip of paper as instruments are freed from their sterile bags. I watch as a young doctor presses his stethoscope to Sally's chest. I smell antiseptic—alcohol or iodine—and see a dozen hands working at once. A decade of *ER* episodes flash through my mind, how the dumb twelve-year-old doctors always screwed up the intubations, how the emergency room always seemed more like a combat zone, where every illness was life threatening and every decision was a dire, last-ditch effort.

The doctor—Indian perhaps—speaks crisply in British English, telling her to administer a drug. The nurse fills the syringe with a clear liquid in a glass bottle, flicks the needle with her finger, and jabs it into Sally's arm before I can even get to her side. Before I can dispense false promises that everything will be okay.

"This is an antitoxin," the nurse says.

"Is anyone in your family allergic to the tetanus vaccine?" the doctor asks, though he says *allergic* like aller-jeck, and my dizzy head keeps repeating his word over and over.

"No!" I say. "I mean, I don't know. I don't think so. I've never heard anything." But then again, maybe. Maybe there's a history that I don't know about. I bobble the question and my answer, because I don't have the words to make this better. The guilt claws at my neck with a thick accusation of *You've done her wrong,* and I nod my understanding because the gravity of my ignorance is life threatening. I haven't just sent her outside to play without sunscreen, or failed to apply bug spray before camp—my not knowing could be fatal.

"She's responding to the antitoxin," the doctor says. He's listening to Sally's chest, her hospital gown is parted, her beautiful tanned skin stretched across her precious ribs. *Make her better, please. Next time I'll know all of the answers. Next time I won't let you give her tetanus or anything else that might hurt my baby. Next time there will be no secrets.*

An hour passes. Sally's face is no longer blotchy. Her breathing is no longer labored. But the doctors still want to watch her.

I step out of the room and call Tom. "Tetanus?" he says. He can't believe she had a reaction. I can hear my mom in the background, clucking her concerns, saying that no one in our family has reacted badly to the tetanus vaccine. Tom says he doesn't think anyone in his family has either, but he'll call his mom as soon as we hang up.

"It's over now," I say.

"Yeah, but we should know," Tom says.

"Tom," I say, laying my hand over my chest, feeling the heavy thumps. "Tom . . ."

"Are you okay?"

"No," I say, "I'm not. I have to tell you something."

I don't know what I'm doing. I don't know what I'm starting. But the ache inside me is cracking my ribs, and I no longer want to hurt. I no longer want the guilt of knowing what everyone else does not.

"Mary?"

"Mom?" I hear Sally call from her room.

I blink, look in on Sally, and now I'm back and my courage is gone. "It was so scary," I say. "That's all. I was so scared."

"She's okay," Tom says. "Thank God."

I know that Tom's crossing himself at the same time I am.

We breathe, listening to each other as if we're holding hands over the phone.

"How long will you be?" Tom asks.

"They haven't said. I'll ask the nurse the next time I see her. I just want to get her stitched up and home for Thanksgiving."

"We all do," Tom says. "But if the doctors want to keep her to make sure she's okay, then you'll just have to stay. Thanksgiving will be here whenever you guys get home." Tom's perspective on everything is infinitely more patient, calm, and reasoned than mine. Tom's the guy who can look at this situation and say, "Who cares? It's just another dinner. What we really have to be thankful for is a houseful of healthy kids."

I know that, too, but sitting in this little room with the fluorescent lights bearing down on me like an inquisition is just too much. What other dangers are lurking around a corner for her? What if there's something else even more reactive out there that could make her throat close like the shutter of a camera? What if it were to happen again when we didn't have a team of doctors outside our room? What if . . . ?

The nurse walks by in her efficient manner, charts stacked in her arms, glasses secured on the top of her head, pen behind her ear.

"Nurse!" I say, and walk to the open door. "How long 'til the doctor comes in?"

"It shouldn't be too much longer. He just finished up with a guy from a car accident."

"Oh, yikes! Is he okay?"

"If you call two busted ribs and a broken arm okay," she says lightly.

"What about the reaction?" I say. "Are you sure that she's out of the woods? Is it possible for her to have another one?"

"Doubtful," the nurse says. "She'll be fine now." The nurse takes a step.

I grab her arm, release it quickly. "What about in the future? How do I keep her safe?"

"Other than doing what you're doing—being a vigilant mom and knowing your family's medical history—there's not much more you can do. With kids, things are going to come up. The doctor will be in soon to suture her wound," she says, and this time walks away before I'm able to ask more.

"Sally, honey. I'm going to step outside and make one more phone call, okay?"

"Can't you call from in here? In case the doctor comes?"

"They really don't want people using cell phones in the rooms."

"But you just called Dad," Sally points out. "Why do you have to call him again?"

"I just need to ask your father something," I say. "Honey, just give me a second. I'll be right back."

"Tell Daddy that I'm sorry," Sally says, her bottom lip quivering. The enormity of the day is finally hitting her.

"It's okay, baby," I say. "I'll stay. I can text instead."

My hand trembles, but I have no choice. For Sally, I need to know. With my phone shrouded in my lap, I punch in the first three digits of the cryptic cell phone. The number populates the screen. I look up at Sal. She's staring at the door, probably wondering when the doctor will arrive. I exhale in a slow stream, look down at my phone, and attempt to put into words this gigantic question I need the answer to.

I need to know if anyone in your family is allergic to the tetanus vaccine. For my daughter—for Sally's sake—she had a reaction. Let me know ASAP.

I look back at Sally—dear, sweet, precious Sally—the sacrificial lamb in this tangle of torment, my daughter who is years smarter than her age, who will someday be blindsided at the hand of her mother. As Greek tragic as you can get.

I read the text again. Hit send.

Two hours later, gone seven hours in all, Sally and I arrive home. Tears are flooding my vision before I even open the door. When I see my mom and dad, Tom and the boys, Emily, Angela and her family, Martina with her daughter, Kayla, I lose it completely. A tray of cheese and crackers sits on the ottoman. Glasses of red wine are in hands and on tables. College football is on the television.

"Hey! There they are! How's our Sally!" Everyone stands, rushes to Sally, examines her wrapped hand, kisses her forehead, offers her a seat.

"Oh, honey," Mom says, cupping my face and kissing my mouth. I fall into her, letting go of the tears I've held on to all day. "It's over," she says. "You're just in time for dinner."

"You came," I say, hugging Martina, my amazing big sister. I hug Kayla and size her up, noting that my niece is a good foot taller than me.

I look at the beautiful table, the golden turkey resting on the rack, and cry some more. The kindness kills me. Everyone is too good. Angie brings me a glass of wine. Emily breaks out in song, an original she's named "I Hope Another Suture Isn't in Your Future!" The boys deliver construction-paper cards to their sister. I'm finally where I want to be. Surrounded. The smells start to fill the air as Mom heats up the side dishes. Pop is carving the turkey. Soon we're all seated for dinner, saying grace, and I'm crying again.

"She's emotional," Angie says, as if the rest of my family doesn't already know that I'm strong through illnesses and injuries but crumble at kindness and pride. Seldom do I make it through one of Emily's recitals, Sally's soccer goals, or moments of pure goodness, like when the boys hug each other in their sleep.

"It was the storm," my mother says. "It set things off balance."

"I'm so glad you're all here," I say in a pitifully grateful voice.

Just as the first dish is passed, I hear my cell phone burble, signaling an incoming text message. I pop out of my seat like a piece of bread in the toaster. "Let me get you some milk," I say to the boys, and once I'm concealed by the refrigerator door, I open the text. It reads: *Poor Sally. Is she okay? I've never heard of a tetanus reaction before in my family, so I don't think she got it from me.*

I had uttered the truth only once before—the day I went to see Landon—the day the photo was taken: the truth that Landon James is Sally's biological father.

In the ten years since, time has obscured the truth as sure as moss blankets the walls of an abandoned house, encroaching upon sacred space without the need to put down roots. Tom has been Sally's steadfast father. The seasons have rotated ten times. We have celebrated birthdays ten times. Christmas, Lent, and Easter. Birth and death and Rising. For the ten years that Tom has been Sally's father, Landon never once tried to be. That was the deal I made: with Landon, with God. *Give me her, give me Tom, and I promise, I promise, I promise . . .* Now, in the form of a text message, the heavy spiral of ten years' time seems reduced to nothing. The contract I wrote has suddenly gone missing.

PART TWO

CHAPTER TEN
Failing to Do Good

DECEMBER REFUSES TO TURN COLD. It's defiant and warm and the kids are loving every minute of it, still riding bikes down the driveway and swinging on their play set. The meteorologists debate the meaning of this warm spell. Some predict that we'll be punished for too much of a good thing, like a champagne hangover or stomachache from polishing off the second half of a pecan pie. Winter will dump on us unmercifully, these grim meteorologists say, as though to remind us that excess in anything will always have consequences.

Angie and her family are the first to arrive two days before Christmas. My girls, little groupies to Angie's girls, traipse after them like lovesick puppy dogs. I hear Kelly, Angie's oldest, murmur something about showing my girls a YouTube video of a talking cat. I look questioningly at Angie and she assures me that it's clean. I'm scared to death of the Internet, YouTube, and Facebook. The thought that my girls could end up on the wrong end of a chat line sends shivers down my spine.

Teresa arrives next with her two boys. Dom and Danny accost their cousins at the door and drag them down to the basement to see their dinosaur collection.

The husbands are outside on the deck drinking beer. We can hear them defending their respective teams. College ball, and Notre Dame football in particular, is their thing. Tom went to Notre Dame, and since neither Loyola (Teresa's husband Paul's school) nor Gonzaga (where Angie and Kevin went) field football teams, it's Notre Dame's fortunes that get analyzed. Paul and Landon James overlapped a few years at Loyola, but their paths never crossed.

My sisters and I settle at the counter and I open a bottle of malbec.

"When's Martina getting in?" Teresa asks.

"Not until late," I say. "They're staying with Mom and Dad, so we won't see them until the morning."

"What's the plan for the morning?" Angela asks while arranging slices of cheese and an assortment of crackers on a breadboard.

"We have the parade," I say.

"What time should we be ready?"

"Please," I say. "Sleep in. Hang around the house. The fridge is packed with food. There's a dozen bagels, bacon, eggs. We'll sneak out in the morning and be home by eleven. Then we can start baking the Christmas cookies with the kids."

Each year my sisters and I bake dozens of cookies with the kids: sugar cookies decorated with icing and silver ball sprinkles, snickerdoodles, linzer hearts, biscotti, snowballs, gingerbread men. It takes us all day and we freeze them immediately. The next day we create platters and tins, some to keep to last us through the holidays, others to give out to neighbors and teachers. Teresa makes them for the shut-in parishioners.

That night my sisters and I lay out a row of sleeping bags and blankets for the kids in the basement: Sally, Emily, Dom, Danny, Kelly, Shannon, Matthew, and Luke. We call out movie choices until we find one agreeable to the four-year-olds up to the teenagers—*How the Grinch Stole Christmas*. I hug and kiss and tuck my way down the line, charge Kelly and Shannon with being the "grown-ups," listen to Sally whine about not being included in their group even though she's ten years old.

Upstairs I load the dishwasher, start a load of laundry, and take out the garbage. Then I lay out a mountain of jackets and mittens and hats for tomorrow's parade, a bag of snacks to get the boys through the inevitable midmorning meltdown, my camera, video recorder, and cell phone. Finally I sit down next to my sisters for a final glass of wine before bedtime. The husbands are in the family room watching a game.

"So, Mare," Angie says, turning into me. "How are *things*?"

Teresa swivels her stool in my direction. The husbands are watching football, but I'm the one with double coverage.

"What things?" I say, thinking immediately that this has to do with Landon James, his running for Senate, the rogue photo.

"*Patrick.*" Angie says Tom's brother's name in a hushed voice, like it's a secret. "We heard he's back in rehab."

My shoulders drop and my fists unfurl. *Phew.* "Yeah, he was in rehab. He's out now, but Kathy went to her mother's with Mia and still hasn't come back."

"Poor Kathy," Angie says.

"Poor Patrick," Teresa says.

"I know he's an addict," I say. "Even in recovery, he's still an addict. I just wish he understood what's at stake, you know? Enough to make him stay clean."

"I'm sure he tries," Angie says.

"I'm sure he tries twenty-four hours a day, seven days a week," Teresa says calmly. "Then he has a weak moment, a crack in his foundation." Teresa is a listener and rarely comments on anyone's life other than mine, so I'm surprised that she's piping in her two cents. "Unless you've battled addiction, I don't think anyone has a right to judge."

"I'm not saying it's easy," I answer. "But he needs to try harder." Teresa looks at me for too long, her deep brown eyes locked on mine, as if to say, "Who made you so perfect?" I'm the first to look away. "It's a *sacrifice* that he needs to make for the sake of his family." I hear myself pushing the point and wonder why; maybe I want to hear what Teresa has to say about Patrick's fall from grace—the crack in his foundation—seeing that he and I are made of the same cement.

"And I'm just saying," Teresa persists, "that you don't know what you're talking about because you've never been in his position. You can't know what it's like to be drawn to something forbidden—even if every fiber in your being is fighting against it. It's hard, Mare. Addiction is something you know nothing about."

I refrain from saying that addiction and I are hardly strangers. While I've never been addicted to alcohol, I've been addicted plenty to people: first Landon, and now Tom and the kids, without whom my skin would have no bones to hang on. Perhaps I could be something other than a wife and mother, but I don't want to be. The risk in losing what's valuable has led me to make a decade of sketchy decisions.

"I'm sure you're right," I say, lightening up. "I'm sure it's much tougher than I can even imagine. I can't even stay away from doughnuts. I'm sure alcohol is just a tad tougher to stare down."

Teresa nods, and then I nod, and then we sip from our wine.

"Anyway!" I say. "Tell me what's going on with you guys. Ang—give me the latest update on teenage girls. Make my head spin."

Angie proceeds to rattle on about Kelly and Shannon. Kelly brushes her hair incessantly until it's as smooth as silk and then secures it in a messy ponytail/bun do that makes her look like she just rolled out of bed. She has a "boyfriend." They text, but Kelly is required to turn in her cell phone each night for her mother's inspection. "Keeps her honest," Angie says.

Shannon started her period and wants to use tampons because she's grossed out by pads. She thinks Lady Gaga is a "poet." She's given up meat on principle but makes an exception for her grandmother's meatballs, since that's "ground beef." We all laugh at that one.

We finish the bottle of wine just as the game ends. We say good night, send Angie and Kevin up to Sally and Em's bedroom, Teresa and Paul up to the boys', and Tom and I head up to ours after checking the locks, turning off the lights, and arming the home security system. As I walk through the hallway, I see Angie in the bathroom brushing her teeth and signaling for me.

"I'll be right there," I say to Tom.

In the bathroom Angie spits and rinses. "Listen, Mare. Are you okay?"

"I'm more than okay," I say. "I'm so happy everyone's here."

"I know *that*, but is there something else going on? Something you haven't told me?"

I look down the hallway. "There is something," I admit. "But it might be nothing. I'm really hoping and praying that it's nothing."

"And you don't want to talk about it?"

"I really don't." I hug my sister and tromp off to bed, anxious to cuddle against my husband while the getting is still good.

I pull on my flannel, pull my hair back in a ponytail, and brush my teeth. In bed we go over the plan for tomorrow.

"I'm going to march with the boys and you're going to stick with the girls, right?" Tom asks. Showing that he knows the plan is one of Tom's methods for getting on my good side. Tonight he's putting forth an admirable effort, probably hoping for a little action or at least a back rub.

"Yeah," I say, "and then we'll meet at the courthouse steps. That's where Emily is going to sing her solo." Emily's choir group will be singing carols tomorrow, and Em's been chosen to sing the first verse of "Silent Night" solo. Then Sally, who has been collecting money for the local food bank, has been asked to introduce the mayor. It is destined to be a big morning for my two amazing daughters.

"We got lucky with this arrangement," Tom says, as if reading my mind.

"I know. What are the chances that they each get to do something special tomorrow? At least we won't have to worry about sibling jealousy for *this* event."

Tom slides over and puts his head on my chest. I rub his back while I settle my head deeper into the soft pillows, exhaling with the satisfying fullness that comes from having a houseful of family, imagining the line of cousins sleeping peacefully in the basement, and eager for the morning to come.

In the morning, the six of us sneak out of the house without waking my sisters or their families. In the car I hand out chocolate-milk boxes and Nutri-Grain bars with promises that we'll eat a hot meal after the parade. The kids hardly seem bothered; they're more excited that they're allowed to eat a junky breakfast.

Once in the parking lot near where the parade will start, I begin the great bundling act. The boys slept in their long underwear last night, giving them an extra layer under their jeans and turtle-necks and wool sweaters. I zip up their puffy down ski jackets, wrap scarves around their necks, push gloves onto their hands, and cover their heads in caps with flaps that make them look like aviators. Tom's holding an American flag and a rolled-up Cub Scout banner.

"Boy, aren't we the picture of small-town America," I say.

Tom smiles. "It doesn't get more wholesome than this."

"Okay, honey," I say to Tom, "I'll meet you and the boys at the end of the parade near the steps to the courthouse."

"I have my phone on vibrate," Tom says over the din. "In case you need to get ahold of me."

"Okay, great. Bye, boys!" I holler. "Stick near Dad, okay? Safety first!"

"Never last!" they holler back.

"No mistakes," I say to Tom.

Once Tom and the boys are on their way, I turn to the girls, who are cozy in the backseat, bracing themselves for the cold that will engulf them in a minute.

"Sally, you ready?" I ask. "Emily, what about you?"

"I don't want to wear a cap," Emily whines. "I'll look stupid while I'm singing."

"Then wear this!" I say, pulling out a surprise Santa hat I picked up at the dollar store yesterday.

"Gorgeous!" Emily exclaims.

"You can wear your winter cap underneath. You'll never see it. You'll stay warm and you'll look adorable."

Sally, on the other hand, couldn't care less about how she looks. Staying warm is her priority. She's bundled in a ski jacket, wool hat, gloves, and clunky boots. The only sign that she's Sally is the amber waves that puddle around the neck of her jacket.

We leave the warmth of the car and brace ourselves against the cold, my girls each holding tight to one of my mittened hands as we walk to the start of the parade. Main Street is already lined with onlookers, hunkered closely against each other for warmth, bundled in blankets and jackets, sipping coffee and cocoa. Once the parade starts and we begin to march, I forget about the cold and relish the moment: my girls in front of me, tossing candy to little kids; Tom with the boys and the Cub Scout troop; my sisters and their families at home in our house; a hot dinner at Mom and Dad's later today. This—small-town quaintness, a community wrapped in Christmas parades, my family's bond as sticky as molasses—is what it is all about. It's bigger than everything it's up against.

In front of us is a float from a local school, a pack of gorgeous hounds from the local hunt club, their master donned in scarlet-red tails. In front of them is a cheer squad, a marching band, a sequined dance team.

Once we wind our way through the parade route and end at the courthouse, I signal for the girls to ascend the steps. The councilman at the top acknowledges me and the girls with a friendly smile, gesturing for the girls to come up.

The councilman taps the microphone, then cheers: "Happy Holidays!" He waits for a crowd to form at the base of the steps. "Thank you, all of you, for braving the weather to join us on this beautiful winter morning, the day before Christmas. For our listening pleasure, I present the St. Andrew's children's choir."

Emily and a group of maybe ten other girls form three lines. Emily is in the front and center and, when the director lifts her baton for the choir to begin, she steps forward and pulls the microphone from the stand. My heart hammers in nervousness for her, an anxiety my daughter doesn't seem to share as she confidently takes another step forward, opens her mouth, and releases a hauntingly pure a cappella first verse of "Silent Night." Her voice is mature and controlled, and it sends shivers down my arms and wells my eyes with tears. I look around for Tom, wanting to make sure that he's seeing her. Emily then steps back and joins the rest of the chorus in the remainder of the song. They finish to a thunder of applause and I furtively wipe the tears of pride from my eyes.

Next it's Sally stepping forward. She has pushed back her wool cap, the same one that nearly covered her eyes a few minutes ago. Now her hair frames her face and the cap is resting toward the back, magically looking like a finely placed beret.

"I'm proud to announce," Sally says into the mic, "the mayor of Woodville, Mayor Gorman!"

Mayor Gorman trots out, shaking his fists in the air in a rah-rah, go-team style. He shakes Sally's hand and thanks her, then turns to the crowd. "Our good citizen Sally was chosen to be up here today to introduce me because of the exemplary work she has done on behalf of the Woodville Food Bank. She raised over five hundred dollars, just in time to feed so many families in need this Christmas season. Sally, we're proud of you! And I'd like to present to you this badge that signifies the importance of being a good citizen."

Flushed bright pink, Sally puts her hand out to take the badge. "Thank you," she says, and steps back amid a swelling of applause.

Next Emily's chorus sings three more songs. Then the mayor is back onstage. "Well, this is a nice surprise. In addition to the Democratic candidate for the US Senate, who will be here soon, we're also fortunate to have with us today the Republican hopeful . . . Landon James!"

The pride and joy I'm feeling for my daughters is replaced instantly by the panic of a cornered animal. Landon barrels onto the stage, shaking the mayor's hand. I look around to see if Tom's nearby. I see him by the moon bounce with the boys, but I can't tell if he's aware that Landon is up onstage, only a few feet from our daughters.

"Thank you, Woodville!" Landon roars. "It's so nice to be here. In June, the people of Virginia will choose their Republican candidate to represent them in next November's election. I want to be your choice! Our country—this land that has made us a great nation full of entrepreneurial spirit and gumption for getting things done—is falling to pieces. We have spent too much. Our children will be burdened for decades to come because of our irresponsible spending. Getting our financial house in order is not just a good idea, it's a necessity to save our country. Our country needs to be vibrant once again! We need our schools to be top-notch! We need our employers to offer jobs and benefits. We need our environment to be clean, our streets safe, our technology and innovation cutting edge. I am passionate about making these things happen. Choose me to be your man and I'll represent Virginia proud!"

I need to get to Tom to quell the jealousy that I'm certain is brewing inside him, but I can't leave the girls up onstage alone. *He got your vote for a lot of years,* I can still hear Tom say. I shake my head, try to steady my vision, and call Tom on his cell. He doesn't pick up, and I'm not sure what that means. I look back at the stage, at my daughters, at Landon. I look back again for Tom. Though I'm surrounded, I feel utterly alone.

CHAPTER ELEVEN
Imperfect

TOM

YOU HAVE GOT TO BE *freaking kidding me.* Onstage with my daughters is Boy Wonder, the egomaniac who strung Mary along for six years and still has the stones to show up in her—*our*—town. Listen to him spewing that crap about a better world, more jobs, less government. Here's an idea for less government: less you! God, that hair. It almost looks styled, like he stood in front of the mirror with a hair dryer. And the fancy suits and shiny shoes. The guy's a Ken doll.

I glance into the moon bounce, get a visual on the boys, who are still happy as can be to jump and fall and jump again. I look onstage again, then at Mary. It appears that she's taken off her ski hat and is combing her fingers through her hair. Since when does she care about her hair? I doubt she even combed it this morning before shoving it into a ponytail. And she's standing on her tippy-toes, like she's trying to make herself taller.

Knock it off, Mary. You're making a fool of yourself.

Mary says that Landon hasn't contacted her in years. Who knows? I want to believe her, but I reserve judgment because she's lied to me before about him calling her. Maybe she didn't lie; she just didn't tell me. Same difference. It was years ago, when the girls were little. The prick actually wanted to name Mary as his beneficiary on his life insurance policy.

Number one: Why? Why the hell couldn't he think of anyone else other than his ex-girlfriend, who was now *married,* with *children,* to name as his beneficiary? Number two: You don't need to notify someone just to name them as beneficiary. He could have done it without telling her. So why'd he tell her? Was it just a lame excuse to contact her? And number three: Why can't the self-absorbed loser get a damn life of his own? And stay the hell out of our town.

CHAPTER TWELVE
Choosing to Do Wrong

LANDON FINISHES HIS CAMPAIGN SPEECH, covering all the major topics: unemployment, national defense, the environment. The crowd roars. Landon takes it all in, nodding and pointing and shaking his fist. Then, when the crowd quiets, he turns toward the choir. "Beautiful!" He claps with a plastic grin on his face—not the real one that used to turn me to liquid.

"And I want to express how impressed I am by this young lady." Landon points to Sally and my heart plummets. "For the work she's done on behalf of the Woodville Food Bank. If only more children, and adults, embraced her commitment to volunteerism, we'd be a better country. I commend you, young lady, and to show my support, I'd like to write a personal check to the food bank for the amount of one thousand dollars."

Sally pops out of her chair like a jack-in-the-box and claps her hand over her mouth. "Thank you so much!" she says with a gigantic smile. Landon walks over to her, holds out his hand for her to shake, and looks into the crowd. The perfect snapshot for the newspapers. My hands quiver as I push my way to the stage, tripping over wires and speakers.

"Sally," I whisper, "sit down!" She looks at me, truly bewildered, as though she's done something wrong. "Sit down," I whisper again. She staggers awkwardly to her seat and looks at me like I've just shown up at her school with rollers in my hair.

I look back and this time find Tom. His arms are crossed over his chest. He's furious. I lift my shoulders and look at him with pleading eyes, as if to say, "I know, this is crazy."

What seems like hours but is probably only minutes later, Sally walks down the steps and looks at me in horror. "What did I do wrong?" she asks. "He gave the food bank a thousand dollars. Isn't that great?"

"Yes, honey," I say, stroking her cheek and kissing her forehead. Sally jerks her head away because she's annoyed at me, and my pawing at her is making it worse.

"I'm so sorry," I say. "I'll explain later. You didn't do anything wrong. I promise." Just then my cell buzzes and it's Tom. He's only about fifty feet away at the moon bounce with the boys.

"Let's go," he says sharply, and I can tell from the clip of his voice that his anger is going to land in my lap.

"I'm sending Sal your way. And trying to get Emily," I say, and then even though Tom hates when I apologize for anything relating to Landon, I say, "Sorry about this."

Tom clicks his phone shut without saying good-bye.

"Listen, Sal. Could you go over by Dad? He's right over there by the moon bounce with the boys. I'll just grab Em and I'll be right there, okay?"

"Mom?"

"Please, Sally. Just go to Dad, okay?"

"Mom!" Sally screams. "You're *ruining* my day! Why are you acting so weird?"

"Go," I say. "Now."

I watch her stomp away and watch Tom receive her. I can just imagine the two of them bonding over how much they both hate me at the moment. I wave, smile, send him a pleading, conspiratorial look. Try to remind him that we're on the same side.

I look onstage, try to signal to Emily. The best-case scenario would be for us to get out of here as quickly as possible without running into Landon. But I can't get to Emily because Landon is blocking the way, jauntily jogging down the steps. I turn away from him, hoping he hasn't seen me, but I feel the tap of his fingers on my shoulder.

"Mary," he says, and for some reason the affection in his voice grabs me by the throat.

"How are you, Landon? Any developments?"

"No, I think we're in the clear," he says. "The PI photographer found a juicier target."

"Thank God."

"You look great."

"No, I don't," I say. "You sounded good up there."

"Still the hamster on the wheel," he says. "Always trying to get somewhere, right?"

"It's who you are."

Our eyes lock. A thousand memories flash through my mind. Meeting him when I was nineteen years old, four years later being reintroduced, the following six years riding a roller-coaster relationship of want and need.

Just then Emily bounces down the steps, kisses my arm, and says, "Hello!"

"You were amazing," Landon says to Emily, and then says to me, "This is your daughter?"

"Yes, this is Emily."

"How old are you, Emily?" Landon asks.

"I'm nine," Emily says.

"Don't you have a sister?" Landon asks.

"Sally," Emily says. "She's a year older than me."

"She's the food bank girl," I say. "The one you were just photographed with."

"That was Sally?" he asks. "I had no idea." He looks over the crowd as if he's trying to find her.

"Emily, honey, why don't you run over to Dad? I'll be right there, okay?"

We watch Emily run to the moon bounce. Even at this distance I can see the vein bulging from Tom's neck, the clench of his jaw, the fury on his face. I wave at Tom, roll my eyes like I'm stuck talking to Landon, send him an exasperated look that says, "Can you believe that he's *here*?"

"That was Sally?" he says again. "I stood onstage with Sally, with *our* Sally."

"She's not yours," I say quickly, shooting a glance back at Tom. "You know that."

"I know," he says. "I just mean . . . you know what I mean. I know I'm nothing to her."

"I've got to go," I say.

"I'll bet you're the best mom, MM," Landon stammers. "I could just see you baking cupcakes and sewing costumes and assembling scrapbooks."

"That's me."

"It must be nice," Landon says. "To be your kid. To be so loved. That must be intoxicating."

My heart squeezes because, all these years later, Landon is still a little boy with no parents.

"I'd better get back to my family," I say. "Good luck, Landon."

"It's nice running into you, Mary. I guess the chances were good," he says, laughing. "It's pretty much what I do these days. Hit twenty small towns in a day. Make appearances. Shake hands with worthy kids." He looks around, nods, then focuses his too-blue eyes on me. "I'm sorry if I've ruined your day by being here."

"It's okay."

"Sally's beautiful. Both your daughters are," he says. "I can't believe I was onstage with them and didn't even know."

"I really need to get back," I say, pointing in Tom's direction.

I've taken a step when Landon says, "My grandmother died. In her sleep, just a few months ago."

Landon shared little with me about his family. I knew the basics: His father left early on, destroying his mother, a young woman saddled with three boys. I knew that he was closest to his grandmother. She was the one who'd occasionally call his cell phone while we were together. Once when Landon was in the shower, his cell phone rang and I saw that it was his grandmother: Millicent James. I answered, introduced myself, and said that I'd heard lovely things about her. In a too-polite manner that reflected her generation, she proceeded to meddle in Landon's and my relationship, hitting the love notes that Landon wasn't able to reach. She told me that Landon spoke of me often; that he was a sweetheart, but that he'd need a "little coaxing," if I knew what she meant. "Don't be afraid to push his hand," she told me. She was concerned about him, wanted him to be happy and married, worried he'd end up old and alone. Before she hung up, she reminded me to keep our conversation to myself.

"I'm sorry," I say to Landon now. I look over my shoulder and see Tom glaring in our direction. "I'm sorry, Landon. But I'd really better scoot along."

"Really good seeing you, MM."

"See you," I say.

Landon exhales, looks down, and then peers up at me from under his flop of hair. "Take care of those beautiful girls."

"Bye," I say, and walk in the direction of my family.

Tom and I barely talk on the way home. Luckily, the kids are nonstop, regaling one another with stories from the morning. Emily belts out "Silent Night." Sally—who has forgotten that she was mad at me—holds her hand to her mouth like a microphone, introducing and reintroducing the mayor. The boys chant "Jingle Bells" over and over.

When we get home, Martina is pulling a frittata out of the oven. Teresa pours Tom and me big mugs of coffee. Angie slides a piece of coffee cake onto our plates, next to the eggs.

"I'll be right back," I say, running upstairs to throw on a pair of sweatpants and a sweater. Tom follows me, and when we get inside our bedroom, he closes the door.

"What were you and Landon James talking about?"

"Basically, nothing," I say. "Just chitchat."

"What kind of chitchat?" he asks. "What exactly did he say to you?"

"That he was campaigning, that he hits twenty towns in a day, blah, blah. Just stuff like that."

"Are you sure?" Tom asks, pressing. "Nothing I'm going to find out about later? Nothing I'm going to find stashed in your desk drawer?"

"Tom," I plead, "come on. Let's not do this. He didn't say anything, just chitchat, I promise."

I look at Tom and shake my head like he's being silly. I know it's unfair of me, suggesting that he is being paranoid, especially since his compass needle is pointed in the direction of something less worrisome—Landon and me talking. It terrifies me to think that his needle would magnetize to true north, where Sally's paternity lies.

"Are you ready to go down for brunch?" I say to Tom, taking his hands.

"I'm ready," he says. "But Mary, you *act* different around him. What's that about?"

"Of course I act different," I say. "I felt weird as hell talking to him, knowing you were right down the road."

"Not weird nervous," Tom says. "Weird happy. You fluffed your hair, did this thing where you shifted your hips."

"*Shifted* my hips?" I say. "What the heck does that even mean?"

Tom attempts an imitation of me leaning back and forth, like a smitten schoolgirl.

"You're nuts," I say, and because the burden of bringing us back to normal always falls on me, I clap my hands on his cheeks and kiss his mouth. "You're nuts, you know? Shifting my hips. Like I'd want to show off my fat ass." I kiss him again, pat him on the butt, and tell him to knock it off. He relaxes a bit, but we're far from back to normal. An uneasy wedge has lodged itself between us, preventing us from closing the door on this.

That night as I curl into Tom, I make a silent promise to him. I vow that the truth is coming . . . soon. *Let us get through Christmas,* I pray, *and then I'll tell you, once and for all.* And because we're the Morrisseys, the proof will speak for itself: our ironclad familyhood, our ardent loyalty, and our profuse love for one another. The evidence will be overwhelming. *There's enough good to overpower the bad,* my defense will show. I may be put on probation, forced to wear a cuff around my ankle, but I won't be taken from my home.

| | |

On Christmas morning it snows—fat, juicy flakes that summon the children. After presents have been opened, the cousins bundle in snow gear and go outside to play. Snowmen are made, fights are had, and sleighs careen down the hill at lightning speed.

PART THREE

CHAPTER THIRTEEN
Confession

THE FIRST DAY OF JANUARY is cold and still. The snow that fell on Christmas morning lingers, covering our lawns, pushed up against the edges of the roads, now slick with a layer of silver ice. As we shuffle up the church steps, on our way to Mass for the Solemnity of Mary, I hold tight to the boys' hands, warn Sally and Emily to watch for patches of ice, keep an eye on Tom, whose dress shoes provide little traction. Once in the church, I relax and smile at my family. I slide onto my knees and pray that this year is going to be a good one, though an uneasy feeling hovers over me, a sticky film of discomfort stemming from seeing Landon James only a little more than a week ago. I wonder how a decade has passed and he and I have managed to avoid each other so successfully. Up until that moment at the parade. Suddenly the metropolitan DC area seems too small for the two of us.

The priest speaks of the Blessed Virgin, her unselfish love, how Christ's birth was made possible by Mary's fiat: *Be it done unto me according to thy word.* When I pray the Hail Holy Queen, I feel consumed with an emotion that's too big to contain in my mortal body. *Let me be just a little bit like you,* I pray. *Let me not hesitate.* But I know that I'm nothing like Mary, a woman who took the ultimate risk so that something great could be achieved. While I have been bold with my risk taking, my motivation has been selfish. I'm aware of the distinction.

After Mass, I stand in line to make my confession. When the person before me exits and the light turns green, I slip into the box and onto my knees.

"Hello, Father," I say. I make the sign of the cross and say "Amen." Then I begin, "Bless me, Father, for I have sinned. It's been three months since my last confession."

"What are your sins, my child?" It's Father Mike and I'm glad. He's more relaxed than Father Tucker, who often borders on sanctimonious, making me feel worse, not better, than before I confessed my sins.

"I'm holding on to a piece of information," I say. "I'm withholding the truth. I guess that's the same as lying."

"What is the nature of this lie?"

Words are too small to describe what I've done. "I've lied to my husband."

"And has this lie hurt him?"

"It hasn't, but if he knew . . ."

"Are you looking for absolution or advice?"

"Both," I say. "I'm thinking about coming clean, of telling the truth. Should I?"

"I can't tell you that, dear," Father Mike says. "My job is to hear your confession. Your penance is three Hail Marys and two Our Fathers."

"But Father," I say. "I want to know how it works. If I tell the truth, what will happen? And if I don't tell the truth, what will happen? I need to weigh my options."

Father Mike chuckles, and the tone of it rings of Teresa— Teresa who accuses me of going at my faith like a lawyer, all bargaining and negotiating. "I have no idea what will happen," he says. "But God does. And if you trust in His will, I'd say that you'll be fine."

"But Father, isn't it always best to tell the truth?"

"It's best to confess your sins, my child. And it's best to tend to your marriage at home."

I make the sign of the cross and say, "Amen." Then I say, "Father? So this is enough, confessing my sins?"

"There is nothing greater than cleansing your soul of sin," he says. "Give thanks to the Lord for He is good."

"His mercy endures forever," I respond, rote, the words from my entire life, but I'm still thinking it through. Did Father Mike just advise me not to tell Tom the truth? I should feel relief, but all I feel is dread, because something inside me knows that the time to come clean is upon me, to confess and hope for leniency.

| | |

Later that night, Tom and I lay in bed. "I talked to my brother today," Tom says.

"How's he?"

"He's working—odd jobs," Tom says. "But I worry, you know?"

"I know you feel that he got a rough shake; that the alcoholism is a curse. I know you worry about him. He's your brother. I'd be the same way with my sisters."

"A lot of it is his fault, of course," Tom says. "He's a grown man. But he's also a Morrissey, and God knows there are plenty of Morrisseys who hit the bottle too hard."

"You're right," I say. "Patrick was made in your father's image. It's a lot to fight against." I snuggle into Tom and pull my fingers through his waves of hair. "You, on the other hand, were made in your mother's image—good and kind."

"What about you?" Tom asks, reaching his arm around my back. "Whose image were you made in? Robert or Regina Russo's?"

"Neither," I say, and mean it. "They're *good* people, my parents. I'm only partially good. Certainly not enough like them to say I'm in their image."

I've plucked up my courage and dropped the bait, and now I wait for Tom to bite. *Crack me open, Tom, so you can finally see my truth.* I squeeze my eyes shut and prepare myself for the blow. It'll hurt, but I'm ready.

What do you mean you're only partially good? Tom will want to know.

But Tom doesn't take the bait. "I think they would claim you," he says.

"That's because they don't know the half of it." I stare at Tom and try to modulate my breathing. My heart is thumping like a gong.

"Mare, just because you lifted Post-it Notes and paper clips from the law firm you worked at ten years ago doesn't make you a delinquent."

On any other day, Tom would have put me on the stand, would have drilled me to explain the meaning of my inflammatory remark "because they don't know the half of it." Today, the one day I want him to press me, prosecute me, force me to come out with it all, he isn't in the mood—his thoughts are elsewhere.

Coward that I am, I luxuriate in the wave of relief washing over me and settle back into cozy chitchat. "It wasn't Post-it Notes and paper clips," I remind him. "It was toilet paper and coffee filters."

"That's right."

"We were on a tight budget. Remember, we were just married and both working and we were living in that little apartment."

"And you were pregnant with Sally," Tom adds.

Pregnant with Sally. "We were saving up for our house," I drift on, though my heart is pounding again. "And eating a whole lot of tuna casserole."

"Hey, I love tuna casserole," Tom defends. "A few potato chips crushed up on the top."

Now all at once I throw myself back on the stand. I can't let this chance pass. I'm so close. "I was pretty stressed back then," I say, the witness leading the prosecutor, taking another whack at provoking him into pressing me for the truth that's all but bursting out of me.

"You were a nervous wreck," Tom agrees. "Worrying that Sally wouldn't be perfect, and then she blew you away by being a thousand times better than perfection."

"I never cared about her being perfect," I say, closing my eyes and sliding out on the easy, loving tide again, remembering what it felt like when Sally somersaulted inside me, when she traced an elbow like a rainbow across my gigantic belly. "I was just so anxious to see her, to hold her."

"Happiest day of my life," Tom says. "Holding Sal for that first time."

"Happiest day of your life 'til Em and the boys came along."

"Of course," he says. "But there's something about your first-born. It hits you harder, that's all."

137

"It was a great day," I admit. "But then you had to put up with me and my roller-coaster emotions."

"I've put up with a lot more since then," Tom says. Here it is—another entrée to the truth. *Say it, Mary. Say it: "The thing is, Tom, there was a reason why I was so wacko after Sally was born. You see, it had to do with Landon James . . ."*

Instead my courage sets sail for good. Gone, just like that. I snuggle my face into Tom's chest. Next time I'll tell him. My heart is racing and my eyes are wet with tears, and I have the distinct feeling that my chest is either swelling or splitting. Sometimes it's just all too much. Too much emotion for my little heart to bear. Too much for just one tiny flawed woman like me. A husband, four kids, my constant worry for their happiness—and the past, the long, deadly reach of my compulsions and mistakes that puts it all at such horrible risk. I'm holding up the dam, though I know there are cracks on the inside, hairline fissures that will soon make their way to the outer layer—and then, an imminent burst.

CHAPTER FOURTEEN

Detesting Sins

ON THE SIXTH OF JANUARY, the children return to school. After I drop the boys at preschool, I cross the church parking lot and enter the parish hall, where I'm meeting with a group of moms who have volunteered to help me put together an Easter retreat for the Sunday school students.

"Do you have the stack of paperwork for the moms who have already gone through the training?" I ask my friend Alice. The diocese won't allow anyone to volunteer in any capacity until they've completed a four-hour training course on working with children. It's the church's too-late, reactionary stance to show that it's now vigilant; that turning a blind eye to heinous acts of decades past won't happen again. As if putting a group of mothers through a four-hour training class will somehow heal the wounds of countless souls who were victimized at the hands of the person they believed to be their most trusted ally.

The scandal makes me sick. I once asked Mom how she did it, how she kept the faith in light of it. She told me that it sickened her, too, but that her relationship was with God, not the Church.

When she said it, I felt a little jealous because what I like about Catholicism is the Church, the *stuff*: the incense, the stained glass, the ritualized standing and kneeling; the purple robes for Lent, the rose-colored robes for Christmas, the stations of the cross. I've never considered myself anything but Catholic, and a happy Catholic at that. But Teresa is right: My belief is conditional, not blind. Her faith—and Mom's faith—loom larger than mine. Their connection with God couldn't be challenged by a nuclear holocaust.

"I'm thinking that they're at the office," Alice answers. "Want me to go check?"

"No, I got it."

"Want to get coffee when you get back?"

"Sounds good!" I holler back.

I slip out of the classroom we're using as our HQ and down the hallway to the church office. My mom's friend of forty years sits at the desk tucked behind a high counter.

"Hi, Dotty," I say, peeking over.

"How are you doing, dear?"

"I'm looking for that stack of paperwork for the volunteers who have completed training."

"It's in the back, hon," she says, then swivels her chair and hoists herself to standing.

"Oh, just tell me where it is and I'll—"

"No, no, don't be silly. I'm off!" Poor Dotty's arthritis keeps her in its grip. I watch as she clutches the countertop and straightens herself, my own back aching in sympathy.

While she's in the back, I glance at her television, which is wedged between her computer and telephone. It's about the size of a tissue box. The news is playing and before I know it, Landon is flashed on the screen—and though the thumbnail photo in the corner is as small as a postage stamp, I know immediately that it's *the* photo. The photo I've been looking for all of these weeks. Landon is facing forward and I'm facing sideways. No sign of Sally, though I can tell from the position of my shoulder that her carrier is hanging from my arm.

I'm leaning over Dotty's counter, my stomach stretched across the cool Formica, my feet airborne. I'm squinting and straining to see the photo, and then, like that, it's gone. The Dow Jones ticker takes its place. I slide back onto my feet, but my hands remain gripped around the countertop. My head swims and I feel like I might vomit. I look again at the television, but now my vision is jutting back and forth, like paint being shaken at the hardware store. Dotty returns with the papers.

"Honey," she says, putting her hand on mine. "What on *earth*? You've gone completely white." Colored spots flash in front of my eyes, and when I look at Dotty, I can't make sense of the words coming out of her mouth.

"I'm not feeling well," I manage to say, but even to my own ears my voice sounds hollow and distant.

"Sit down, honey," she says.

I shake my head but the motion makes the room spin. "I've got to go."

I list out of the room and find myself jogging unsteadily back down into the parish hall. Though I've been here a hundred times before, it now seems awkward and unfamiliar to me—like I'm the new kid on the first day of class, looking for the library, or is it the gym? Where'd everybody go? The empty hall seems to be echoing. Then I hear Alice's roaring laugh, remember where I am, duck in and grab my purse, then mutter something about having to go.

"Hey, Mare!" Alice calls. "What about coffee?"

I shake my head again and run, with the sound of her voice echoing "Mary!" through my head.

I drive home without noticing whether there are other cars or red lights or pedestrians or stop signs. I charge through the front door and grab for the remote controls. In fifteen minutes I've seen my photo appear half a dozen times. I'm pressing in my stomach with the palms of my hands, fighting for breath, trying without hope to imagine which way to run. I'm helpless, trapped. I literally don't know what to *do* with myself.

The phone starts to ring. I can see from the caller ID that it's Mom, Angela, Martina, then Teresa. My neighbors, some church friends. Then, almost in unison, numbers I don't recognize. I suspect without answering a single one that it's the reporters starting to call. The networks, the cable stations, magazines and blogs I've never heard of. I ignore them all. The only person I want to talk to is Tom, and he's not calling and not answering when I call him. I don't know what to do.

I pace the house. My fingernails bitten to nubs, I scrub the kitchen until the smell of bleach makes me dizzy and my newly gnawed fingertips are burning and throbbing. I sit on the sofa, but it doesn't feel right. I stand back up, but my legs feel weak and spindly. My *skin* doesn't feel right. It's tight and tingly and I slap my cheeks so I can feel the warm vibration that follows. I pace some more. Somehow I end up in the master bedroom closet, under the drape of clothes, my knees pulled tightly in to my chest. I'm now gnawing down on my cuticles, the insides of my cheeks. I'm too petrified to cry. *Tom, Tom, Tom, dear sweet Tom. What have I done? Why didn't I tell?*

At eleven I splash water on my face, pinch my cheeks, and slide into the car to pick up the boys. A paranoia as sticky and thick as the summer humidity adheres to me. It seems that everyone is staring: the teachers standing outside of school at pickup, the other parents, the fellow drivers. It's as if I am covered in chicken pox.

The boys are oblivious. They chatter on about their day.

"We did paper machines!" Dom says.

"Mâché," I correct, and when I see in the rearview mirror Dom's mouth turn down because he said it wrong, I hate myself a thousand times more because I'm the worst person on earth. "Tell me about it!" I say in my most cheerful voice.

"You just dip paper in gluey water," he mumbles, but his enthusiasm is gone.

"That's awesome, buddy," I manage.

"I'm hungry," Danny says.

"Got anything left in your lunch box?" I ask, knowing he does.

"Just my chips and grapes and half my sandwich and my cookie," he lists proudly.

"Eat some of that stuff," I say, and then even though I feel as though my face is made of plastic, I turn and flash the guys my biggest smile because not one minute of their innocence deserves to be sullied by me.

At home I stick the boys in front of the television with a bowl of Goldfish crackers and a bin holding their dinosaur figures to play with. I check the caller ID and see that Tom still hasn't called. More calls from friends, family, and more—many more—strange numbers and names. The media. Listening to the messages on the wildly blinking answering machine isn't even an option. When the phone rings again and it's Angela, I finally answer it.

"Hi," I say.

"What the heck?"

"I went to see him one day," I blurt, startled by the sound of my own voice. "We needed to talk."

"About what?"

"I can't say. Tom's going to kill me."

"Jesus, Mary, and Joseph," Angie says. "What's going on?"

"Oh my God," I say. "Tom."

"Have you talked to him?"

"Not yet."

"Call him!" she says. "Face this head-on. Whatever this is."

"I am," I say. "He's not answering."

"Do you want to talk about it?"

"Not yet."

"Call me," she says. "Promise?"

"Yeah, okay."

"Promise me that you're okay."

"I'm not going to jump off a bridge, if that's what you mean."

"Mare, what's this *about*?"

"Just do me a favor, Ang. Call Mom and Dad and Teresa and Martina. Just tell them to stop calling. That I'm okay but can't talk yet, all right?"

At three thirty the boys and I walk down to the corner to pick up the girls. My neighbor Susan, who says whatever is on her mind, blares, "Was that *you* on the television, Mare? What gives? Out leading a secret life?"

"That's me," I play along. "Not enough to do at home!"

"Seriously, Mary, what's with the photo?"

I'm in the outdoors, but suddenly I feel like there's not enough air. I inhale, but my lungs have turned into cocktail straws, narrow and unyielding. I lean over at the waist, rest my hands on my knees, and look up. "It's crazy!" I say in a voice that's not my own. "I was downtown one day after Sally was born. I was waiting for my friend to show up. We were going to have lunch. Then, *what do you know?* I happened to run into Landon James. Not sure if you know this," I say, making a visor with my hand, gauging Susan's reaction, "but he and I used to date. Anyway, I was talking to Landon when all of a sudden I start to . . . *leak,* you know, *breast milk,* and I realize that I've forgotten to put the pads in my bra. Long and short of it, Landon took me up to his hotel room to get cleaned up. That's it! Sorry, nothing too juicy!"

"Oh," Susan says, clearly disappointed, her eager face falling glum. "Because on the news they're wondering about your relationship with him. They're referring to you as the 'mystery woman.'"

I pull my mouth tight and raise my eyebrows while shaking my head back and forth. "Some mystery. A leaking mom!"

That gets a laugh from her. She believes me. "But at least you're on TV like it was truly a scandal, right?" Like this is something I might aspire to.

Just then the bus pulls to a screeching halt and Sally and Emily pile off. We walk home immersed in everyday chatter, and for a moment everything feels excessively normal, so average I wonder for just a split second if it is going to be all right. Tom's at *work,* I remind myself. There's a chance that he hasn't even seen the photo. There's a chance that he *won't* see the photo. As long as he's stuck in meetings all day, as long as he's tied up on the phone, as long as today is one of those days when he barely looks up from his desk. This could be yesterday's news before it gets to him.

But by six o'clock I have dinner on the table and still haven't heard from Tom. I've left three messages for him, texted twice, e-mailed once. Clearly my naive notion of Tom not seeing the photo was just that—naive.

"Blessing," I say, and cross myself. "In the name of the Father, the Son, and the Holy Spirit, amen."

"'God our Father,'" Dom begins to sing.

"I want to do 'We Are Thankful,'" Danny whines.

"'God our Father'!" Dom screeches, an angry furrow pitched between his eyebrows.

"'We Are Thankful'!" Danny rebuts, equally determined.

"'Bless us, O Lord,'" Sally chimes in, steamrolling over her brothers.

"Just say whichever one you want!" I snap, pounding my fist on the table.

All four children look at me like I've just yanked the Easter Bunny by his ears.

"Sorry, guys," I say. "Mommy's so sorry. I'm a little tired today. Go ahead and say your blessing to yourself tonight, whichever one you want. Your choice!" I pull my face into a smile, but it feels strange, like too-elastic pizza dough that doesn't want to be stretched. Lord only knows what it looks like to my children. I wonder how many days, weeks, or months I'll be faking happiness in front of them. What if it's forever?

"Where's Dad?" Sally asks.

"Working late."

"Dad never works late," she says. "He's *always* home for dinner."

"Daddy loves dinner!" Emily says. "Remember when Daddy won us free dessert for eating that gigantic steak?"

I can't help but smile because it's true—once Tom did polish off thirty ounces of a porterhouse just to win a free brownie sundae for the kids. He lay in bed that night, sick as can be, grinning ear to ear, saying that it was worth it to see the joy in the kids' faces.

We eat dinner and the children fill the silence, thank heavens. Sally's irritated with me, I can tell, but still doesn't want to miss her opportunity to talk about her day. She chatters on about her literature class. They're reading *Tuck Everlasting*. Though many of her classmates beg to differ, Sally's certain that immortality would be torture.

"I wouldn't mind being Aphrodite," Emily says. "Being an immortal goddess would be awesome."

Before Emily even finishes, I brace myself for Sally's rebuttal, a know-it-all response that will criticize her sister.

"These are humans, not gods, Em. There's a difference in living a human existence *forever* versus a divine existence."

"I don't see the difference," Em says as she rakes lines in her mashed potatoes.

"The difference is *expectation*," Sally says. "We're humans. It's our expectation that we'll someday die. That someday all this will be over. It's natural. It's not natural to live forever. Besides, some say that our human existence is hell on earth. The goal is getting out of here . . . moving on to the next world."

"Moving where?" Dom wants to know.

"What's hell on earth?" Dan asks.

"What's wrong with you?" Em asks her sister.

"What's natural?" Dom pipes in.

"Where's the next world?" Dan interrupts.

"Never mind," Sally harrumphs, as if her siblings are too beneath her intellectual acumen to engage in conversation.

"I still think it would be cool to be Aphrodite," Emily says.

"There are better goddesses." Sally sighs, exasperated. "Ones who hunted and lived with their animals, ones who didn't choose to bet everything on *love*."

"Why *wouldn't* you want love?" Emily wants to know.

Because love can kill you, even if you don't die, comes to my mind.

"Love's fine, I guess," Sally concedes. "But it's not everything. A woman needs to be her own person, first."

When Sally looks at me, all I see is indictment, as if she knows that I was never such a woman.

After dinner I send the kids up to get ready for bed.

"Why don't we have to do dishes tonight?" Emily wants to know.

"I've got them, honey," I say. "Go ahead up."

"But it's only seven thirty," Sally balks, and her snotty tone hits me wrong. It's all I can do not to lash out at her.

"Please, Sal," I say. "Just take some quiet time tonight."

"I don't want to."

"Since when do you not want to read a book?" I ask, feeling the heat fill my cheeks.

"I just want to stay down here," she says. "I don't want to go upstairs yet."

"Do it anyway!"

"I want to wait for Dad! Where's Dad?"

"J. C., Sal. Can you possibly pick up on the fact that I'm not feeling well tonight?"

"'Not feeling well,'" Sally repeats skeptically. "I thought you said you were tired."

"Either way," I say.

Sally stomps away in a huff. I listen to her exaggerated heavy footsteps pound up the stairs. Hear her flop onto her bed.

I stand at the kitchen sink, staring into my own reflection in the window. The eerie lighting makes my face look drawn and ugly, like I'm looking into a fun-house mirror. I hate that I talk to Sally like an adult, that our relationship is already *there*, that I expect her to pick up on my nuances and facial expressions like one of my sisters would. I hate that she knows *not feeling well* or *being tired* is code for something worse.

I stare out the window into the darkness. *Where are you, Tom?*

By nine o'clock the children are all asleep, and my nerves have passed through jittery and are well on their way to panic. I sit on the floor with Tom's dresser drawers dumped out in front of me, neatly folding his undershirts, T-shirts, shorts, boxers. I lay each one out flat, smooth it with my hand, over and over, until there's not one wrinkle. I fold and press. Fold more, press more. Perfect. Make it perfect for him. Show him how much I care, with my expert folding. He'll come home, he'll open his drawers, he'll see the tidy stacks, he'll know how much I love him. I hold my hands out in front of myself. Watch them shake.

In his top drawer I find a stack of cards that I've given him over the years, for Valentine's Day, his birthday, our anniversaries. Each one gooier than the last, words underlined for emphasis, my handwriting at the bottom: *I love you so, so, so, so much! Forever and always, Mary.* Hearts drawn in pink and red, pierced with arrows. An abundance of smiley faces.

When Tom and I met it was like breathing fresh air after being stifled in a muggy, hot jungle. Tom was easy; we believed in the same things, we wanted the same things. He loved family, wanted one of his own, treated his parents well, didn't carry self-aggrandizing aspirations. My parents loved him the first time I brought him to dinner. Without preamble and coaching, he held the chair for my mother, devoured three servings of stuffed shells, and cleared the table afterward.

Only months into our relationship, we were talking about getting married and buying a house. After years of being with Landon, it threw me for a loop when Tom considered me part of his plan. *What's wrong with this guy?* I remember thinking in the beginning. Maybe he just wants to get married and I'm the girl he happens to be dating. Then, later, I found out that there was an abundance of low-hanging fruit dangling from Tom's little black book. I'd heard of Tom's ex-girlfriend Cassandra, a willowy waif with giant doe eyes who liked to cook but never ate. The realization that Tom *chose* me came to me one night when we were snuggled on the sofa watching a movie. *I'm not just the right girl at the right time. He really wants to be with me.*

Being with Tom was easy, but he wasn't predictable. After only three months of dating, he swept me off my feet, flying me to Napa Valley and proposing on the hillside of an olive grove. I remember feeling such a rush of gratitude for his showing me that a relationship could glide along easily; that it didn't have to be a battle, an uneven power struggle in which one party wanted one thing and the other something different altogether.

Thank you! I wanted to say in the most appreciative way. It was as if the curtain had been drawn back and behind the small life I had been leading was an entire city, an entire world. I remember thinking about my college philosophy studies, and Plato's Allegory of the Cave, how the prisoners down below believed that the shadows on the walls *were* reality; that they hadn't a clue that there was actual *life* being lived only steps away from where they sat.

"I'm ready," Tom had said the night he proposed on that Napa hillside. "I'm all in. I want to marry you, Mary, but I want to be real. We need to acknowledge that you've just gotten out of a long-term relationship. I'm all for getting engaged, but I think we should take it slow."

I took Tom's hands and squeezed them, looked him in the eyes. "I think we should take it fast. I've wasted enough time with the wrong guy. I don't want to waste another minute." Then I tiptoed up to him and kissed him hard on the mouth. I must have been convincing because we were married three months later. Had I not answered the phone when Landon called only weeks before my wedding, had I not gone, had I the courage to refuse him, I wouldn't be sitting here now, waiting for the earth to open up and swallow me whole.

CHAPTER FIFTEEN
Heartily Sorry

IT'S ELEVEN O'CLOCK WHEN TOM finally pulls into the driveway. I'm sitting in the living room on the sofa in the dark, his plaid flannel shirt wrapped around me like a cape. Before I know it, he's standing in front of me. His eyes are bloodshot, his face is blotchy, his jaw is clenched. His fists are balled and he smells of whiskey. *Whiskey!* The poison that corrupted his father and brother. The poison he swore he would never touch.

"I've been calling you for hours," I say. "Where have you been?"

Tom finds a dusty bottle of whiskey under the cupboard, a bottle we'd bought for a party years ago. Pours a few inches. Downs it in one sip. The curse of the Morrissey men, wrapping her slimy arms around Tom's neck. On a night like tonight, it doesn't seem that Tom needs too much coaxing. He's ready to jump into bed with the alcoholic seductress.

"I've been at a bar, obviously," Tom says. "Sitting and thinking and trying my hardest to find one *logical,* reasonable explanation for why there is a photo of you and Landon James flashing across every television in America. A photo of him kissing your cheek as you two come out of a hotel room."

"It's not what you think! I had Sally with me. She was in her carrier. We were just talking, Tom," I plead.

"I'm not a stupid guy," Tom says. The coolness in his voice makes me shake harder. "And I feel that I'm a reasonable guy, a guy who doesn't jump to conclusions without considering every possibility."

"You are!" I agree. "You are the most reasonable person I know. I love that about you."

"But I couldn't do it," Tom says. "I sat there for hours and I couldn't think of one good reason why you would have seen Landon James." He looks up at me briefly. His eyes are red and swollen, his mouth pursed tightly. I want to go to him, put my hands on his face, assume his suffering. "So let's have it, Mary. What gives?"

I had rehearsed this exact moment a thousand times in the past few weeks. Would I play dumb? Would I deny that it was me? Would I feed him the story I had fed our neighbor Susan? Or would I just come clean? I decide on telling the truth. All at once my defenses slough from my body. I have nowhere to run and the truth is my only way out, even if it leads Tom out the door.

"I met him that day," I say, "because we had some business to discuss."

"Business? What the hell does that mean? Were you giving money to his campaign?"

"No."

"What kind of business did you have to discuss with Landon James?" Tom's only inches from my face. I can feel the heat from his breath. This is my doing, I think. I've driven him to drink just like his good-for-nothing brother and father.

"Can we sit down?" I ask.

"Please, Mary," Tom scoffs. "Just tell me what the hell is going on."

"I saw Landon that day. After Sally was born. But I also saw him one other time. The month before our wedding."

"You saw Landon James two times. After you were with me?" The words slip through his teeth like smoke.

"Just those two times," I say, swallowing back the flood of tears. "I swear to God, Tom. Since the day you and I met, I only saw Landon those two times."

"Okay," Tom says, pulling at his hair. "Let's take them one at a time. Why the hell did you see Landon before we got married?"

"That was forever ago. He had called and was in really bad shape. He had given up his Virginia senate seat to run for attorney general, and he didn't win and he was feeling really bad."

"So what?"

I take a breath. *Say it.* "So . . . he was begging me to come back to him."

"Come *back*!" Tom says in disgust.

"I know."

"And you were considering it?"

"God no!" I say. "That was the last thing on my mind. It was the opposite of what I was feeling." I take another breath, unable to look at his face as he waits for me to go on. "For the first time, I felt highly superior to Landon. He was down and out, and I was getting married in a month to the best guy in the world. For the first time in ten years, I had the upper hand with him. I know it's stupid and juvenile, but there was a part of me that wanted a little revenge for all of the years he strung me along. So, yes, I went to see him. I went to flaunt my good fortune in front of him. I went to show him that I was finally truly happy."

"Okay, *fine*," Tom says through clenched teeth. "So you went to wave your engagement ring in his face. What happened when you saw him?"

"He was a mess!" I say. "He said he'd made a huge mistake letting me get away. He said he didn't care if he lost everything as long as he could have me. I actually felt sorry for the guy, but I also felt so proud that I was about to start the life I always wanted."

"Then what?"

"Then my plan of kicking him while he was down flew away. You know me," I say, wiping my face with my sleeve and then forcing myself to look him in the eye. "I'm not like that. I ended up feeling *bad* for him. So I sat with him and tried to make him feel better. We discussed a plan to get him back on his feet. I cheered him on, like an idiot. I sat there and told him that he could do it; that he could make his dreams come true; that he'd be back up on top before he knew it."

"Then?"

"He started to feel better and asked if I'd stay for dinner."

Tom's face darkens, and when he speaks his lips don't move. "Did you?"

"It seemed harmless. You were out of town. It was just dinner. We talked about old times—I mean, hell, Tom, I'd known this guy since I was nineteen years old. He asked about you. And I told him. I told him how great it was to finally be in a relationship like ours. I told him that he should try it sometime."

"Then what?"

I swallowed. "I had a couple of glasses of wine," I say.

"What happened, Mary?" Tom says, knowing what a light-weight I am—two glasses of wine leave me silly and affectionate.

"I can't say it," I say.

"Say it!" he demands, eyes snapping now.

"You know what happened!" I yell, stepping back. "Don't you? Can't you guess?"

"Did you sleep with him?"

The words alone are apocalyptic. A wave of nausea engulfs me. I run to the toilet and vomit.

Tom stands in the doorway, offers me nothing. I wipe my mouth with a wad of toilet paper, stand up, and push myself back into the corner of the small room.

"Oh, God, Tom, I'm so sorry," I cry. "Please, you've got to know how sorry I am. How sorry I've been *all* of these years. I don't know what I was thinking. I just wanted him to feel bad for the rest of his life about losing me, and it just happened, Tom. You've got to believe me. I'm so sorry."

The look on my husband's face is indescribable, devastating. I know I'll never forget it, like I'm disgusting to him.

"Please, Tom," I beg. "I made a horrible mistake."

"A mistake?" Tom says, his voice a broken, raw whisper. "A mistake is forgetting to send in a mortgage payment, or . . . or . . . bumping the fender of the car in front of you. Sleeping with your ex-boyfriend when you were engaged to me . . ." He can't finish. Can only slowly shake his head.

"I know, I know! I can't even explain why it happened. You've got to know I was young when I met Landon, and he had some strange power over me—it's like he pulled my strings. I hate to say that. It makes me seem like such an idiot."

Tom cocks his head and releases a shell of a laugh. "Believe me, Mary, you're not helping your situation. Telling me that you were helpless to Landon James's charm."

"It wasn't charm. I don't know what made me do it. I just wanted him to feel like he'd missed out. That he lost his chance with me."

"So you thought you'd give him one last fuck to remember you by."

"God, Tom!" I cry. "This is *me* you're talking to. The mother of your children, and you're talking to me like I'm a whore. I don't deserve the f-word."

Tom stares at me; the stone-cold look back on his face begs to differ.

"I can't say anything right." I'm panicking. "Whatever I say is going to be misconstrued. It shouldn't have happened, but for God's sake, Tom, haven't I been a good wife and mother all of these years?"

"Not the point."

Finally we both stop and take a moment to breathe. Tom settles down a bit, his fists unclench. But this is only round one, the easy round, the one that might be forgiven. Round two promises to be much worse.

"Let's get through this," Tom says. "What business did you have to discuss with Landon James the second time you met, after we were married? When that photo was taken?"

I sit down, and for the first time in hours my breath flows easily. It's over and I know it. My defeat is certain and there's a calmness in the retreat. Tom once told me that being knocked out in the ring felt like surrender, the acceptance of knowing it's over.

I've waited ten years to say the words that are about to come out of my mouth. I look at Tom, knowing that I'll never see him again with the same eyes and, more important, that he'll never see me the same way again. I reach for his hands, but he knocks mine away. I cover my mouth and swallow a decade of tears.

Here it is: the end of life as I know it. I can only hope to God that finally telling the truth will offer at least a shred of solace. Just to have it out in the open for once, not to have to suck on the bitter lie for another day. I take a deep breath, will my heart to hang in there, and stand in front of Tom.

"Business about Sally," I say in almost a whisper.

"Sally?" Tom says, confused.

"Yes, honey. About Sally."

"Is this a goddamned riddle?" Tom yells venomously. "What does this have to do with Sal?"

I look at him with pleading eyes. I want to say it, but he gets it on his own, and when the earth shifts under his feet I can almost see him crack down the middle.

"No! *No*, no, no, no," Tom says, shaking his head. "Don't you even tell me what you're about to tell me. No!"

"Tom," I sob. "Please."

"Say it!" he roars.

"I can't!"

"Say it, Mary. So help me God, you say what you're getting at. Say it!"

My ears are ringing. My mouth won't operate . . . and then it does, "It's true. Landon James is Sally's biological father." I have said the words that I have said out loud only once before—to Landon.

"*My* Sally?" he says in a gravelly yelp. "You're telling me that my Sally is not *mine*. Is that what you're saying?"

"Oh, God, Tom. I'm so sorry. But she *is* yours. You *raised* her. She's your girl. You're her daddy. Please, Tom."

"You were knocked up when we walked down the aisle and we acted like it was our little secret, but all along you knew it wasn't our secret—it was your dirty little lie. You've been lying to me our entire marriage. Our entire marriage!" Tom yells. He walks toward the wall next to the fireplace, braces his hands against it, and taps his forehead—a metronome tapping to the beat of his grief. Then he pushes himself to upright, and punches his fist straight through the drywall.

Instinctively, I look up toward the kids' rooms; cannot even imagine how I could explain the racket, the discord between their parents.

"I didn't know whose baby it was, Tom," I cry. "I prayed so hard that she was yours, and when she was born it was the happiest moment of my life when I saw her swirl of amber hair, because I thought for sure that she was yours. But then the nurse handed her to me, and even though she was a squishy newborn, I saw something in her eyes—a resemblance to Landon—and that's when I suspected."

"You didn't know whose child you were carrying?" Tom's voice disintegrates as he says this, and he begins to sob.

"Tom, please. We have a wonderful life. We can't let this ruin what we have."

"You fooled me into loving Sally more than myself and she's not even my girl. I would have done anything for her, and you just let me believe my feelings were true." Tom sobs, storming across the room. As I watch, he lifts from the mantel the porcelain vase we bought in Napa Valley on the day of our engagement and hurls it into the fireplace. Then he punches another wall, leaving a fist-sized hole. He examines his bloody knuckles and falls onto the sofa, crying into his hands. "Sally," he whimpers. "Sally. Sally. Sally."

I go to him, kneel beside him. Pull his hands to my mouth, hold his knuckles against my lips, kiss soft, moist kisses onto them. "She's your girl, Tom. You can't blame her for any of this. I know you'll never forgive me, and I don't blame you, and I'll spend the rest of my life trying to make this up to you, but Tom, for God's sake, we have four children and they're all yours, and you cannot take this out on Sally. She'd be devastated if you changed how you treat her."

"Stop lecturing me on what I do and do not need to do!" Tom barks darkly, pulling his hands away from me. "You don't have the right to tell me *anything*."

I sit down next to him on the sofa. Watch him suffer through the torture and pain. Watch him writhe while the truth snakes through his mind and heart. Watch him hurt and know that I caused it. *Through my fault, through my fault, through my most grievous fault.* The words echo in my head as I pray for mercy for poor Tom.

He looks up, presses his lips together, then smirks. "The life insurance policy that Landon named you as the beneficiary, that was for Sally?"

"Yes," I say.

"Your relationship with him never ended," Tom says in the saddest voice. "In one way or another you've been carrying on with him all these years. I was just the dumb sap who didn't know it."

Then he's on his feet and out the door. A few minutes later I hear the screech of tires as Tom backs up his car, then the punch of the accelerator issuing a hot-rod squeal down the driveway.

CHAPTER SIXTEEN

The Pains of Hell

TOM

I HOP ON I-66 HEADED west. I pull in enough air to fill a basketball, push against the steering wheel, and watch the tendons in my forearm pop. I ball my lacerated hand into a fist and pound it down onto the center console—the compartment between my seat and the passenger's. I hear it crack, feel the gash on my hand bust open again. Damn it, it's going to cost a bundle to get that thing replaced. "Screw it," I say, furious at myself for worrying about being responsible at a time like this. Since I already broke it, I punch it again. And again. I gun the engine, grit my teeth. A deer is nibbling grass on the side of the road. It looks up at me and flinches a bit. *Stay,* I warn it, because right now it is looking an awful lot like Landon James—and Mary, for that matter.

There's no other way to describe it. I'm filled with *hate*. Hate. For my wife, for the mother of my children. At this moment I hate her and want only one thing: to make her hurt as badly as she has made me hurt. Pure vengeance. She is anathema to everything I believe in. Landon James? Hell, I'd knock his lights out with a quick right jab. He'd feel the crack of his jaw a split second before he was on the ropes, then flat on his ass. But I don't feel hate for him like I feel for Mary. Landon James is disposable, inconsequential in so many ways. But Mary, God, Mary. She broke my heart.

All these years I've known there was something up, something I couldn't quite put my finger on. I always felt like I was second string when it came to Mary and Landon James, but I just thought it had to do with the two of them: lingering feelings, a shared past, a decade spent together that couldn't easily be erased. But no, there was more. There was a secret. A roll in the hay right before our wedding.

And Sally, dear God, Sally. My girl, who everyone says looks like *me*! Our hair, it's the same color, the same texture. And she's so competitive, so athletic and determined. I thought she got all that from me, but she didn't get anything from me. I'm nothing to her.

I look at the speedometer. I'm pushing 90 mph. If I get stopped, the cop will check my blood-alcohol content. Who knows what it would register. Maybe I'd get thrown in jail. Maybe I could make a case for rehab. Patrick and I could room together. He could teach me how to say "screw you" to a responsible life. We'd spend our days in the rec room, shooting hoops. Then we'd take turns talking to the shrink. I'd tell her how my wife is a cheating, lying whore who ruined my life. She'd listen and nod and offer me a tissue. Later, Patrick and I would sit with all the other losers in the art room, making crafts out of macaroni and glue like we're kids. Maybe at night the nurses would knock me out with some strong-ass meds that would put me into a coma sleep in which I wouldn't stand a chance of thinking about Mary or Landon or Sally.

The exits fly by. I'm already past Manassas. I'm happy to see the speed limit increase to 65 mph. At least now I'm speeding only twenty-five miles over the limit. *You're allowed to be irresponsible once!* I hear in my head. Everyone else has been. My father, my brother, even my mother, whose complacency is a type of irresponsibility. Mary, Landon—they were irresponsible. "Good ol' Tom!" I say aloud, gunning the engine again. Always the guy to count on: dependable, reliable, honest. Screw that!

I'm in the country now. I took the boys camping up here once, to the Shenandoah Valley. We pitched our tent right off Skyline Drive. The two little guys sat on my lap and we looked out at the brilliant sunset, a view that extended to heaven. "God made everything beautiful," Dom said that day.

"That's right," I told them. "God's pretty awesome."

"No one's gooder than God," Danny said.

"Yep," I said. "God's the best. But you know who else is really awesome? Mom."

"Because of the love," one of the little guys said.

"Yep, because of the love," I said that day. "And because Mom is true-blue. That means that she's honest and kind and always tries to do the right thing."

"Mommy never lies," Danny said.

Truth. I know now that there is no such thing. If Mary—the one person I believed to be good and true—is a dirty, rotten liar, then everyone is. Everyone.

CHAPTER SEVENTEEN
The Nature of Wrongdoing

I STAND IN THE KITCHEN, staring out the window, stunned. *What happened did not just happen. What happened did just happen. Tom knows that I saw Landon, that I slept with Landon, that Landon is Sally's father.* The enormity of it makes me dizzy. For a decade I imagined this moment in time, but now that it's here, it's worse, bigger, more sickening. What I did, the lie I've been living, telling it to Tom, is eviscerating.

We'll never come back from this.

I stand at the window for an hour, just staring, like a dog waiting for the return of its master. When I'm finally able to break my gaze, I begin to clean, wiping down the counters and appliances, standing atop a chair to get the dust from the top of the refrigerator. I say Hail Marys, Our Fathers, over and over and over again, but I feel like a hypocrite, like the idea of me praying is indulgent and hopeful when I should feel nothing but sorrow and guilt. I don't deserve God's help right now, but Tom does, so instead of praying for me, I pray for Tom. I pray that God will heal his pain, that God will soothe his hurt, and mostly I pray that God will protect Tom behind the wheel, a man fueled with anger and whiskey. I shake my head at my stupid self because I'm doing it again, negotiating agreements: *Protect my husband and I'll absorb his pain.* I imagine God laughing at my stupid self with my stupid deals, reminding me that He provides whether the terms are good or not.

Kneeling before the fireplace with the garbage can at my side, gathering shards of porcelain that once made the vase Tom and I bought on the day of our engagement, I pause to look up at the wall, at the two battered spots that were assaulted by Tom's fist. I stand and place my hand on the deeper hole, see a smear of Tom's blood from his knuckles. Unthinking, I reach into the bin for a shard of porcelain and run it across my palm until I draw blood, then place my blood on Tom's. *I'm sorry, baby. I'm so sorry, I whisper,* rapping my forehead against the wall.

The bookcase is only a foot or so from the larger of the two holes. I brace my back against the side of the fireplace and push the bookcase with my legs until the hole is covered, hidden away from my children's sight. The other hole isn't as deep, so I relocate the framed mirror atop it. With the evidence covered, I feel creepy, as deceitful as a crook.

By the time I sit down on our bed, it's two o'clock in the morning. My hands are still shaking and my teeth are still chattering, though I'm covered in a heavy sweatshirt. I watch the time on the clock turn minute by minute. When I go to the bathroom, I catch a glimpse of myself in the mirror. My eyes look sunken, like a refugee's, like those of someone who will never come back from where she once was. Years ago I volunteered at a shelter where most of the women had been abused. They all had the same ghostly eyes. My eyes look like theirs, though I don't deserve to have the eyes of a victim since I'm the abuser.

In bed I wonder about Tom. *Where are you, honey?* Did he find a diner, plop into a corner booth, nurse a tenth cup of coffee, his eyes rubbed red and puffy? Or did he continue on with his initiation into the land of whiskey, where his father and brother roam? Where would he go for comfort? What would he do? It's not like he has a support system like I do, my three sisters, my adoring parents, all skilled in the doting and hovering department, an arsenal of stuffed shells and stuffed pastries prepared and ready, whether for crisis or celebration.

Tom has his parents, who, while supportive, are avoiders. I can already hear Sean, who pretends everything is dandy, even if Patrick is in rehab or Colleen is in chemo for breast cancer or his blood pressure has topped two hundred. "Oh, son! God bless you, son," he'd say. "This is just a glitch. You and Mare will work this out, you'll see. How about spending the day with your old man?"

And Colleen is no better, the way she reasons and rationalizes but never sits down, addressing adversity through motion. I can see Tom sitting at his mother's table in her immaculate kitchen while she sorts silverware and refolds perfectly square napkins. I can hear Tom flipping roles, telling his mother to sit down, that it is going to be okay. Colleen would bend down, kiss Tom's head, and agree. "Of course, dear. It's going to be okay," she'd say, and then begin cleaning out the refrigerator.

And then there is Patrick, the guy whose premonition about me was spot-on. "It's not too late to bail," Patrick had said the morning of our wedding. "I've got a twelve-pack in the trunk." I now wonder whether Tom remembers his brother's prophetic quip, considers the possibility that Patrick's soulful eyes could zero in on his future. Tom must wish he'd heeded his brother's warning.

At four o'clock in the morning, I hear the garage door open and the sound of footsteps making their way downstairs to the basement. Then I hear the shower turn on, sending a high-pitched whine up the pipes. Half an hour later Tom enters our room for clean clothes. I slip out of bed and stand in front of him. "Tom," I plead.

"Not now," he says.

"When?"

He shakes his head at me in disgust, as if to say, "Never."

CHAPTER EIGHTEEN
Cornerstone of Faith

TOM DRESSES QUICKLY AND THEN leaves the house. I lie in bed, waiting for the boys. With clockwork predictability, they crawl in with me at six o'clock, finding perfect fits in impossibly small spaces. Dom's head is resting on my neck, his silky hair tickling my nose. Danny's on my side, softly singing a song he learned at Sunday school, "Peter, James, and John in a Sailboat."

"That's nice," I tell him.

"They're possums," he says.

"That's right," I say. "Apostles."

Domenic stirs, stretches wildly, smacks me in the face. "Where's Daddy?"

"He had to go to work early," I say, smoothing his hair across his head.

"I wanted to crack eggs on his back and give him chills," Dom says.

"Do me," I say, rolling onto my stomach so that my son can snap and smack his little fists on my spine.

"Did it give you chills?" he asks, and I nod yes because since last night I've had nothing but.

An hour later we're down for breakfast, four kids lined up at the counter, slumped over their bowls of cereal, trying to fight the sleepiness that still has a hold on them like a Benadryl hangover. I stare out the kitchen window with a coffee cup held to my lips.

When I turn around and Sally finally looks up, wiping the sleep from her eyes, she gasps. "Mom! What's wrong with your face?"

I reach for my cheek, which feels thin and slumpy. I know my eyes must be swollen and lined. I consider how to explain the worn and crumpled look on my face to my children.

"I didn't sleep well," I say. "So help me out, okay, girls?"

The girls eat their cereal and drink their hot cocoa and then head up the stairs to get ready for school. I coax the boys upstairs and today they actually comply. Maybe I look so scary they're considering that since I've magically transformed into a monster, they had better listen to me or else. I get the boys dressed, hair and teeth brushed, a quick trip to the toilet. Sally and Emily are packing their backpacks on the kitchen counter.

"Why'd Dad leave so early this morning?" Sally asks. "Another trip to Chicago?"

"No, honey, he just had work to do."

Sally squints her scrutinizing eyes at me. "You sure you're okay, Mom?"

"I'm fine, honey," I say, and then blow my nose for effect. "Let's get going, okay? Want me to drive you today instead of taking the bus?"

I drop the girls off first and then the boys. Back home I sit on the sofa, chewing on my cuticles, staring at the wall, wondering how much deeper I'll fall into the abyss, how much hotter things can get.

Angie calls, Mom and Dad, Teresa, and Martina. I can't talk; I let them go to voice mail.

The turn of the door handle tells me that Tom's home. I stand and face him and find that his anger hasn't abated; his face isn't any more forgiving today than yesterday. His fists are still tight balls, his jaw is still a wire pulled taut.

He stands before me and says, "I'm not leaving my house and my children. I thought about it, leaving you and the kids, but screw that, Mary. They're my kids, too, and I'm not going to leave. If you want to, you leave."

"Tom!" I plead, and again my heart slams into my chest like the recoil from a shotgun. "Stop talking that way. No one is going anywhere."

"I want to make sure that I'm clear, Mary," Tom says with pure, cold hatred. "You and me, we're finished."

I stumble back into the sofa and fold at the waist and cover my ears, because they're ringing as though a bomb has gone off and I can't tell if I'm still whole or blown to bits. I look up. "You can't possibly mean that."

"For the children's sake I'll be cordial to you, and if you want to stay we'll find a way to live in this house together. If you want to leave, I'll find a way to take care of the kids. Either way, I'm staying. And for now, the children will know *nothing*. Nothing! Do you understand?"

"This is crazy," I say, and again start to cry. I slide off the sofa and fall at Tom's feet and grab his ankles and cry teardrops onto his shoes.

He pulls his feet away. "There are things that I need to know,"

Tom fumes bitterly. "The day Sally was born . . . you delivered a lie as much as you did a child. How'd it *feel*, Mary?"

"How do you think it felt?" I croak, sitting back and covering my face. "Knowing the truth and wanting it to be something different. I can't describe what it was like to see you with her. You were the proudest father in the world. You cradled her like she held the keys to the kingdom. She was your girl from the start." I stand, look him in the eyes. "Love's love, Tom. You can't possibly think that you no longer love her."

"Of course I still love *her*!" Tom yells.

"I get it," I say. "*I'm* the one you no longer love." I look at Tom, wait for him to argue, try to find something in his eyes that tells me he still loves me, but he's stone-faced and cold and when it sinks in, my legs almost buckle. He really doesn't love me.

"Tom, dear God, you have to know how sorry I am. I *fell*. After all those years of Landon not choosing me, he finally did, and I fell for it. That's all I can say."

"That's not enough," he says.

"Please, Tom, we have to work this out. We're a family. For God's sake, we're a family."

"Leave God out of this, Mare. If you recall, adultery is a sin."

"Well, aren't you the picture of perfection!" I yell.

"I've never claimed to be perfect," Tom says. "But since I've known you—for eleven years—I've never once lied to you."

"That's only because you've never had anything worth lying about!" I holler, taking a stab at a rather iffy argument. "You've never had a gun put to your head like the one that was put to mine! How could you possibly know what you would have done in a similar spot?"

"That's your argument?" he roars. "That everyone has a break-ing point? That everyone has a price?"

"Don't they?" I cover my face and begin to cry because I know my argument sounds lame, like trying to acquit a murderer be-cause he was *really mad*. "How can you possibly know how far you would go if it had to do with the kids, with your brother, their health and survival? My lie has given you a family! If I had told you what happened, where would any of us be?"

"It wasn't your choice to make alone!" he yells. "I should have known the situation. You should have told me the truth! Maybe we would have still ended up a family, maybe we wouldn't have, but at least our lives would have been honest. So cut the moralistic bullshit about how your lie has given me a life. There is no silver lining to your lie, Mary! No matter how hard you try to convince yourself that there was virtue in what you did, there's not!"

"What are you saying, Tom? That I'm unforgivable? Unre-deemable? That there is no getting past this?"

"There's a lot that I could get past, but you know the most un-believable part of all of this?" I stare at him, but my vision is be-traying me, making the features on his face grow larger and then smaller. "The most unbelievable part is that Landon knew Sally was his and I didn't. Why was that, Mary? I don't agree with it, but I could at least understand why you didn't tell me—you thought I would leave. I could understand even more why you wouldn't tell Landon—he'd never know if you hadn't told him. But here's the kicker, Mare: You told Landon. You sought him out and told him. Why? What were you hoping for in telling him? Were you hoping he would sweep you off your feet, and you and Sally would run away with him?"

"No! God, no!" I scream. "I never once had that thought. That's not why I told him."

"Then why?"

"Because I was going to tell him and get his word that he would stay out of our lives. And then I was going to tell you! That was the plan. To come clean. To live the truth. But I told him, got his word, and then I never told you. Never could. I tried a million times, but I could never get the words out."

Tom walks to the mantel, lifts a framed photo of the kids from a few years back. I brace myself for him to pitch it into the fireplace, but he doesn't, just stares at it, traces his finger across their younger faces.

"You say you never chose Landon over me, but Mary, there's no denying that you did. You trusted your secret would be safer with him than it was with me. That's all there is to it."

With that, Tom storms out the door, and the next thing I hear is the shriek of rubber on the driveway.

For the rest of the morning I sit on the edge of the fireplace with my face in my hands. The flue is open and an icy stream of air has chilled me to the bone. In my daze, I rock back and forth until a new thought collides with the one I had clung to all along. That I have been lying to Tom for ten years, I knew. What I didn't know was that I was lying to myself, too. *Why* did I tell Landon? What was I hoping for? Was it what Tom said? Was I hoping for Landon to steal me away from Tom? Not once had that thought knocked on my door . . . until now.

CHAPTER NINETEEN
All My Heart

AFTER SALLY WAS BORN, AFTER I saw her resemblance to Landon James, after I had fallen into a deep depression, I picked up the phone and called him. We made plans to meet at the Mayflower on Connecticut Avenue.

We sat awkwardly in the gigantic lobby chairs.

"I was very surprised to hear from you," he said.

"I'm sure," I answered, lulling Sally by rocking her carrier.

"Did you want to see me for any reason in particular?" Landon asked. "I mean, you don't need a reason."

"I have a reason," I said.

"Oh, okay. Great."

"I have something I need to tell you."

"Okay."

"Is there somewhere more private where we could talk?"

Once inside the hotel room, Landon asked, "Would you like something to drink?" He waved to the mini-refrigerator.

"Sure," I said. "A soda, something without caffeine. I'm nursing."

Landon opened a Sprite for me and set it on the ledge by the window.

"So what's this all about, MM?"

I turned to him, took an enormous breath, and looked down at Sally. "We named her Sally," I said.

"She's adorable," Landon said, reaching out with a finger to touch her hair.

"I don't know why we chose the name Sally," I said. "It just seemed nice, not too pretentious, not too cute."

"I like the name," Landon said.

"It fits her."

"Uh-huh."

"Landon?"

"Yeah, Mary?" he said, still fingering Sally's silky hair.

"You're Sally's father . . . biologically."

"W-what?" Landon stammered, pulling back his hand. "I *am*? How's that *possible*?"

"The last time we saw each other, remember?"

"Of course I remember," he said, sitting down and bending at the waist. "How do you know?" he said, his eyes on his shoes.

"Look at her," I replied, and turned Sally outward in his direction, hanging her from my forearm like a floppy newborn cub.

"What?"

"Don't you see it?" I asked. "Can't you see the resemblance?"

"To me, she looks like *you*."

"It's easier for someone else to see," I said. "But that's why I need a DNA sample. Just so we're sure." I reached my hand into my purse, pulled out a little kit I had purchased on the Internet, a cluster of Q-tips and sterile envelopes.

"Whoa, hold on, Mary, you're nearly giving me a heart attack. Give me a second to breathe."

"Sorry," I said. "I've had time to think about this. I understand that it's a shock."

"What about the test?"

"You just swab your cheek, and then I send it off. I'll make up a fake name. None of this will be 'on the record.'"

"What about your husband? Tom, right? What did he say?"

"I haven't told him yet."

"Are you planning to?"

"Of course," I said. "I just wanted to tell you first and have a discussion about how we're going to handle this."

"How *are* we going to handle this?"

I took a deep breath and released it, looked at Landon with pleading eyes, and kissed the top of Sally's head. "I want you to stay out of her life."

He stood and walked to the window, placed his forehead against the cool glass, and breathed little clouds of fog onto the pane.

"I want to raise her with Tom," I went on. "With the other children we're going to have. I'm asking you to give up any right to her, Landon. I mean, my God, you're running for attorney general again. You have your law firm. The last thing you need is an 'illegitimate' baby, right?" As the word *illegitimate* floated from my mouth, I felt guilty instantly for my little innocent baby, who was anything but illegitimate.

Landon exhaled noisily, furrowed his brow. "Goddamn, MM, why'd you tell me, then? What kind of man would give up his right to his own child?"

"She doesn't fit into your life, Landon. And she fits perfectly into mine. I'm asking you to let me have her. You owe me, Landon. For a decade of my life when you promised to love me and you didn't. You owe me. Let me get on with my life."

Landon covered his face with his hands, and when he removed them his eyes were red and puffy. "I know I owe you," he said. "But still, what you're asking . . ."

"I know, Landon," I said. "It's a lot. But it's not like you want a baby in your life right now, is it?"

"No, God no," Landon said. "It's the last thing I want. It's just the point of it: giving up any claim to a child I fathered. It makes me feel like my good-for-nothing old man, that's all. A de facto lowlife."

"You're nothing like him."

Landon stared into space, as though trying to will that to be true. Then he turned to me. "You didn't have to tell me," he said. "Why did you?"

"I don't know," I said. "For some reason, I just had to."

Landon walked briskly toward me, and my first thought was that he was storming out of the room, but instead he lifted Sally from my arms. He held her awkwardly in front of himself, and then he sat in the chair and draped her across his legs. She didn't seem to mind. Tears welled in his eyes, then he shook his head, wiping them away. "Goddamn, MM. She's . . . she's really *my daughter*."

"No, Landon, she's not," I said. "A daughter belongs to the father who raises her. Biology doesn't matter. You, of all people, know that. I want Tom to raise her."

"What if I say no?" he asked. "What if I want to be her father?"

"Do you?" I asked, because I knew from experience that Landon James didn't want to be a husband, much less a father.

He didn't. Landon agreed to my terms, and then a few months later he was elected as attorney general. That was when I learned that Landon's success was my ticket to freedom. The more successful, the more public his career became, the less likely the chance that he'd want anything to do with Sally and me.

CHAPTER TWENTY

Loss of Heaven

THE DAYS THAT FOLLOW ROLL through like a heavy fog. I'm a stranger in my own home. My children think I'm acting weird. I'm despised by my husband. I can see in his eyes the raw disgust he feels for me, and I don't know how to act. I'm torn. On the one hand, I still need to be Mom to my kids. They need me to be up and happy and cheerful and here. They need me to be present in every minute of their days. Running away, crawling into a hole, seeking shelter under a pile of thick blankets isn't an option.

But on the other hand, Tom needs me to be sorry. He wants to see me suffer. He wants me to hurt as badly as he does. And then there's Sally, my intuitive lawyer-to-be daughter, who is scrutinizing me and analyzing my every move as though she's a forensics expert, ready to testify as to the competency—or lack thereof—of our family.

The needs of my children are at odds with the needs of my husband. The two are incompatible, and every move I make feels wrong. If I laugh at something the boys say, I feel as if I'm betraying Tom's pain. If I'm gloomy and quiet for Tom, I feel guilty that I'm not the mom my kids need. I'm being pulled, and my heart—the anchor that once rooted me against the tugs—has given up, separated from the rope.

Each day Mom and Dad call. "It's fine, I'm fine, everything is fine," I whimper over the phone. I don't have the vocabulary to put this crisis into words, can't craft a sentence around this catastrophe, can't even begin to explain *what I have done.* On the third day, they show up at my door. I collapse into my mother's arms and fight for breath, because at the sight of her I lose it and cannot breathe. I want to breathe in, but the cries are forcing their way out. There's a traffic jam in my throat and just as Dad's going to get a paper bag for me to breathe into, I fall to my knees and catch some breath. "I'm okay," I say, and then start to cry again.

For the next hour I cry and my parents hold me without saying a word. I lie across them like I did when I was a kid. Dad strokes my hair and Mom draws shapes on my back. I soak Dad's pant leg with tears and snot, but he doesn't seem to mind. Maybe I can go home with them, move back into the room I shared with Angie, organize my shelves of stuffed animals, write in my key-lock diary, and pretend I never grew up and built a life on a lie.

Mom's loving and caring, but she's also efficient. "Okay, then," she says. "Let's sit up, get a cup of coffee, and talk this through."

Once Mom has started the coffee and we're back on the sofa, I say, "I saw Landon."

"Saw him?"

"I was *with* him."

"With him . . . in the biblical sense?" Mom asks.

"In the I-was-a-giant-idiot sense," I say.

"Recently?"

"God no!" I say, shocked, forgetting that this is their first time hearing a story I've known for a decade. "A long time ago. Before Tom and I got married." I swallow. "Right before we got married."

"Oh, honey," Mom says in a sad voice, like she pities her stupid daughter who couldn't say no to Landon James.

"Did it happen again?" Dad asks.

"Of course not," I say, offended, but Dad's question is valid; if I did it once, why not twice?

"And Tom knows," Mom says.

I nod. "But there's more. It wasn't just that I slept with him."

Mom and Dad look at each other. My poor parents, who raised me with perfect morals, who took me to church every Sunday, who said the Rosary with their girls every night, who focused on family and gratitude and making smart choices.

"He's Sally's biological father." I say the words, and though I said them to Tom the other night, today—in the light of day, not fueled with adrenaline—they seem dirtier, more tawdry, like seeing a seedy nightclub in the daytime. A creepy feeling fills me, like watching the sex scene of an R-rated movie with Mom and Dad in the room.

Mom and Dad nod, rock backward and forward, fiddle with their hands, and pull their mouths into tight lines. "Well," Mom says. "Saints preserve us. That's big."

"I know," I cry.

She puts her arm around me and I bury my nose into her neck. Dad reaches over, too, and rubs my back. After a while Mom goes to the kitchen to pour us coffee. When she returns, she says, "Her hair. Tom's hair. You'd never guess that he wasn't her father."

"The hair," I repeat. "Same color as Tom's."

"But also the same color as my mother's."

"It had to come from somewhere," I say, because the jig is up and there's no point saying that it came from Tom anymore.

"My mother, your grandmother, was widowed early with two small children—my older brothers. When she remarried, to my father, he was a widower, too, with a daughter. When they got married, they went on to have three more children—my brother, Mike, my sister, and me. So they had yours, mine, and ours, if you will. But they never once treated any of us different and we never talked in those terms. We were all siblings. We never said 'your dad' or 'my mom,' and it wasn't until we were older that we used to sit around and sort it through. We were just a family."

"I know, Ma," I say. "I can never remember who belonged to whom in your family."

"That's the point," Ma says. "We all belonged to each other. So much so that we couldn't remember either. We were just a family, brothers and sisters all the same."

"I love that story. I wish Tom had known the truth from the beginning. Maybe we still would have gone on with our lives, had our children. But I didn't play it that way. I was too scared he'd leave."

| | |

Day four of our new coexistence, and nothing much has changed. Tom wakes up, heads to work early, is home in time for dinner. He spends more time than usual outside with Daisy, our golden retriever, throwing her a tennis ball. We barely speak to each other, yet we still sleep in the same bed and all sit down as a family for dinner every night. Pretending.

"Blessing," I say, snapping my fingers at the boys. Instinctively my four children make the sign of the cross while Tom says grace. Then the craziness begins, and the kids start barking out what they need, what they're missing. Tom cuts a piece of pork chop into bite-sized pieces for the boys. I pick at the salad bowl with tongs, like playing Operation with the kids: cherry tomatoes for Sally, red peppers for Emily and Danny, just "leafs" for Dom.

Sally pops out of her chair looking for pepper, then Danny pops out of his booster seat.

"Gosh darn, Sally!" I say. "He watches you get up and thinks it's okay."

"I needed pepper," she says.

"Missing the point," I snap.

Out of the corner of my eye I see the side of Tom's lip turn up, and I'm not sure what it means: that he's happy to see the children disobeying me? That he no longer finds Sally's brand of wit funny, now that he knows of her biology?

Once meat has been cut and doled out, bread buttered, milk poured, dressing passed, I take a bite. A minute later the twins proclaim that they're finished, even though Danny's only picked at his food.

"Dom, go play. Danny, sit down," I say. "You need to eat five more pieces of meat."

"I don't like it," he whines.

"Eat it or no dessert."

"I don't want dessert anyway," he says, blowing my negotiation. He runs off to play.

"That's so funny," Sally says. "Danny, who *needs* to eat, is punished for not eating by not getting dessert, and Dom, who eats a ton, eats his meal and, as a reward, gets dessert. So the one who eats gets *twice* as much food, and the one who doesn't, loses an opportunity to eat." Sally's sitting up proud, like she's just won a case.

"Yes, Sal," I say. "I get the irony."

"So, you should think about it," she says in her know-it-all voice.

"I swear to God, Sally," I seethe at her.

"You shouldn't swear to God."

"Go to your room!" I holler, pointing upstairs.

"Why?"

"Because I'm sick and tired of your snotty comments. Enough!"

Sally harrumphs and doesn't budge, and before I know what's happening, I've taken a step in her direction and slapped her across the face.

"Mom!" Sally cries, reaching for her cheek.

"Mary!" Tom says, rising from the table.

"I'm done," Danny says, dropping from his seat.

"Sit down!" I scream, lifting the little guy and planting him firmly in his booster seat.

"You *hit* me!" Sally yells.

"Mary," Tom says again.

"He needs to eat his five bites," I hiss in Tom's direction.

"He'll eat if he's hungry," Tom says. "Stop badgering him. You need to take—"

"Sally, room! Danny, eat! Dom, go play!" I look at Emily, and she's staring at her plate. "Finish up, Emily!" I holler.

The room is spinning and my cheeks are hot and I can't breathe. I open the door to the deck and walk into the yard, looking for Daisy. Rarely have I had the instinct to strike the kids and I ponder why tonight Sally looked like such an easy target—and I wonder if on a subconscious level I saw her as Landon's proxy, and smacking her in front of Tom was the same as smacking him. *For you, Tom.* I pray that that wasn't my motivation; I pray that I wouldn't do such a thing. But the days have begun to blur and I no longer know who I am, so why not, what would stop me from being *that* person?

"Good God," I mutter, at last finding Daisy's ball. I lift it and aim it at the tree but miss by a mile, stupid me with my stupid girl throw.

| | |

After dinner Tom sits in front of the television. A game is on, but I know he's not really watching. His eyes are fixed on the middle of the screen, and when a commercial comes on he doesn't flinch, just keeps staring. A few minutes later, Sally exits her room and stands at the top of the stairs.

"Can I come out?" she asks with a tremor in her voice. "I'm finished with my homework. And I'm sorry." I nod at her, and when she gets to the bottom of the stairs, I lift her and hug her, hoping that my regret is evident in the wrap of my arms. "I'm sorry, baby," I whisper, and she nuzzles her acceptance in the crook of my neck. Then she leaves me and heads toward Tom, sliding easily next to him. She rests her head on his shoulder and flops her long legs over his.

I watch from the kitchen, chew a cuticle on my thumb. *Please,* I beg, *please.* Tom stays put, wraps his arms around her, and kisses the top of her head, but I can tell that he's tense. He's seated awkwardly, like a guy in a doctor's office waiting to receive blood results. I know that he won't last long; that he won't be able to slouch into the sofa with her. A minute later he removes her legs, kisses the top of her head again, and walks out to the backyard. I step into the laundry room and shut the door. I cover my mouth with my hand and fold at the waist. The pain of Tom acting uneasily with Sally is physical, a punch in my gut, an explosion in my stomach shooting shards of glass into my heart. Dear God, what have I done to her? What have I done to him? What have I done to our family?

Back in the kitchen I'm relieved to see that Sally is unfazed by Tom's departure. She's spread out on the sofa and is watching the game. I open the door to the backyard and walk out to Tom, who is squeezing Daisy's tennis ball in his fist.

"I'm sorry," I say. "About dinner. About everything . . . but you already know that."

"Yep."

"What are we going to *do*?" I plead.

"About what?" He throws Daisy's ball deep into the trees. We watch her scurry for it.

"About *everything*."

"You know where I stand," he says, reaching down and pulling up a clump of grass.

"I know where you stand on us, but what about Sal? You can't turn your back on her. You can't do that, Tom."

"I'm not turning my back on Sal," he says. "She's too old to be climbing all over me anyway. Time we all grow up a bit."

The next day is Sunday, and like we do every other Sunday, we go to Mass. Tom ascends the steps, holding Dom by the hand on one side, Danny on the other. Sally and Emily walk together. I bring up the rear and wonder what it will be like before Communion, when the priest asks us to offer one another the sign of peace. Our family is a little silly when it comes to this. We lean into one another, kissing and hugging, shaking hands. Will Tom skip me altogether, or will he fake kindness for the sake of the children? We squeeze into the pew, our four children a hearty buffer between Tom and me.

When the time comes, Tom opts to skip me when offering the sign of peace. He lingers with the boys, taking longer than usual, before reaching across to the girls. Then he shakes hands with nearly every person in front of us and behind us. Peace offered to one and all! Just not his adulterous wife.

We stand for Communion and when we return we're back on our knees. Somehow our order has gotten jumbled, our buffer thinned. Danny has scooted over to an edge and the girls are at the end of the row, next to me. The only person separating Tom and me is Dom. My eyes are closed and I'm praying when I feel Dom fiddle with my hand. Then he yanks it toward him, and I see out of the corner of my eye that he is also fiddling with Tom's hand. He stretches our arms until my left hand and Tom's right hand and Dom's two little hands are a cluster in front of him, a Rodin sculpture of the infinity of space and movement.

My heart hammers as I wait out this uncomfortable moment. I can see Tom's jaw clenching, can sense his wanting to pull away. He does just that, but Dom is having nothing of it. He yanks back Tom's hand and once again places it on mine. He weaves my fingers in between Tom's, and then he bends over and kisses our hands, back and forth, back and forth, whispering his mantra: "Mommy, Daddy, Mommy, Daddy."

I glance at Tom, who meets my eyes with his. He shakes his head, just barely, a slight wave of accusation that says, "You ruined us." *Tom,* I beg with my eyes. *It's me. It's still me.* But then I realize that Tom met me post-Landon and I've never been anything to him other than that person, the person who willfully and maliciously entered into marriage under false pretenses. The hate I feel for myself is consuming, so much so that there isn't an ounce of me left with a clear conscience.

| | |

That night, as we're getting ready to go to my parents', Tom claims to have a migraine. "Go on to Nana and Pop's without me," he says to the kids.

The kids look at him skeptically, digging back into their memories, wondering whether this has ever happened before, whether Daddy has ever skipped dinner at Nana and Pop's.

"Why don't you just take a Tylenol?" Sally asks.

"And drink a cup of tea with sugar and a square of chocolate," Emily suggests.

I stifle a smile because that's my formula for headache relief, down to a tee.

"It's a bad one," Tom says. "I know I'll feel better if I just lie on the sofa and rest."

The kids whine and whimper for a few more minutes and try to get Tom off the couch, but finally they relent. They kiss him on the cheek and tuck the blanket around his body.

"There's chicken noodle soup in the fridge . . . ," I say.

"I'm fine," Tom snaps before I've gotten it out.

When we get to Terrace Circle, Mom and Dad are sitting at the table with cigarettes and Diet Pepsi. Once they extinguish their butts in the tray, I begin to smell the roast resting on the rack, sauce on the stove, bread baking in the oven. My thoughts turn to Tom, how much he'd love this meal, how unfair it is that we're here and he's at home on the sofa when I'm the one who should be ousted, not him. He should be surrounded, coddled, nourished. He should be here with Mom and Dad doting over him, stuffing his belly with good food, offering their support.

The kids crowd around Mom and Dad, covering them with hellos, hugs, and kisses, helping themselves to a handful of the peanut M&M's that are always in a glass dish on Mom's table.

Once the kids are downstairs playing, I settle in with Mom and Pop.

"So," Mom says. "How are things? How's Tommy?"

"The old Tommy's gone," I say, and start to cry. "I killed him, and the guy who has taken his place is mean and cold and distant."

"He's *Irish,*" Mom says, as if that explains everything. "He's got a lot of anger to work through."

"Give him time," my father says.

"It's not going to matter," I say. "I've ruined everything."

"It feels like that right now," Mom says. "Because none of us can see the forest for the trees. But just wait, you'll see. Tom'll come around."

"Why would he?" I ask. "Why would he want to get over this? What I did—it was such a betrayal."

"He's mad," Dad adds. "Soon enough he'll remember that being a dad has nothing to do with DNA."

"I believe that," I say. "I think he couldn't stop loving Sally even if he wanted to. I think, eventually, *they'll* be fine. But I don't think that we will."

"Families are built on much less than what you and Tom have," Dad says. "You kids have a great marriage and a great family. You're going to get through this."

"How?"

"It's going to take a lot of time," Dad says. "You're going to have to be very patient with Tom. Let him do what he needs to do. Let him work through it in his own way."

"But why would he forgive me?"

"The same reason why other people forgive," Ma says. "The weight of carrying the pain gets to be too much. At some point we have to do what God asks of us and let go."

CHAPTER TWENTY-ONE
Sin No More

TOM'S LEAVING TOMORROW MORNING FOR Chicago, but this time it isn't his usual two-night trip; this time he has volunteered to travel on to Phoenix. He'll be gone a week, maybe ten days. The kids are throwing fits, none of them used to a dad who travels for a week at a time. My kids have never had to try on an arm's-length dad, the kind who works late, golfs on the weekends, and demands obedience at the dinner table. The kind of dad who goes off to war for a year at a time, watches sports in his recliner rather than playing catch in the backyard, drinks a fourth beer instead of reading his boys a bedtime story. My kids have been spoiled by their twenty-first-century dad, the sweetest guy in the world who hasn't once caused them pain, gives his time and love in abundance, and would lay down his life for any of them. *Any of them.*

"Let him *be*," I say to the kids, who are hanging from Tom like fishing weights. The display of love is so uninhibited it's almost hard to watch, to see how our kids adore their father so, how *on the hook* they are for his return of affection. My instinct is to warn the children to keep their distance; that there is a risk attached to getting too close. "They're fine," he says in a cheerful voice, though his eyes are looking at the kids, not me. His inflection is for them. "How about we go get some ice cream?" Tom says.

The kids hoot and holler, already planning their order.

"I'm going to get a milk shake!" Sally says. "Can I?"

"You *may*," Tom says.

"And I want a banana split!" Emily exclaims.

"I want the dip thing," Dom says.

"Me, too," Danny calls.

"The dip thing?" Tom says in a silly voice.

"He means chocolate ice cream on a cone dipped in chocolate," I explain.

"*Obviously*," Tom says, glaring at me briefly. "I've taken them to get ice cream a million times."

"Sorry," I say. "Just trying to help."

"We'll be back," Tom says.

"Aren't you coming, Mommy?" Dom asks.

"I guess not, buddy," I say, throwing it back to Tom for once, tired of just closing my eyes and clenching my stomach while Tom punches me in the gut.

"Come *on*, Mom," Emily says. "Don't you want your root beer float?"

"I would," I say. "But it looks like Daddy wants to have some special time with you before he leaves for his trip."

"That's right," Tom says. "Let's go, kids."

Before I can object, he ushers them out the door and loads them into the minivan.

The next morning, I watch from the kitchen window as Tom loads his suitcase into the trunk. A new emotion—anger—rises, pushing sadness and regret out of the way. A surge of heat warms my neck and behind my ears. I run outside and into the driveway in my bare feet.

"Tom!" I holler, just as he's backing up. "Can I ask you something?"

"What?" Tom says, shifting into park.

"Why is it that you can forgive your father a thousand indiscretions and your brother, too, but not me? Patrick so much as stubs his toe and you go running! He falls off the wagon and you make every excuse for him in the world. *Nothing* is his fault! He doesn't need to take any accountability. You forgive, forgive, forgive him a thousand times. How about throwing some of that Catholic charity my way?"

"It's different! In a million ways it's entirely different," Tom seethes. "I never chose Patrick over you. No one got hurt by my helping my brother."

"I didn't choose Landon!" I say. "This is madness. You've got to know how it was back then. I loved you, of course, I loved you so much. But we had only known each other for six months. I had known Landon for ten years!"

"So you were sure enough about me to marry me—put your name on my retirement account and health insurance—but not sure enough to give me your loyalty, your fidelity. That only comes with time with you?"

"Never mind," I say, wiping my eyes.

Tom squeezes the steering wheel, then looks at me hard. "You know, Mary, I'd love to know what you're most sorry about: the fact that you slept with Landon when you were engaged to me. Or is it the fact that you got caught?"

I gulp for air, pull back tightly with the slingshot of a litigator's response, but my projectile falls flat. "Wait!" is all I can come up with.

"For what?"

Tom shifts into reverse and backs out, and then drives, leaving me alone. "No mistakes," I mutter to no one at all.

| | |

The nights that follow are quieter than normal. Tonight I slip into Sally's room. She's sprawled across her bed with her myth book on one side and a book of Bible stories on the other. Emily's lying across the foot of her sister's bed, flipping through a catalog. When I ask Sally what she's up to, she tells me that she's trying to find similarities between Greek myths and Bible stories. Never having considered such a parallel, I ask if she's found any.

"A lot," she says. "They both talk of floods, of wars, of power."

"I guess that's true," I say. "Anything else?"

"Well," she says. "Men fell—like, you know, in both—because of trickery, deceit, and temptation."

"Oh, yeah," I say, as my eyes well up with tears. "Be right back. I need to blow my nose." Out of her room and into my bathroom, I make it just in time to cover my face to hush my bawling cries. I sit on the toilet and sob into my hands. The guilt of Tom's being gone at my doing—at my trickery and deceit, because of temptation—makes me want to kill myself. I think of the pride and propriety of fatherhood, how men define themselves by what they create; how for Tom, losing his claim to Sally has robbed him of something he considered his. The elusiveness of fatherhood, how it requires a faith that's not required of women, who witness their bellies swell and blossom into nine months of evidence.

My deceit robbed Tom of something that was his.

My trickery betrayed him.

He trusted that Sally was his. He trusted that I was true. Now our masks are off and we're revealed as something different altogether. How does a man maintain his faith, his beliefs, his convictions, when the premises themselves are false?

|||

After I wash my face, I return to Sally's room, call the girls onto my lap, and though there are knees and elbows and too-long legs, we find a way to perfectly cluster together.

"I love you girls so much," I say. "You have no idea how much I love you girls."

"Mom," Sally says. "We know."

Then I go to check on the boys, who are nestled together watching *Toy Story*. At the sight of me, they stand on the bed, so instinctively it makes my heart lurch, and climb their way into my arms. They sing their "I Love Mommy" song, and because I can't stand the thought of my gigantic bed without Tom, I carry the boys into our room and allow them to sleep next to me.

I worry the beads on my rosary, let my fingers slide down to the cross. I finally see how deep my betrayal goes. This isn't just about us as a family, or Tom and me as a couple; I've rocked the foundation of Tom's core belief system. I've forced him to question his faith.

|||

When Tom returns home the following Friday, the boys leap into his arms and the girls coil around his waist. He stands there like a pillar, supporting each of them. The first time we make eye contact it's held for maybe a second, and I swear that I see the glimmer of a smile in his eyes, but then he looks away.

"Did you bring us anything?" Dom wants to know.

"Bring *you* anything," Tom jokes. "Now why would I bring you anything?"

"Come on, Dad," Danny says.

Tom unzips his computer bag. "Let's see, I have shower caps for the girls and bars of soap for the boys."

"Dad, really," Sally says. "We know you're joking."

"Okay," Tom says. "Let me look again." This time he pulls out giant lollipops for the boys, inside each of which is a real scorpion. The boys ooh and aah, daring each other to eat his. And for the girls he pulls out little cardboard boxes, with silver-and-turquoise earrings inside.

"Thanks, Dad!" Sally and Emily cheer.

"What about for Mom?" Danny wants to know. "Did you bring her anything from Arizona?"

"Mommy always says not to spend money on her, so this time I listened," Tom says. "You guys want to go play a game of H-O-R-S-E before dinner?"

The four children and Tom slip into their coats and then rush outside. In no time I hear the bouncing of the basketball, the jeers and cheers of the kids, the words of encouragement from Tom. And once again, I'm left inside the house, alone.

What once seemed unfathomable—a tangible divide between Tom and me—has now become our reality. It's unnerving how quickly reality shifts, the pace at which we all adjust to new circumstances. Just weeks ago, we were a family, embarrassingly loving, demonstrative family members who crossed all boundaries of personal space to get closer to one another. We were once a family that crowded onto one sofa to watch a television program even though there was ample seating elsewhere. We were leg drapers, arm wrap-arounders, food, drink, and joy sharers. Now there is a force field around Tom and me, a barrier cloaked in polite indifference. Who we were has been replaced by who we are—actors in a commercial, portraying a happy family.

CHAPTER TWENTY-TWO
Above All Things

THE DAYS ARE OBLIVIOUS TO my crisis, and with perfect predictability they continue to pass. February and March push through,
one cold front after another. Snow, then ice, then snow covering
ice. It's cold outside and it's cold inside, the way Tom and I live
alongside each other with no warmth. I walk through my days
with the icy-cold shrapnel of my past pressing into my chest.

Tom has found a nifty loophole to being home. He spends
each weekend in Virginia Beach with Patrick, who is now sober
and back at work. With Tom's help he's opened a handyman
business, offering services from cleaning gutters, painting, and
roofing to building decks and sunrooms. He's swamped with
jobs and Tom has become his partner, helping him with the
labor as well as managing the money aspects of the business.

When Tom started his routine of leaving for the weekends,
the kids were intolerable, wailing for him to stay. But kids adapt
and by the fourth weekend they were used to it, and they no longer pitch a fit when he leaves. When Tom returns and takes the
kids to dinner at Friendly's on a school night just for the hell of

it, they burst with excitement, as giddy as children of divorce who only see their dad every other Sunday. The scarcity of him has increased his value like that of a sought-after commodity.

Each time he returns home, I look for signs of forgiveness. But he continues to be the same: cold and distant and nowhere near forgiving me. He wakes up early, returns from work late. On Friday night he packs his bag for the weekend.

It's Friday now and because Tom's packing and I'm folding laundry, I offer him a stack of T-shirts from the load. He takes them without looking up.

"What are you and Patrick working on this weekend?" I ask.

"A deck," Tom says, slapping the T-shirts into his duffel bag.

"How is Patrick?" I ask.

"Fine."

"Kathy and Mia?"

"Fine."

"Do you need anything else?" I ask, offering him a pair of jeans and socks.

"Whatever," he says.

"Well, do you or don't you?" I ask, balancing the jeans and socks in my hand.

"If you don't feel like putting the laundry away, just give me my stuff."

"Screw you," I say under my breath.

"What?" he says.

"I said screw you. I was asking if you needed clean clothes, not trying to get out of my wifely responsibilities of putting laundry away."

"My bad," he says.

"So this is it?" I say. "This is our life. This is how it's going to be. Forever!"

"Don't know."

"You know, Tom. It is customary for the punishment to fit the crime. Don't you think you're being a little cruel and unusual?"

"I don't," he says, zipping his duffel and leaving the room.

I race down to the basement. Tonight I won't be there when Tom leaves our house, helping him disengage from the children. Let him peel the children off his own legs. Let him say good-bye to them. Let him close the door on their four beautiful, wide-eyed faces. I'm done helping him leave us.

In the basement I head into the back room that's full of exercise equipment. In the corner hangs Tom's punching bag from college. It's heavy and as immovable as a side of beef—and daring me to give it my best shot. I assume a stance with my left foot forward and draw back my right arm, then make a fist, re-membering how Tom once showed me, with my thumb on the outside, dummy, not the inside. I punch at the bag. It hurts like hell, the pain shooting all the way into my shoulder. I pull back my arm again. Ready, aim, fire. Again, again, again. I punch with my right hand, then my left. In seconds I'm hurting and dripping with sweat, but the pain is welcome, sharp and bracing like being smacked by a wave, not dull and aching like the incessant rub that's left me raw. My knuckles are red and some of the skin is peeling off. I punch again, harder, harder. I want to see blood. I punch once more, fall against the wall, and spin with the room as I suck on my knuckles. I can't decide if the throbbing hurts or feels good, my lines are now so blurred. I know that later it will hurt more. Everything always hurts more later.

CHAPTER TWENTY-THREE
To Do Penance

ON ASH WEDNESDAY WE ENTER Lent, a period that forgives darkened pasts and welcomes in a future of light. We sit for Mass and receive a smudge of dirt across our foreheads from last year's burnt palms, to signify that we are all sinners; that we are repentant creatures. We participate in the Holy Eucharist and head into Lent with pure hearts. Only my heart is anything but pure. It's burdened and dark and damaged and neglected. With each day that passes and Tom and I share a house but not our lives, I feel my heart grow even tighter, like a hand clenched in an arthritic fist.

My emotions open and scab over and reopen again, like wounds that cannot heal. I continue to ache for Tom's pain, but I also feel like I'm worthy of forgiveness. Short of public humiliation or wearing a scarlet *A*, I feel that I've expressed a more than adequate level of sorrow. What I need now is to be absolved of my wrongdoing. What I need now is for Tom to stop beating me up every day with his creepy politeness and icy distance and offhanded jabs. *If God can forgive me, then why can't you?* I want to scream at Tom. My insides are so bruised, I'm surprised my skin doesn't shine purple.

I wake up every morning, like the littlest kid in the school-yard, defenses up, feet dancing, dukes flying. Each day I'm ready to say, "Enough!" I'm ready to call Tom out, insist on a little re-spect, demand a trace of dignity, for God's sake.

But then I see Tom, and though he's still flaming mad, he's also hurt, a hurt that has built a home in his eyes. I see it, even when he's playing with the kids. That's the only time I get to look at him these days. When he doesn't know that I'm watching. And when I do—*see him*—all my toughness turns to fluff, and I'm gooey and sorry and reduced once again.

When we at last celebrate Easter, a calm that is closer to apa-thy spreads through me the way tiny drops of water seek thirsty roots. I continue to be sorry to my bones, but I can't fall on my sword another day. I need a break from hurting.

|||

The days continue to pass and the kids are busy in school. Sally is reading Anne Frank and writing a paper of her own for her composition class. She's chosen to write about Daisy, our dog, and Sally's fear that she'll someday die. I speak briefly with her teacher, who assures me that this is typical, that this is the age when children start pondering the death of family members, pets. It's the age when children learn that sad and bad things can happen: sickness, the loss of a parent's job, a move to another school. Her teacher tells me, statistically speaking, that this is the age of divorce. Many parents make it to the ten-, twelve-year mark and then call it quits. In the blink of an eye, children go from a stable two-parent family to splitting time with Mom in one place, Dad in another, often a stepparent not far behind. Unfortunately, her teacher tells me, it's the end of an innocence in many regards.

I listen, nod, and process the notion that Tom and I seem quite likely, or almost certain, to contribute to this sad statistic, our solid family tree splintering into two, the strength we've found in numbers gone forever.

To think that Sally is growing up, that she has dipped not just a toe but an entire foot in the waters of a mature life. To think that she comprehends, on some level, that a girl like Anne Frank had feared for her life, that a holocaust was reality. I don't want Sally to have these thoughts. I don't want her to worry about sad and bad things. I don't want her to know that six million innocent people were killed just because of who they were. I don't want her to know that terrorists are capable of flying planes into our skyscrapers, that creeps lurk behind corners, that her mother's indiscretion could rob her of her two-parent childhood. I want her childhood to be pure and perfect. I want her to have 100 percent confidence that her parents will always be here and her grandparents' door will always be open, with them welcoming her in with the smell of sauce on the stove and bread in the oven.

But then I think, well maybe a little dose of reality is a good thing, because clearly Sally's life won't always be cannoli at Nana's and a game of H-O-R-S-E with Dad. Surely the time will come when something bad will happen: a friend will get hurt, a family member will be stricken with cancer, her dog Daisy will die. Surely the time will come when she will learn a truth that will hit her so hard it will flip her inside out. My thoughts blur and render—back and forth—at the reality of this. And then a thought

I've never wholly allowed myself to consider bubbles to the surface: Sally might someday learn the truth about Landon James.

Emily has said good-bye to the ancient history of the Greeks and Romans, stepping eagerly into the Middle Ages, an era that appeals to her with its lords and ladies and colorfully dressed minstrels. She's learning about the rise of Christianity, the role the Church played in people's lives, providing for them in the way the city-state no longer could. One night she's regaling us with the characteristics of a castle, how there are layers and layers of defense: the moat, the stone, the tower, the keep. "Why do you think they needed so much protection?" she asks. Sally answers before Tom or I have a chance to sugarcoat a response. "If you hold the keys to the kingdom, you're a target," she says flatly, drawing a finger across her neck in a cutthroat gesture. "People want what others have, and they're willing to fight for it."

My girls, and their capacity to learn, floor me. I marvel at their ability to memorize lengthy poems by Longfellow and Kipling, just as easily as they can reduce fractions and measure angles. I don't remember learning, when I was in the third and fourth grades, what they're learning. I remember practicing swearwords in the bathroom with my friends, talking about boys, and holding a stick to my mouth, pretending to smoke a cigarette like bad Sandy in *Grease*. My girls are so mature, so *smart*; their capacity to take in so much hits me hard. The pride I feel for their accomplishments is excessive, like water boiling.

And the little guys. They're learning to hold their pencils correctly, write in giant block letters, identify the days of the week, the months, the seasons. They proclaim their jobs each day. "I was the weatherman!" or "I was the book selector!" I adore that they're small, and it pains me in a certain way that they long to be big like their sisters. I want to tell them to slow down. "Just wait!"

I want to holler. "You'll be there soon enough." But the way they emulate their older siblings is too adorable to interrupt.

"We need to do our homework, too," the boys will say, pulling out their workbooks and crayons, sliding their chairs next to their sisters, basking in their oldness.

Then I do the math. When the boys are ten years old—the age Sally is now—the girls will be fifteen and sixteen. Then I want to cry, thinking that by the time the boys are oohing and aahing over Roman torture and gladiators being thrown into the ring with lions, my baby girls will be begging their father to teach them to drive, rolling their eyes at me every time I say no, and confiding in their girlfriends their darkest secrets. A few years later, they'll be on their way to a college dorm room, dragging with them an overstuffed duffel and a hot pot. The thought that Tom and I and our children might weather these years separately—two homes, joint custody—makes me ache.

CHAPTER TWENTY-FOUR
Restore Sanity

TOM

I NOW UNDERSTAND THE APPEAL of alcohol. It shouldn't be a revelation, but it is, as I've always done my best to keep my distance. If you drink enough of it, it dulls the pain to a manageable level. If you drink more than enough of it, it makes the pain go away altogether. For two months now I've been driving down to Virginia Beach on the weekends. Patrick and I work all day Saturday and Sunday, cleaning gutters, building additions, finishing basements. By six o'clock my back feels like metal rods have rusted inside it, my feet throb, and my arms hang like heavy strips of wet blanket, but there's something intensely satisfying in seeing progress. Something measurable.

Patrick and I are getting along great. We've switched roles. He's taking care of me for once. He's strong and sober and back together with his family, and I'm the brother who crashes on his sofa. Most nights, after Patrick and I have cleaned up from our day's work, Kathy cooks a nice dinner and the four of us sit on the back porch, eating, drinking iced tea. It's wild seeing Patrick so put together, taking care of his family. Mia cracks me up. She squeals and giggles when I tickle her tummy, reminding me so much of the little guys right now, but also of Sally and Em when they were five years old. God, it's like it was yesterday. Walking them to school on their first days of kindergarten. Mia makes me ache for my kids, but being away for the weekends is the only salvation I have.

After dinner I usually tell Patrick and Kathy that I'm going for a walk. Patrick offers to come, and I always say no, *spend some time with your family*. The fact that I'm gone for hours isn't exactly crafty on my part. Patrick must know that I've gone for a drink. I never say so, and feel guilty as hell that I do it, when he's trying so hard to stay sober. But hell, this is my time of need, and if I can't get a drink or two every night, the crappiness of the situation will bury me.

Each night I head in the same direction. Straight down the boardwalk to Sandy's Bar, a dark dive with pool tables and a jukebox.

There's a bartender there named Chloe. She wears tight, cutoff jeans and a halter top. One time I asked her if she grew up around here, and she took it as an invitation to tell me her life story. She's never been married. She's a single mom of a five-year-old daughter. The father of her child hit the road at the sight of the first ultrasound. He came back once, Chloe told me, held Ava—their child—and then shook his head, saying that fatherhood wasn't for him. In high school Chloe wanted to be an artist. Sometimes she draws sketches of the bar patrons on the back of cocktail napkins and gives them to the guys like a parting gift.

Chloe doesn't know a thing about me. It's almost like she senses that it's better not to ask. The way she rambles on about her life is exactly what I want, exactly what I need. By any standard she's had a tough life, yet she's always smiling, always bubbly and cheerful, like she's just grateful to have made it this far.

By the time I get to Sandy's tonight, Chloe's outside, pulling the door closed with a heavy thud.

"Closing up already?"

"You'd never believe! Our water went out," she says. "We had no choice but to close. They promised we'll be set by tomorrow."

"You have the night off then?"

She looks at me with a sidelong glance, and I realize what I said could be misconstrued. "I do!" she says cheerfully.

"Well, have a good night," I say. "See you tomorrow."

"Yes, definitely!" she says. "If they deliver the water, anyway."

"It'll be fine," I say, smiling. "See you." I start to walk away.

"Hey, Tom!" she says. "What are you going to do now? Hit another bar?"

I freeze, rooted in my footsteps. I don't know what to say. Is she asking me to do something? Go somewhere? "I guess," I say.

"Just curious," she says with a wave.

"What are you up to on your big night off?"

"I haven't even *thought* about it," she says. "I'm never off this time of night." She looks out at the ocean, at the sunset. "God, I'm cooped up in that dreary bar every night, and just look at the sunset. I can't believe what I'm missing."

Her cheerful expression shifts a bit, like she really gets it: the regret in missing a sunset every night.

"Do you . . . want to go down on the beach? Watch the sun set?" I'm Tom, married Tom—husband, father, and provider—Mr. Responsible. I don't typically ask twenty-five-year-old bartenders to watch the sunset. I'm slightly exhilarated, but mostly I feel like a creep, unable to shake the fact that this girl was once Sally's age.

"I'd love to," she sings. "Let's go!"

We walk down the boardwalk for a while until we reach an entrance onto the sand. She pulls off her sequined flip-flops but I keep my work boots on. It's only April, but it's unusually warm, though not warm enough for a dip in the ocean, so I'm taken by surprise when Chloe starts to run toward the shore. In no time she's up to her waist, her saturated cutoffs turned a dark indigo blue. Then she dives into a wave, comes up, flips back her wispy blond hair, and adjusts her tiny halter, which is clinging happily to her breasts.

A minute later she's standing next to me. "That was awesome!" She shakes her head and I get a sprinkling of her wet hair across my face.

"What are you going to do now?" I ask, because I'm a dad and I'm responsible and I'm looking at this young woman who is now in wet clothes.

"Enjoy the sunset!" she says with a flourish, missing my point altogether.

"You're wet," I say, and wonder why the hell I care about her being wet if she doesn't.

"I'm good," she says flippantly, lying flat on her back in the sand with her arms anchored behind her head.

Feeling odd standing over her, I take a seat beside her. All I can think about is the sand that will be stuck to her when she stands up. Sally does that all the time—emerges from the ocean and then plops on the sand. When she gets up we call her a cinnamon doughnut.

A while later Chloe claims to be dying for a drink, so she gets up and dusts herself off, though it's a futile attempt, and then we walk to Bart's, another local dive. She goes to talk to the bartender, whom she clearly seems to know. He hands her a Bart's T-shirt, which she puts on over her wet and sandy halter. Then she shimmies the halter down until it puddles at her ankles.

She sees me watching her. When she pulls the halter from the ground, she twists her body and raises her arms above her head with a theatric "Ta-da!"

"Very talented," I say.

The bartender shrugs off his leather jacket and gives that to Chloe, too. I'm guessing they went to high school together—maybe as recently as a few years ago. We order beers and a plate of nachos. On the back of the paper menu, Chloe sketches me with a pencil. The likeness is striking. Though I feel younger at the beach, I clearly don't look it, as Chloe has captured my forty-year-old mug perfectly with lines meandering around my eyes, a map of dead-end roads framing my mouth. I look rugged, which is how I feel most days when I'm working with Patrick hoisting two-by-fours. But my eyes look sad and I wonder how she's managed that with only a piece of graphite.

She's a talented artist, and I get a twinge of sadness in my chest that she's tending bar when she possibly could have done something different with her life. I stop short of suggesting that she sign up for classes at the community college. It's none of my business. *She's* none of my business.

A few beers later, we end up throwing darts and shooting pool.

Somehow we manage to drink ten beers between the two of us. Somehow Chloe ends up in my car, claiming she needs a ride home. Somehow Chloe explains she doesn't have to pick up her daughter from her mother's tonight. Somehow I end up in Chloe's apartment, on her couch, with another beer in my hand.

Chloe walks around the apartment, flipping on some lights, switching off others. She turns on some music, picks up some of her kid's toys, and throws them into a basket. Then she stands directly in front of me and does a little twirl, as if she's announcing herself. Almost in slow motion, she shimmies her still-wet cutoff shorts off her tight twenty-five-year-old body. I watch her, entranced, my heartbeat suddenly loud in my ears.

Then she slips down her panties, which are tiny little strings, and I swallow hard, pushing the endless questions and images from my head. *Enjoy this,* I tell myself. Don't worry that she's a good fifteen years younger than you. Don't worry that her little undies are smaller than your daughters'. Don't—*don't*—think about Mary, because she doesn't deserve to be thought about. She betrayed you and lied to you, over and over. Don't think about Mary.

Chloe shifts her hips, putting on a show, and then crisscrosses her hands across her Bart's T-shirt, grabs it from the bottom, and lifts it over her head. There, standing in front of me, is twenty-five-year-old Chloe—hot, tight, tanned, young—exhibiting herself for my benefit.

Her eyes slip down from mine and then back up, lit by a new kind of smile. Decisions have been made by at least parts of me. Heart hammering, I swallow hard, seek to find some dim, functioning corner of my cerebral cortex. I'm at a hell of a crossroads. This moment will define who I am for the rest of my life. Will I continue on as Tom—Mr. Responsible, Mr. Do-the-Right-Thing—or will I become *that guy*? Or am I already that guy? Is that who Mary has made me? Hell, maybe I've always been him, and now he's just been freed to stand up and take his due. That can't be . . . but, maybe.

Then I do think of Mary, how the month before we were married, she was at a similar crossroads. She was alone with her ex-boyfriend and, rather than doing the right thing, she did the wrong thing.

Why not? I tell myself. Mary's *that girl,* the one who slept with her ex-boyfriend when she was engaged to you.

Payback. Yes, payback.

Before I've even had a chance to think it through, Chloe walks toward me, swings one long leg over my two, and sits astride my lap. Inches from my face, her naked body gives off heat and a fresh, salty tang. She reaches for my hands, lifts them to her breasts, which are so small and perky they fit in my cupped palms. I hold my hands there, frozen, afraid to move, afraid to feel her little energetic breasts. She scoots higher in my lap, flips her hair to the side, and lowers her mouth to mine. When I feel her lips, I am all of a sudden an addict—just like Patrick and my dad, at the taste of whiskey. I want nothing but more. More than anything in the entire world—at this moment in time—I want Chloe, and don't care if it means that I never again have Mary, and if I never again see my children.

Goddamn! Mary, Sally, Emily, the boys. *Goddamn!*

I pull away from Chloe's lips, though my entire body is thrumming, begging to take her. *Goddamn!* I lift her off my lap, stand stock-still as she rights herself into sitting on the sofa.

"No?" she asks, almost kindly, almost like she knew she was taking a chance.

"I want to," I say. "You have no idea."

"But you can't?"

"I can't," I say. "I can't."

"I kind of figured," she says.

I stand at ease now. My mutinous body back under my control. "I'm going through a tough time." She deserves to know something. "Wife, kids. It's difficult."

"Yep."

"How did you know?"

"You're a nice guy, Tom. You're a good guy. I work at a crappy bar. You're not my usual customer."

I want to tell her not to settle, that someday she'll meet a great guy, someone who will treat her well and care for her daughter as if she were his own. As I think this thought, my mind turns to Sally, the daughter I raised because I believed she was my own. Would I have been good enough to raise her as my own if I had known she was Landon James's? Did Mary's lame-ass rationalization hold water: Did her lie give me a life? I push the thought from my head with a decided *not now*.

"Sorry, Chloe . . . and thanks," I say as I walk to the door. By now she's slipped the oversize Bart's T-shirt back on and pulled her hair into a ponytail. Now she barely looks old enough to order a beer, much less twenty-five, much less old enough to be involved with a guy like me. I step outside, inhale the sea air, and pull the door closed. Then I open it back up, turn the bottom lock so that it'll catch when I close it. "Lock the top bolt when I leave," I say.

She nods.

I can't help it. She's a young woman living alone. I want to make sure she's locked in for the night. As it turns out, I'm *that guy*, not the *other guy*.

CHAPTER TWENTY-FIVE

Relapse

LANDON IS STILL IN THE news. The primary election will be held in June. It looks like he's got a good chance, not just at the primary but at the entire senate race. The incumbent Republican senator has announced his intention to retire, and so far only a handful of hopefuls have thrown their hats into the ring. The photo of Landon and me held the press's attention for less than twenty-four hours before it was overshadowed by news of another candidate's sordid Internet wanderings.

I'm just pulling into the grocery store parking lot when my cell burbles, alerting me of a text message.

Can I call? It's from Landon.

No!!!! I text back.

Before I can collect my thoughts, the phone rings. I ignore it, but he calls again. And again. On the third try, I slide my thumb across the phone to answer it because I know if I don't, he'll keep calling.

"You can't call," I say.

"I'll only be a minute."

"What do you want?" I ask.

"I want to know how you are, *obviously*," Landon says. "I can't stop thinking about what you're going through."

"Don't worry about me," I say. "I'm not your concern."

"You are."

"I'm *not*," I say, as the anger in me burns fiery red. "I've hurt the people I love the most, but lucky for you, the photo didn't seem to interest anyone but my husband. Already yesterday's news. Once again you've come out unscathed, smelling like roses."

"It's not like that," Landon says. "I know you're going through hell."

How to describe hell? I think of Sally's Greek mythology, of Procrustes, "the stretcher," how he stretched or amputated the legs of his tricked captors to make them fit in his iron bed. That's how I feel, like I am anything but right, and trying to fit is pure torture.

"Listen, Landon. I'm hanging up. *We* cannot talk on the phone. Ever. You've got to understand that."

"This is hard on me, too," he says in a rush, trying to get it in before I cut him off. "Knowing what that photo represented. The day I essentially signed away my rights as a father to Sally."

"Landon," I sigh. "It was for the best."

"Who's to say?"

"Who's to say?" I say incredulously. "*I'm* to say. It's not a subjective matter. It's a fact. You were in no position—never were—and Sally has had the *best* father in the world all of these years." I think about Tom playing soccer with Sally in the backyard, the two of them at Tom's workbench building a birdhouse from scratch, Tom explaining how to solve for x in a tricky prealgebra problem.

"I'm not arguing that," Landon says. "And obviously it was what I wanted back then. I didn't want anything in my way. Still don't. But this year, ever since I saw her last Christmas . . ."

"Ever since you saw her last Christmas *what*?"

"Nothing, nothing," he says. "It just made it real for me, that's all. Seeing her."

"Yes, Landon, you saw her. You saw her with her sister, and you know she has brothers and a mother and father. She has a family. She's a happy girl surrounded by family, so whatever it is that you're thinking, don't!" My heart is racing. This is the one thought that Landon James is not allowed to have, ever.

"Take it easy, MM. I'm not thinking anything. I have the election coming up. That's all I'm thinking about."

"Then why are you calling me?"

"I don't know!" Landon shouts with a strain of desperation. "Because I care if you're okay. Because I feel bad that I damaged your marriage. And because I think of Sally now. I can't help it. I think about her now."

"You can think about her, Landon, but you *know* it can't go further than that, don't you?"

"Is your marriage going to survive this, Mary?"

"My marriage *has* to survive this."

We both hold on the line but say nothing. Just breathe.

"I'm hanging up," I say. "Don't call again."

The phone is already away from my ear when he says, "What's it like, MM? Being a mom?"

"Good-bye, Landon. Don't call again." I hit end. *What's it like being a mom?* Are there actually words that describe what it feels like to put my mouth on that sweet, velvety spot behind my sons' ears, the feel of the tender arrows that are their shoulder blades, the vine of pebbled jewels that run down their backs? Are there words for the way my heart rises and tumbles at my daughters' accomplishments and defeats, how I sometimes need to sturdy myself when they're dressed in jewelry and heels, the way looking into my daughters' eyes is like looking into a magic mirror that reflects back pieces and parts of everything I am and ever wanted to be? Are there words for the way the pillow feels against the back of my head each night, knowing that the four of them are safe and sound and tucked in and asleep?

If I were to have answered Landon's questions, I would have said, "It's like winning an election every day. It's an *honor.*"

I stare at my phone and am unsure if I should cry or scream. Landon is the last person in the world with whom I should be having a conversation, but my husband is no longer talking to me, and in a weird way it feels good to be talking to someone who knows me—well, at least someone who *knew me,* once upon a time. Twenty years later and Landon James is still leaving me unsettled.

CHAPTER TWENTY-SIX

Admitting

AFTER LANDON AND I WERE reintroduced by our mutual friend David Kaye, we went on to date for the following year. And while it was only a year of dating, I marked our relationship as having started five years earlier, from back when we met for the first time. Our tree began to grow rings, dating its age, from the first moment Landon kissed me.

By now I was in my second year of law school and Landon was working eighty hours a week at the corporate law firm of Myers & Jones. He'd call me every night on his way home from work. Maybe he would stop by once during the week. Around Thursday he'd say, "Are we on for Saturday night?" We'd go out to dinner, we'd sit at a bar listening to music, sometimes Landon would cook, sometimes I would. Occasionally we'd meet up with friends, or Landon would introduce me to a colleague, always quick with a compliment: "This is the brilliant legal mind of Mary Russo," or "This is the beautiful and talented Mary Margaret." He was full of it and I knew it, but there was no denying that he made me feel like a million bucks when he slung his arm around me and claimed me as his own.

It seemed like we were doing normal couple things, moving in the right direction. Each Saturday night we'd end up at Landon's apartment. Landon was sweet and vulnerable and when he looked me in the eyes I swore, oh how I swore, that in those moments, I could see his vulnerability, could see how ready he was to commit to me. That gentle look I saw in him always seemed to me like his true nature, like if he weren't so afraid, he'd open up more. A few times he told me about his father, who left, and how his mother never recovered from it.

On many nights, it seemed that Landon—with me—had found the tonic to his painful childhood. With me, he had found safety. At least that was how I saw it. Wrapped in his arms, I was convinced that Landon James was on the brink of an emotional breakthrough. I would lie awake the entire night, wondering what he was thinking, where this relationship was going, praying that God would make him love me back.

Looking back now, I do believe I was a safe haven for Landon, someone with whom he could be entirely himself. But I can also see how it was mostly about him. He was the one who did the talking, rattling on endlessly about politics, the local government, how within the next year he'd want to get his foot firmly in place down in Richmond. He already had a platform, he already had slogans. He was sure that his law firm would back him. *And the law firm represents some real heavy hitters, Mary,* I can still hear him saying. *With their support . . .*

Because he never said it, I filled in the blanks for myself, imagining being by his side up on the podium as he delivered his acceptance speech. I imagined his career, how years later it would be told that Landon James's wife, Mary, was an integral part of his success, how Landon leaned on her more heavily than on any of his advisors. I once shared this vision with my sister Angela, who quickly rebutted, "Mary, has Landon ever mentioned you being part of any of this?" No, I said. But we're dating. We're together. What else could it mean?

It was the Saturday that marked the year Landon and I had been dating. He hadn't mentioned anything along the lines of our "anniversary" and I didn't bring it up, hoping secretly that he had planned something big, a special dinner punctuated with a piece of jewelry to signify his commitment. I bought him cuff links, more expensive than I could afford, but they were beautiful gold squares with a red ruby in the center of each. Very GOP, I thought.

"I could really go for a burger," Landon said that night, seemingly oblivious that I was squeezed into a little black dress with three-inch spike heels.

"Well, okay," I said. "Maybe I should change."

"Go ahead," he said, clicking on my television and finding the news.

So I changed out of my black dress and stockings into jeans and a sweater, and dumped the contents of my little black clutch into my everyday shoulder bag, watching the wrapped cuff links tumble from one bag into the other like a prize from a gumball machine. All the while I continued to think that this was Landon being coy, setting me up for a big surprise at the end of the night.

Dinner came and went, messy bacon cheeseburgers and fries and pint after pint of beer. We walked back to his apartment. A block from it, Landon reached for my hand, swaying it gently forward and back, like one would do with a child. "Not much of a dinner," he said. "We should have gone somewhere nicer."

"No big deal," I said, and gulped in a gallon of the crisp air, because now I thought maybe he was just being coy, that he did know about the anniversary.

Once inside his apartment, he turned on the teakettle and made me a cup of tea without my asking. He brought it to me and set it on the nightstand next to the bed. I had drunk too much; my head was tipsy from too many beers and the confusion of the night. It felt good to just lay my head back against the cool stack of pillows. Landon slid into bed next to me and placed his hand on mine. I curled toward him so that our faces were only a kiss apart. He looked into my eyes, brushed his fingers across my cheek, and opened his mouth as though he were about to say something.

"What?" I whispered.

"Nothing," he responded.

"Tell me," I said, but he shook his head no.

"I'm sorry," he said. "About tonight. You looked so pretty. I should have taken you somewhere special. Sorry I'm such a dope."

And while I was aware that this moment in time—half drunk and lying next to the man I wanted—was hardly the time to divine what he was feeling, I swore that I could see love in his eyes.

"Happy anniversary," I said in almost a whisper.

"Is it?" he said, pulling his hand back.

"We've been dating for exactly a year. I guess you didn't have it marked on your day planner."

"I'm sorry," he said. "I guess I'm not the kind of guy who would think to do that."

I looked at him. "What are we doing? Seriously, Landon. Don't you think this is weird? I mean, here we are, we see each other a couple of times a week. I end up in your bed every Saturday night. What's going on here?"

"What do you want me to say?"

"I want you to tell me how you feel," I said. *I want you to say that you love me,* I thought. I want you to say that you see us together, fulfilling each other's dreams. I want to promise to help you become whatever you want and I want you to promise to build a life with me with a houseful of babies.

"I don't even know what you feel for me," I said. "If you care for me. I mean, you never say *anything.*"

Landon's body had stiffened. His chest now felt more like a rock than a cushion. I could feel his shoulders inching toward his ears. I rolled farther from him, and onto my pillow, staring at the ceiling.

"I'm not an emotional person," he said. "Emphatically not."

Emphatically not. Like he was writing his thesis, like he was addressing a courtroom, like he had a thesaurus under his pillow.

"I get that," I said. "But you've got to give me *something.*"

I lay there, waiting for him to toss out something trite and meaningless to appease me. An "of course I like you" or "I'm having a lot of fun" or "you're a really nice person." Feed me a line! Tell me a lie! Say something that will keep me on the hook a little longer, because I really don't want this to end, but I really don't want to feel foolish for another day either.

"My father left, my mother checked out, and I've been on my own since I was a kid. I just don't know if I love you," he said, looking at me briefly and then back at the ceiling. "How would I know? How does *anyone* know for sure?"

His admission left me halted. At that moment, all I wanted to do was to love him; to love him so fiercely that I'd heal his entire childhood, that I'd restore what was taken from him.

"I'm serious. How do you make a case for love?" Landon went on. "I mean, where's the empirical data?"

"There is none," I said. "It's a leap of faith."

"I'm short on faith."

"I have it in abundance."

Landon and I lay side by side, looking up at the ceiling, considering. Perhaps this—a small admission on his part, that love for me was even possible—was the first layer peeling back. If I were able to continue peeling back more and more layers, maybe this relationship could take root. Maybe.

"Try?" I said, placing my hand on his chest, sneaking a glance at his eyes, which looked nervous and worried. "*Try* to love me." I hoped my plea to him to love me would sound passionate yet steady, as if I—the one endowed with a keen ability to love—had wisdom to impart to him, the fledgling. But even to my ears it sounded closer to begging.

"I don't know if I'm ready."

"I know I love you," I said. "And I'm willing to take the chance if you are. Just try, and if it doesn't work out, we'll survive, *I'll* survive. I'd rather mend a broken heart than go on like we're doing."

A thick fog of silence descended on us, and we lay there sipping for air, for fear that if we moved or spoke we might choke. Finally I closed my eyes and recited Hail Marys. Landon must have taken me for sleeping, because a while later he rolled into me and brushed the hair out of my face and whispered, "I do love you, Mary. I love you so much." I feigned a noisy exhale and kept my eyes shut, because the dissonance of the moment had me in a stranglehold. Without knowing, I knew that Landon would retract his statement, that he'd take back what he had given, because for him, it was asking too much.

When I woke up in the morning, Landon was already in the shower. I went to the kitchen and poured a bowl of Cheerios just as he was walking out of the steamy bathroom.

"Good morning," he said, his voice as formal as that of a lawyer addressing a courtroom.

"Hi," I said, taking a bite of cereal.

"I've got an early meeting," he said. "Take your time. Just pull the door locked when you leave." Five minutes later he was dressed in his suit and tie, his hair still wet, leaving little droplets on his shoulder. I stepped in front of him and reached up to kiss him, but he turned his cheek. "We'll talk later," he said, and was out the door.

Before I let myself out, I placed the wrapped box of cuff links on his dresser.

Five days went by without my hearing from Landon. Five days of bone-aching, heart-wrenching pain. He'd done it again; he'd killed me again.

On the sixth day, he sat in front of me in my apartment.

"First of all," he said, "I want to say—for the record—I *knew*. I knew it was our . . . our, you know, *anniversary*."

"You did?"

"I did," he said. "I bought you a necklace." He dipped his hand into his coat pocket and pulled out a box, handed it to me. Inside was a heart-shaped locket on a gold chain. "I wanted to give it to you. I wanted to take you to dinner at Angelo's."

"But you didn't."

"I froze," he said. "That day, all day long, I thought I was having a heart attack. I couldn't breathe. I thought about canceling, but I thought that would be worse. So I just acted like a jerk. Like I hadn't remembered."

"What about now?"

Landon walked to the window, pressed his forehead against it. When he turned and looked at me, his face was composed in perfect lawyer fashion. "I can't do it," he said. "I can't be in the type of relationship you want to be in. I'm not ready for commitment, marriage, children. I know that's what you want, but I can't."

"I see," I said, sitting down and cupping my face with my hands. "Then why have you been dating me for a year? What did you think was going to happen?"

"I thought it would end. Like every other relationship in my life. I never considered that we'd still be together."

I looked up at him. "But we are."

"Why does everything have to *lead* to something more?" Striking a cooler tone now, turning toward the window again. "Why can't two people just enjoy each other's company?"

Because Saturday night dates had run their course, that's why! Because I had bigger plans for myself. And while they didn't include appearing on *Larry King Live*, or having the title Congresswoman in front of my name, they did include marriage and babies—lots of babies—and birthdays and anniversaries, and milestones and traditions.

"Why does everything have to lead to something?" I croaked. "You've got your entire political career planned for the next twenty years. You already have slogans for your campaigns! You're the one with a ten-year plan, aren't you?"

"I'm sorry," he said. "You know how much I enjoy being with you."

I wiped my eyes and reached for a tissue. "Is it so wrong to want to connect with someone?"

Landon just shrugged, as if he didn't know the answer to the question but knew it didn't apply to him.

"What now?" I asked.

"I don't know, Mary," Landon said. "You know where I stand. I've got to focus on work, the upcoming campaign. We want different things and I don't want to hurt you more than I have. I am sorry."

I was sorry, too. Sorry that I had wasted a year of my life. Sorry that I had been thinking about Landon James for five years. I was a twenty-four-year-old girl who had been pining over a guy who just couldn't do it. Classic.

"Then . . . ," I said, all of a sudden filled with a rush of power. A new start! I'd get right back out there and start dating, find a guy who shared my dreams of a house and babies and Hallmark cards and gaudy Christmas decorations; a guy who would celebrate every milestone; a guy who had already held a baby in his arms, maybe a niece or nephew, and had become addicted to the smell of baby shampoo and talcum powder; a guy who would care about me as much as I cared about him.

"Then what, Mary?" Landon asked. "What now?"

"I guess this is good-bye," I said. "We're done."

Only we weren't. I just didn't know it at the time. I didn't know that Landon would continue to darken my door, offering me just enough to keep me on the hook, for another five years.

PART FOUR

CHAPTER TWENTY-SEVEN

Awakening

THE NEXT FRIDAY NIGHT, TOM stays for dinner before heading to the beach. He tells the family he'll be taking another trip. This time to Ireland. He glances at me briefly, then looks at the kids, explains how it's for work, how his company is doing work for an Irish company. How there are a lot of tech companies in Ireland these days. Maybe he'll bring them a souvenir. The kids squeal at the thought. Emily wants an Irish jig dress. Sally's hoping for a soccer jersey. The boys will take anything.

I jam my hands under my legs, feel my lips press together, can see the rise and fall of my sweater as my heart fills with smoke. Ireland, really?

Once again, Tom's playing chicken with me. At each end of the dinner table we're two cars headed toward each other at full speed. Who will be the first to swerve? In this case, who will be the first to leave the table? He's poking at me, taking easy shots, hitting me where it hurts, but I'm not budging.

"That's nice," I say in my forced-pleasant voice. "When's that?"

"In a few weeks," he says. "Next month."

"When *exactly*?" I ask through clenched teeth pulled into a smile.

"The first week in May," he says. As he says it, his tone loses a bit of its edge. Even he feels crummy about this, I can tell. "Girls, do me a favor and take the boys upstairs to get ready for bed," Tom says.

"What's going *on*?" Sally says. "Why are you guys acting so *weird*?"

"Sal, please." I look across at Tom. He's staring at his plate.

"We're part of this family, too," Sally says. "We deserve to know what's going on."

"Sally, now," Tom says. "Take the boys upstairs."

Sally stomps her way up, Emily follows, and the boys crawl on their hands and knees, barking like puppies, panting with their tongues out.

"Interesting timing," I say.

"Hmm?" Tom asks, poking at his food.

"Just ironic, because that is the week we had blocked off for celebrating our anniversary."

"Well," he says, "a lot has changed since January. And this is for work."

"I wasn't implying that we'd still be celebrating our anniversary."

"Right."

"I was just commenting on the timing."

"Just a coincidence."

"Crappy coincidence," I say.

"It's for work."

"Got it."

Tom stares at his plate, then looks up.

"I thought I'd bring Patrick along."

"Your brother? To Ireland?" Tom's gone out of his way to hurt me this time: Ireland, our anniversary, his stupid brother.

"That's right."

"And . . . why are you doing that?"

"I'll have some downtime. It won't be all work. Thought it would be fun to have him there. He's always wanted to go."

"You think that's a safe bet?" I say. "Patrick? To the land of whiskey?"

"Temptation is everywhere," Tom says. "Isn't that right?"

"Oh, God!" I say. "Is this *never* going to end?"

"Listen, Mary, I just thought it would be nice to bring him along. He never has an opportunity to go anywhere."

He's always wanted to go. . . . He never has an opportunity. . . . Never mind me, the mom who has been raising four kids for ten years and has not once been outside the United States.

I plaster on a smile that is gigantically too big for the moment, but it's the only way to mask the blood-boiling anger that's pulsing through me. "Well, that's just *wonderful!* I hope the two of you have an excellent time together."

"He might not be perfect," Tom says in a cool voice, "but he's never lied to me. At least there's that."

"Hooray for him," I say, getting up, stacking the plates, and walking toward the sink. I stop and turn. "Maybe you'll find some nice Irish girls at the local pub, just so you can jab the knife a little farther into my chest."

Tom slips into the backyard and I see him throw Daisy's ball so hard and far, she can't get it. It's beyond her invisible fence. Tom stomps and pounds his fist into the palm of his other hand, and then climbs into the brambles to fetch it.

I can't breathe. My chest hurts, my *heart* hurts. I want to scream and break things, but I'm not *allowed* to because I'm the mom and everyone—everyone—is watching me at all times. I can't even lock myself in the bathroom for five minutes without one of the kids pounding on the door with some dramatic entreaty that requires my immediate attention. I consider the stack of plates sitting in the sink. I eye the mallet on the counter that I used to pound the chicken. I hold it in my hand, squeeze the rubber handle, pretend to hammer it down onto the plates. Then I think about the *mess,* the cleanup; it would take an hour to make sure I'd gotten every tiny shard of glass. Forget it.

I run down to the basement and head to the corner of the exercise room. I punch at the bag. Again, again, again. "Screw you!" I whisper through clenched teeth. *Screw you,* I whisper through my cries. *Screw you.* Then I fall onto the ground and push my face into the carpet. I roll over onto my back, scoot my body until I'm lying directly beneath the bag, and then nudge it with my hand. Daring it. I look up at the chain atop the bag, connected to a carabiner clip, swinging from the hook in the ceiling. *Crush me,* I think. *Who cares?*

| | |

The following week is quiet. Tom's news of a trip to Ireland has sent me into a depression, one that makes me pull back and draw inward. I'm tired of putting forth so much effort. I need a break. The more I retreat, the more attentive Tom becomes. An interesting seesaw of emotion and guilt between us. A few times during the week he tries to smile at me. Once he pours me a glass of wine. He says good night before edging to his side of the bed. He senses that I'm brittle, that if he blows too hard I might turn to dust.

The next week I'm feeling better. Working through the stages. Acceptance has taken the place of depression. Or maybe it's more apathy. I find myself shaking my head at the thought of Ireland, a pervasive feeling of *whatever* running through me. Take your stupid trip with your stupid brother. See if I care.

Tom's anger has turned intermittent, like the slow setting on the windshield wipers. He has his moments in which he borders on nice, then sometimes the fury fills him, and I get the feeling he'll never reach forgiveness, like it's an actual place, a remote village in the mountains of Nepal. A Sherpa is needed to lead him in.

The night before Tom leaves for Ireland, I'm lying in bed next to him. He's asleep on his side, facing my direction; one hand is on his face, the other curled into his chest. I reach out my hand and cover his, touch his skin for the first time in months, let our palms adhere. I scoot a little closer, lift my hand and use it to brush the hair out of his eyes. He used to love that. "Run your fingers through my hair," he'd say each night, with his head in my lap as we watched a *Seinfeld* rerun before bedtime. His hair is silky and the amber waves slip through my fingers. His hair, same as Sally's. "Your daughter looks just like her father," so many people have said over the past ten years. That was God helping me out. *I'll give you this. I'll make her in his image.* But a likeness only masqueraded as the truth, only made the truth so much harder to bear.

Tom opens his eyes, sees that I'm touching him, matches his eyes with mine. We peer into each other's sadness for a second, maybe two. I keep running my fingers through his hair, saying a prayer each time, something like *Please, please, please.*

"I miss you," I whisper.

Tom reaches for my hand, sandwiches it between his, and squeezes it gently. I think I see the corners of his mouth edge up, just so slightly. Then he blinks, closes his eyes, and turns over. He scoots farther away, hugging his side of the bed, leaving a gap between us as large as the Arctic tundra, but maybe not as cold. I roll over to my side, hugging my pillow into my chest, and think, *Well, maybe.*

In the morning, I check my list. Even though Tom's sadness and anger masked as cruelty has left me undone, I still can't help myself when it comes to packing for his trip. I'm a wife and mother. It's in my job description. I've gone on the Internet to research the weather, how it could rain in Dublin at any time, how layering is his best bet. Aside from his work clothes, I've packed long-sleeved shirts, sweatshirts, jeans, socks and underwear, and two rain jackets (knowing that stupid Patrick would never think to bring one).

When Tom says good-bye, the boys cry and the girls issue dramatic statements of love and devotion, like their father's shipping off to war.

"We'll miss you *so much*!" Emily cries.

"We *LOVE* you *so much*!" Sally says, throwing herself into Tom's arms.

There are hugs and kisses and more hugs and more hanging and more proclamations and declarations of the best and biggest love *ever*. Finally, Tom leans into me and gives me a friendly hug—one of those where two people don't really touch, just hover around each other like scaffolding, patting each other quickly and briefly, as if the other has a skin disease.

"Good luck to you," he says.

The kids may have gotten Tom's undying pledge of love, his loyalty, a piece of his heart to squeeze tight like a security blanket, but me, I got a buddy's pat on the back and a good luck!

"Dad," Sally says in a hushed tone. Tom turns, looks at her. "You are coming back, right?"

Tom lifts her into his arms, as naturally as he did when she was a little girl, hugs her tightly and kisses her cheek, over and over again. "I love you, Sally," he says. "And yes, I'm coming back."

CHAPTER TWENTY-EIGHT
Deserving of Love

THREE HOURS LATER, I FIGURE that Tom's finally on the airplane, following a half-hour drive into DC, parking and security, and a two-hour wait to get onto the plane. I close my eyes and imagine that he and Patrick are settled in, Tom with his folded newspapers, Patrick with his jumbo coffee. With any luck, Tom remembered to buy them some snacks and maybe a sandwich. I can see Patrick staring out the window, his jittery leg bouncing. I'm certain Tom's wearing the airplane headphones, listening to the pilots chat and navigate. I'm thinking all of this when the phone rings.

"Mary . . . It's Colleen."

"Hi," I say carefully, because I haven't spoken to Colleen since Tom and I went off our cliff. While Colleen has always treated me like a daughter, what I've done to her son is a game changer. One night, as Tom and I brawled, he went too far and used his mother as evidence against my wrongdoing. "Even my mother— my mother who loved you *like a daughter,* my mother who has forgiven more than her share of indiscretions—said that what you've done, and the fact that you've lied about it for so long, was inexcusable."

"Mary, dear," Colleen goes on.

I think I detect that Colleen is crying, and Colleen, who is always perfectly composed, never cries.

"Are you okay?" I ask.

"I need to get ahold of Tom. Or Patrick. I tried Kathy . . . but she wasn't home."

"They're on a plane, Colleen. What's going on?" Now I'm sure. There's no way there's not something wrong with *that* voice.

"Honey, oh, Mary . . ." Colleen's dam breaks, and all of a sudden she's sobbing.

"It's Sean. He's in the hospital."

"What happened?" Before she even answers, I think of Tom, locked on an airplane over the Atlantic.

"He was just *here*," she cries in a frantic, shrill voice. "We were watching our programs. I had taped *60 Minutes* from the other night. I went to get him another cup of coffee. When I came back, he was slumped in his recliner. *Slumped!* Oh dear, Mary. I only left the room for five minutes." Colleen sobs, and I can't even imagine the heavy tears pouring from her: perfectly put-together Colleen, my mother-in-law who toughed out breast cancer with a stiff upper lip and five miles of walking each day.

"What did you do?" I ask.

"I called 911. The ambulance was here in less than five minutes. They put him on a *stretcher*," she cries. "Then they drove away."

"How is he now?" I ask, reaching for a pen and a pad of paper.

"I don't *know*. They just left a few minutes ago. He's probably still in the ambulance." Colleen releases a giant cry, and I can imagine her finely manicured hand covering her eyes as her shoulders bob up and down.

"Is there anyone there who can go with you to the hospital?"

"I'll drive myself."

"Are you sure that's a good idea?"

"I'll be fine. It's only a few miles."

"Colleen," I say as strongly as I can, "I'll be there in four hours. I'm leaving right now." I'm already slipping on my clogs and reaching for my keys and purse. "Your only job is to get yourself to the hospital safely and to be with Sean. I'm coming!"

"Oh, Mary. *Thank you,*" she cries. "I know you and Tom . . ."

"Don't worry about that now," I say. "I'm on my way."

I'm in jeans and a T-shirt and haven't yet brushed my teeth or hair for the day. I run upstairs to my bathroom and do the minimum: brush teeth, a swipe of deodorant, a hair band wrapped around my wrist for later. I grab a pair of undies from my drawer and an extra T-shirt, and in less than three minutes, with only my purse and cell phone, I'm in the car and heading toward the interstate. I call Mom and explain. She says she'll coordinate with Dad to pick up all the kids. I'm rattling nonsense about the girls' homework, how Emily needs for you to literally *stand over her* while she does her math. Whatever it takes, I tell Ma. Set a timer, reward her with mini-marshmallows, but don't let her get away with not doing her multiplication. Sally, on the other hand, is Miss Efficient and Miss Cocky, so much so that she'll do her work too quickly, making careless mistakes. She's working long division. I tell Ma to make sure she multiplies them back to check her work.

Mom says yes to everything, but I know her. She'll feed the girls tea and cannoli before homework and then sit with them for hours, making a fun game out of it. I go on: Whatever you do, don't let Dom or Danny fall asleep on the way home from school or you'll never get them to bed tonight. Again, Mom agrees, but I know her. Her adage is: never wake a sleeping baby. She'd rather slip into bed with them at three o'clock in the morning and sing them back to sleep than deprive them of their afternoon nap.

"What about Tom?" Mom asks.

"He's on a plane for the next ten hours. I'll call him as soon as he lands. Hopefully, we'll know something by then."

I fill up at the gas station and drive through McDonald's. Other than that, I don't stop, zipping my way south.

Thanks to a heavy foot on the gas pedal and the lucky absence of cops, I make it to Colleen in three and a half hours. I jog through the parking garage and the hallways until I reach the surgery waiting room. When I see Colleen, I stop short, because all of a sudden my self-confidence can be measured in ccs, barely enough to fill a syringe. *Hi, Colleen, it's me, the woman who ruined your son's life.*

"Colleen," I say carefully.

"Oh, Mary!" She rises from the brown tweed chair and rushes to me. "Thank God you're here!" She collapses into my arms, and any feelings of ill will she might be harboring against me are put at least temporarily on hold.

"How is he?" I ask.

"He's in surgery," she sobs into my chest. "Triple bypass!"

"A heart attack?"

Colleen pulls back, covers her mouth, nods.

"When's the last time someone's come out to talk to you?"

"About an hour ago. He'd already been in surgery for a couple of hours."

"Did they say anything? About his prognosis?"

"I don't know, dear. I don't remember. It's all such a *blur.*"

"Okay, okay," I say, leading her back to the chair. I sit beside her, still holding her hand, stroking the soft, thin skin stretched across her delicate veins. "How about some coffee? Are you hungry?"

She shakes her head no, so I sit with her, pull her into me so that her cheek is on my shoulder. I check the clock, one thirty. Tom's plane doesn't land until seven o'clock tonight.

For the next two hours, Colleen and I avoid land mines as if we have metal detectors. The children are safe ground, so I tell Colleen everything: what the girls are reading, what the boys are learning, field trips and projects, upcoming events at school. I tell the least about Sally because all of a sudden I wonder if Colleen loves her first grandchild less now that she knows the truth. That can't be true, but . . .

When the surgeon pushes through the double doors, he removes his glasses and rubs the lenses on the bottom of his scrubs.

"He's out of surgery," he says.

"How is he?" Colleen asks hesitantly, as if she assumes he'll say, *Not good.*

"He did very well."

"So what *exactly* did you do?" I ask. "What exactly happened?" I know Colleen is in no shape to take notes and that Tom will need to know every detail when I call him.

"The blood vessels that supply blood to the heart can become blocked, and that blockage prevents enough oxygen from reaching the heart. Thus, coronary artery disease. In your father's situation, there were three vessels that were blocked. We were able to take vessels from his legs and graft them onto the heart, thus creating a detour for the blood flow."

"So he's going to be okay?" I ask, marveling at the doctor's simple explanation: *The road was closed, so we made a detour!*

"He should be just fine," the doctor says. "Of course, when he's back to full speed, he's going to want to make some lifestyle changes."

"What about drinking?" I might be overstepping my boundaries as the daughter-in-law, but Colleen's so spacey, she won't remember.

"Drinking too much alcohol can definitely lead to a rise in triglycerides. It can also cause high blood pressure. Like anything," the doctor says, "moderation."

Two hours later, we're called back to see Tom's father. Colleen collapses into his bed rail. She wails his name, *"Sean, Sean . . . ,"* like he's a wounded soldier on a battlefield. He's barely lucid, still groggy from the anesthesia. I close my eyes and think it through. Colleen has loved Sean throughout their entire marriage, throughout his infidelity, his excessive drinking. Here she is, nearly reduced to rubble at the sight of her ill husband. I can't help but wonder where she puts it. Where does she put the anger and resentment and pure animosity she must feel for this man? Is it compartmentalized—still there, somewhere, tucked away, for her to pull out when the mood suits her? Or has her love, her devotion, her lifetime commitment to this man *overwhelmed* the bitter feelings, like a strong wave engulfs a sand castle or too much garlic overpowers the sweetness of basil, or confessing our wrongs and praying an Act of Contrition absolves us from sin? How can she be so undone by a man who has hurt her so deeply?

Would Tom even care if I was in the hospital? Would his former feelings of love for me supplant his seething anger? Would he ever find a place to tuck my indiscretion into? Does absolute forgiveness really, truly exist? Is there something higher, beyond "I forgive you, but . . ."? Is there a place in the heart that ends with "I forgive you, period"?

A few hours later, Sean wakes up slowly, blinks and coughs, struggles to sit up. He's disoriented and confused. When Colleen smooths the hair on his forehead and tells him it's okay, the furrow between his brow unknots itself. His gaze locks onto hers like an anchor, like her sapphire eyes alone have the power to buoy him in troubled waters.

"What . . . ?" he croaks. "Where . . . what . . . ?"

"You're in the hospital," Colleen says gently. She's straightened herself, wiped her eyes, plastered on a smile. Her composure has come back before my eyes, like a Polaroid developing into focus. I'm astonished. She was able to let go with pure, uninhibited love and emotion when he was in surgery and after, still groggy, but now that Sean's coming to, her strength is erected again. Is it that she feels he doesn't deserve seeing her reduced to tears? She'll cry for him, but she won't let him know it. Hmm. The dignified lady she is has politely yet firmly kicked the frantic lady in the butt with a solid *I'll take it from here.*

I'll forgive you, but . . . That's Colleen's caveat, it seems. She forgives Sean, but she won't let him see her vulnerable side. She won't let him see how much she truly cares. That's her armor, her protection. *I'll forgive you, but . . .*

Sean looks at me, scans the room, baffled and worried. "Where's Tom? Where am I?"

"You had a heart attack, Sean," Colleen says. "A heart attack. The surgeon had to do a triple bypass on you."

It takes a moment for Sean to process the enormity of this, like trying to get a good grip around an awkward piece of furniture. Then he begins to weep, jagged little gulps of sobs.

"I'll be right out here," I say to Colleen, and then step into the hallway. The doctor is walking by. "Excuse me!" I say. "Sean Morrissey, in this room." I point. "Is he really going to be okay?"

"Your father should be better than he was before."

"My father-in-law," I say. "Not that it matters."

"You're right," he says. "It doesn't. When you're married, it all gets thrown into the mix."

I check my phone, call Mom, call Tom's boss, Chuck. By the time I'm finished with the phone calls, I do the math and figure that Tom should have landed by now. I dread dumping this on him when he's so far away. I know how helpless he's going to feel. I dial.

Tom answers on the third ring. There's the commotion of the airport in the background. I hear Patrick say something about getting something to eat.

"How was your flight?" I ask stupidly, trying to spare Tom for another minute.

"Long, very long," Tom says. "You'd think there would be some more legroom on an overseas flight, but no luck."

"Yeah," I say, "did they feed you?"

"Just one of those boxed lunch things. It wasn't too bad."

"Probably anything tasted good on a flight that long." I smile and realize that we're having a conversation. I close my eyes and wish that we could just *talk*, have some inane conversation about legroom and airplane food, but I know that I need to tell him. "Listen, Tom, first let me say that *the kids are fine*. In fact, *everything's fine*." It's in the parents' code: Never start bad news without the reassurance that all of the kids are fine. A parent's heart can only withstand a few seconds without air when there's a possibility of harm to one's child.

"What happened, Mary?" Tom says, his voice breaking.

"Your father, Tom. He had a heart attack."

"What?"

"He had a heart attack, but he went through surgery—triple bypass—and the doctors say he's going to be fine."

"How'd this happen? Where's Mom? What did she do? Is anyone with her? God, we're both *here*! She's all alone. Are her sisters coming?"

"Tom, stop!" I say. "I'm here. I'm with your mother. She's fine. And yes, I've called her sisters and they're coming the day after tomorrow. But I'm here and I'm going to stay for as long as they need me, so don't worry."

"You're *there*?" he asks in a little boy's voice. "You're in Virginia Beach?"

"Of course, Tom. I left the second she called."

"And the kids?"

"Mom and Dad have it covered."

"And Dad is out of surgery and he's doing okay?" Tom clarifies.

"That's right. I just saw him."

"He hasn't been feeling well," Tom says. "For a while."

"I know," I say, because it's true: For months now Colleen has told us that Sean has been subpar.

I hear Tom sniff, clear his throat. "Well, *thank you*, Mary," he says in a very official voice, but I know better.

"Okay, then," Tom says. "Let me make some calls and see if I can get on a plane back tonight. Maybe the plane I came on just refuels and heads home. I'll have to go to the counter and ask. And I'll have to call Chuck. Let me make some calls and I'll get back to you."

"Listen, Tom," I say. "I know this is your dad and you're going to do whatever you feel that you have to do, but I talked to Chuck and he said of course he'll bring you home immediately, and that he would reschedule the presentation and send another guy. But I told Chuck to hold on. I told him that I'd try to convince you to stay, *just for tomorrow,* to do the presentation. Here's the thing, Tom. Your father is in a hospital bed recuperating.

He's going to be here tomorrow and the next day and the next day. The heart attack is over. The surgery is over. So why don't you at least stay and do the presentation? You've been working on it for a month and some other guy isn't going to be able to do it as well as you. What do you think? Trust me, Tom. Everything is fine here. If it weren't, I would tell you."

I hear Tom take in a gigantic breath and exhale noisily. "I don't know, Mary. I mean, my dad just had a heart attack. I should be there."

"And you will be. All I'm saying is that I don't think it matters whether it's tomorrow or the next day. It's up to you, honey." I say *honey* before I'm aware it's exiting my mouth. It's been months since Tom and I have used any term of endearment for each other. We stick purely to our very formal Tom and Mary Show.

"Okay," he says. "Let me think about it. I'll call you back."

We say good-bye, but neither of us hangs up.

"Mary," Tom says finally.

"Yeah?"

"Nothing," he says. "I'll call you back."

CHAPTER TWENTY-NINE
Principles

TOM

I STARE INTO THE AIRPORT, but my vision is messed up, like I can't remember how to read. I'm looking at the signs above baggage claim and I can't seem to remember what flight we were on, what city we came from, the name of the airline. Tourist billboards are plastered on every wall, the castles, the green hills, the mossy cliffs. Patrick's outside, I guess, smoking. I look around for the shoulder bag he brought on the plane because, knowing Patrick, he probably left it on a bench somewhere, but then I realize that it's hanging from my shoulder, along with my computer bag. I can't think! What else did I have with me? Aer Lingus, that's it! Where the hell is the Aer Lingus counter? Upstairs, likely. Where the hell is Patrick, smoking an entire pack? *Oh God, Dad.* My father, a heart attack. *Oh God, Dad.*

And Mary's there. Of course she's there. She's there taking care of my parents and I'm way the hell over here with my brother instead of her. I'm hurting, God, I'm hurting, but I didn't need to be such a bastard to Mary. Hurting was what I fed on, but that cold hardness with her was just gluttony. It wasn't necessary. I stuffed myself on meanness, and now Mary's there, taking care of my parents. Of course she is.

How do you measure what's real, what's true? How do you stack up all that's pure against all that's evil? Even if I want to, how do I forgive Mary for crushing my heart? How the hell do we get beyond this?

Patrick's walking toward me. I can smell the Camels before he's even near me, thanks to some pocket of air traveling in front of him.

"Where's our luggage?" he asks.

"I don't have a clue," I say. "I've been on the phone with Mary."

"Kids okay?"

I clutch Patrick's biceps and tell him the news. I tell him that Dad had a heart attack, that he's going to be all right, that Mary thinks I should stay for a day. I tell him everything I know and when I'm finished, Patrick asks, "How does Mary know all this?"

"Because she's there, Patrick," I say, and even though I would expect nothing less of Mary, the fact that she's there and I'm here lodges a boulder in my throat.

CHAPTER THIRTY
Offend Thee

NIGHT FALLS AND SEAN SLIPS back into sleep. Colleen and I are playing a game of Scrabble and she's kicking my butt, coming up with words like SQUIRES and ZOOLOGIST on double- and triple-point squares. Tom called earlier in the night and said yes, hesitantly, he would stay and do the presentation tomorrow and then he and Patrick would hop on a plane. I promised that I'd let him know if anything changed with his father's condition.

I call home and Mom puts the phone on speaker. "Nana's teaching us how to make biscotti," Sally says.

"And she let me paint my fingernails," Emily adds.

The boys brag that Pop let them pound nails into a board, *just because!* The kids scurry back to their business, forgetting that I'm listening. I hold the phone to my ear and absorb the sounds I craved for so long and cherish every day. My children: happy, secure, confident. Thriving individuals whose hearts are not only whole but strong, the muscle fortified with an abundance of love's nutrients. "We'll talk to you later, hon," Ma says. I nod, clear my throat, croak out a pathetic "Okay, Ma. Thanks." I hold the phone to my ear until they hang up.

A day and a half later, I've sent Colleen home to catch a shower and a few hours of shut-eye. I'm sitting with Sean, slumped in one armchair, my feet propped onto another. With a pen poked behind my ear and the local paper's crossword puzzle in hand, I ask my father-in-law, "A four-letter word for a Greek god, starts with E?"

"Where's my Sally when I need her?" he says.

"I think it's Eros," I tell him, remembering Sal telling me the story about Aphrodite and Ares, Eros's mother and father. I stand and stretch, hold the water cup with a straw for my father-in-law to take a sip, adjust his pillows. "How 'bout this one, a four-letter word for an extinct bird," I say, sitting back down.

"A dodo," a voice says.

I turn and see Tom standing in the doorway. My heart plunges. He looks as rumpled and disheveled as I know I must, after his days of travel, but adorable, too, in that just-off-the-mountain type of ruggedness. I wonder what he thinks I look like, still in my jeans and T-shirt from two days ago.

"Tom," I say, my eyes welling. I look away, as if taking a precaution against staring into the sun. "Look, Sean!" I say. "Tom's here. I imagine Patrick's not far away."

"He's outside," Tom says, leaving out the obvious: smoking a cigarette or two before facing *this* situation head-on.

Tom approaches his father hesitantly, places a careful hand on his shoulder. "Hi, Dad," he says. "How are you?"

"Better than new, son," he says. "New blood vessels and all."

"Look at all this stuff," Tom says, pointing to all the machines.

"This is the heart monitor," I explain.

"Mare watches it like a hawk," Sean says, and Tom's mouth smiles, but his eyes are sad.

"This is his blood pressure, his oxygen level," I go on. "The IV is just saline, to keep him hydrated. A little bit ago we ate some applesauce and Jell-O, didn't we, Sean?" I look over at my father-in-law and rub his shoulder. It's been hard to see a strong man like Sean reduced to a feeble, childlike state, even temporarily. The thought of my own parents turning the corner into old age and diminished health nearly kills me. It's frightening to see how easily pillars crumble.

I stand up and take Sean's water cup to the sink. Rinse it, fill it again, poke through a fresh straw. "Drink," I tell him. "He's a good patient," I say to Tom. "Sometimes a little obstinate, but I guess that runs in the family."

Tom sits in the chair I had been in, leans into his father. "Good God, Dad," he says. "You scared us all to death."

"Thank God for Mary, here," he says. "She's a tough little cookie. Watching over the doctors and nurses, making them check the medicine twice before they shoot it into me. Poor doctors probably haven't answered so many questions since they took their boards."

"Well," I say, a mix of pride and embarrassment, "you hear horror stories."

"What's next?" Tom says to his dad. "When do you head home?"

Sean looks to me to answer. That's how he's been these past couple of days, unsure of his footing, deferring to me or Colleen most of the time. "A few more days," I say. "Then he'll head home and start a whole new life of healthy living, right, Sean?"

"Broccoli and water," he snorts.

"And a shot of whiskey on your birthday," I add. Sean and I have made up a calendar of ten days during the year when he'll indulge in a glass of whiskey. His birthday, St. Patrick's Day, Thanksgiving, and Christmas topped the list, along with a handful of holy days of obligation.

"How was your trip?" I ask Tom. "And the presentation, did you pull it off?"

"It went well," he says. "They're definitely on board."

"Good," I say, morbidly thinking we need Tom to be successful at work, we need him to bring home a big bonus at the end of the year, especially if his anger is interminable. If he never forgives me and one of us needs to move out, we'll have two households to support. I'm *assuming* Tom would continue to support me as well as the kids. Maybe just the kids. Maybe I'd be forced to hit the pavement, looking for a job, competing for a first-year associate position against twenty-five-year-olds fresh out of law school. How would I fare compared to the new lawyers who know how to use iPads and smartphones and who are willing to work until midnight on weekdays because they don't have to monitor homework, confront a new mound of laundry each night, and put four kids to bed?

After a while, Tom says, "Well, Mary, I'm here now. Do you want to head back home? Get back to the kids?"

"Oh! Yeah, well, sure," I stammer, feeling entirely kicked out of the show I'd been running for the last forty-eight hours. It hadn't occurred to me that I'd leave *immediately.* "I guess I could do that."

"Mare, honey," Sean says, winking at me when Tom's back is turned, "do you think you can stay another night? That night orderly is a little rough on the old man. He's liable to yank my cords out if you're not here to monitor him while he changes the sheets."

"I can do *that,*" Tom says. "I'll be here, Dad."

"Oh, son, that's true. But Mary has a way with these guys. Wait'll you see her in action. And she'll get me an extra pudding with dinner, too." Again Sean winks at me, like he wants to be sure that I get what he's up to; that forcing me to stay another night will bring Tom and me back together.

"I'm happy to stay," I say. "If it's okay with Tom."

"Whatever Dad wants," Tom says, sounding as though he feels slighted, like he flew all the way across the Atlantic—twice—just to be relegated behind the woman who ruined his life.

While Tom sits with his father, I run home to Sean and Colleen's house. Colleen is just slipping into her car to head back to the hospital, looking fresh and revived in a salmon-colored twin set and white linen pants.

"Tom's with him," I say.

"Mary, dear," Colleen says, reaching her little peach of a hand to my cheek. "I don't want to pretend that there isn't an eight-hundred-pound gorilla in the room. I admit I'm not happy about your situation with Tom."

I begin to cry like a child because being admonished by a parent—any parent—is crushing.

Colleen reaches her arms around me. "But I believe that you love Tom. . . ."

"I do!" I blubber. "More than anything. Colleen, you have no idea how sorry I am."

"I do," she says. "Suffice it to say that I've seen such sorrow in the eyes of my husband before."

I'm split down the middle because being grouped with Sean isn't exactly what I was hoping for, but then again, at least Colleen is extending an olive branch.

"I have the most luxurious bubble bath under my sink,"

Colleen says, making it clear that our heart-to-heart is over. "The tub was just scrubbed. Get yourself a glass of wine, light some candles, pour in the bubble bath, and take a well-deserved rest."

CHAPTER THIRTY-ONE
Persons Harmed

I DO AS COLLEEN RECOMMENDED and soak for a good hour in the tub, under a foot of lavender bubbles. I sip from my glass of chardonnay and try, try so hard, to breathe and relax. But relaxing is a luxury, a pleasure reserved for deserving people, and at the moment—even five months later—I still don't feel that I deserve much in the way of pleasure. I've hurt Tom on so many levels: the most basic—I was with another man when I was committed to him. A level deeper—I carried, delivered, and passed off as his own a child who wasn't his. Sink lower—I kept my infidelity a secret for the entire duration of our marriage. Hanging by my thumbs—I never came clean; the truth was revealed as the unfortunate side effect of a stupid photo, not from my stepping up. I had ten years to find the courage, to do the right thing, and never did.

I think of Tom, what he said that day. *I'd love to know what you're most sorry about: the fact that you slept with Landon when you were engaged to me. Or is it the fact that you got caught?* It was a crappy thing for him to say, a *mean* thing. But now I wonder about my motives, whether there was any purity to them or just selfishness. There are two types of contrition, Mom taught us: perfect and imperfect. *Perfect,* stemming from our love for God, for our sorrow for having offended Him. And *imperfect,* arising from other motives, such as the loss of heaven or the fear of hell.

If I'm honest, I have to admit that my contrition was the imperfect kind: the fear of being caught. I believe that I've been a good wife and mother, that I've made my family a happy home, but it was a house built with stolen bricks. A charity funded with drug money. A test aced by cheating. I had ten years to make my contrition perfect, but lying was the steroid that kept me in the lead. A position I wasn't willing to give up.

When I dry off, I see that Colleen has laid out some clothes for me. They're actually mine, an outfit I'd left in the dryer the last time we'd visited. I gather my clean undies from my bag and pull on the capris and T-shirt that Colleen left. Then I return to her bathroom. I rummage through her top drawer, knowing that she always has samples from Clinique and Estée Lauder during their free-package period. I find a new mascara, some blush, and a rose-colored lipstick. I blow out my hair until it's smooth and find my toothbrush, then brush until my tongue and cheeks feel raw.

As I look in the mirror, I gaze into my own eyes and think, *Please, please, please, Tom. Love me again.*

By the time I get back to the hospital, Sean's room is filled with visitors. Patrick is on one side of his dad, Tom is on the other, and Colleen is holding court for her two sisters, who have just flown in from Albany, explaining the triple bypass procedure in exacting detail. Sean roars when he sees me, "There's the best nurse in this whole hospital!" He goes on to regale Colleen's sisters with the same stories he told Tom, how I keep the doctors hopping, how I score him extra pudding.

I examine the aunts and smile oddly because I'm unsure what Colleen has told them about me. It seems they are oblivious to my and Tom's problems, so when we all settle in for a visit, they ask the obvious. They want to know about the kids. I look at Tom, and he smiles and shrugs, urging me to give the aunts the lowdown.

I prattle on about the girls, how Sally is playing travel soccer, is the tallest girl in her class, and is a voracious reader. "She has the vocabulary of an adult," I say. "Currently her favorite word is *extraneous*. In her estimation, most of what I say is extraneous, like an unnecessary and annoying bother."

The aunts laugh, remember their own children as they went through the know-it-all stage, nod and laugh and wipe tears from their eyes. "It goes so fast," they lament.

I tell how Emily is rehearsing for *The Wizard of Oz*, still singing in the church choir, and is on a spiritual quest for "truth and beauty." "When she's older she'll either break my heart by moving to New York City to be an actress or running off to the hills of India with her poet boyfriend to seek transcendence."

"And the twins," I say. "They're still so little, but they think they're big. They just beam with pride when they do things themselves."

"You're blessed," Aunt Elaine says. "God smiled on you and Tom with that wonderful family of yours."

"I agree," I say, looking at Tom and offering him a sad smile.

Then the aunts ask Tom about Ireland, what he was able to see in his one-day trip.

"I saw the inside of the hotel and the inside of the conference room where I made my presentation," he says wryly.

Patrick tells of his one-day excursion through Dublin while Tom was working.

"You'll go back," Aunt Deirdre says to Tom. "Next time you'll take Mare. And you'll visit County Clare and see the Cliffs of Moher and sleep in a castle."

Aunt Elaine looks at me, her eyebrows raised high in excitement for us.

"Definitely," I say. "I've always wanted to see Ireland. Hopefully, that'll be in our cards someday." Again I look at Tom, gauge his reaction to see if he believes our cards hold a future.

Then Sean launches in, telling stories about his time in Dublin, and breaks out in a croaky rendition of "Molly Malone." We're all laughing, and before you know it the childhood stories come out. Colleen tells of when Tom and Patrick were kids, the stunts they'd pulled playing Evel Knievel and TV heroes like those in *The Six Million Dollar Man* and *The Incredible Hulk*. Soon, Tom's laughing and I want to cry because I haven't seen him laugh in *so* long and he has the best laugh, the kind of roar that emanates from his belly, a smile that transforms his face, a joy that forms crinkles of diamonds in the corners of his eyes. He wipes at his eyes, remembering the carefree times as a child, when he and Patrick were just two boys, before the alcoholic DNA in Patrick's body had coiled around him, before Tom flicked on the television one day to find out that his wife was a liar and a cheat and a thief.

Visiting hours are just about over. For Sean's benefit, I give a stern talking-to to the night orderly who is preparing to change his sheets. Then I turn my back to Sean and give the orderly a wink and a smile and a ten-dollar bill, mouthing the words *Thank you*. Colleen and her sisters are talking about a Chinese restaurant not too far from the hospital one of the nurses said was decent. Patrick says he's starving and could go for some kung pao. Tom agrees. I hang back, unsure if unredeemable me is invited to the party.

"Ready, Mary?" Colleen says.

"Maybe I'll just grab something in the cafeteria," I say, because among this crowd of Tom, his brother, his mother, and her sisters, who really wants me along?

"Don't be ridiculous," Colleen says, looking at Tom with raised eyebrows, as if urging him to get on board. "You're coming."

The aunts look at Tom for an explanation for my hesitation. "Maybe she doesn't like Chinese?" Aunt Elaine says, and I smile because it's obvious they don't know what I've done.

Tom looks at his aunts, his mother. "Of course, Mary. Come have dinner."

Tom and Patrick had taken a cab from the airport, so they're without a car. Colleen says she has room for her sisters plus one. She slings her arm around Patrick and tells me and Tom that they'll meet us there. She is being far from sneaky, trying to play cupid with us.

We walk to the car in silence. As I'm pulling out of the lot, Tom says in his careful, formal voice, "Thank you again for coming. That was good of you."

"Of course I came," I say.

"Not, 'of course,'" he says. "You didn't have to come. It wasn't your family. And it was big of you that you made the effort."

"I didn't do it for points," I say. "And just so you know, they *are* my family. Just because you and I are on rocky ground doesn't mean I no longer love your parents. They may not be my blood, but I consider them my family nonetheless. I don't need the DNA to match up."

"And neither do I. Don't question my love for Sally," he says. "That's *never* been the issue."

"I know," I say. "I know you love her. I'm sorry I said that. This is no time to make things worse. I have no business laying into you now, or anytime, for that matter."

"I'm sorry, too," he says. "I shouldn't have said that they're not your family."

At dinner I drink three beers and I'm nearly drunk. For about half an hour I relish the cloudy space I'm occupying, where I'm not constantly examining faces and scrutinizing comments for subtext. I relish being altered, how it makes the plum sauce on the moo shu pork taste richer, sweeter, how it makes Aunt Elaine's eyebrows seem cartoonish and drawn on, how it warms my cheeks and wraps its arms around me like an electric blanket. Tom drives us back to Colleen's. I fall asleep in Sean's recliner in my clothes, the underwire of my bra digging into my ribs, a chenille blanket tucked into my sides. I'm lucid enough to consider getting up to go to the bathroom, to run a toothbrush across my teeth, but I can't move, literally cannot move, like I've swallowed cement.

At three o'clock in the morning, I wake up. My tongue is fuzzy and my eyelashes are goopy, stuck together. I tiptoe to the bathroom, put my mouth under the faucet, and drink what seems like a gallon of water. I wash my face, brush my teeth, and use the toilet.

I stand there in the dark hallway outside the bathroom, wondering where everyone is. I imagine the aunts are in the guest bedroom with the two twin beds, and Tom and Patrick must be in the family room on the sofas. I sneak into the family room and see Tom sprawled on the leather sofa. Patrick isn't on the other one. Maybe he went back to his house. I consider lying down on the vacant one, but first I kneel next to Tom, run my fingers through his hair, over his shoulder. He opens his eyes, looks at me, and pulls back the blanket covering him to make room for me.

Inviting me in.

I am a woman dying in the desert, and Tom has offered me water.

I slip in next to him, my back curved into his stomach, his arm over mine. I lay there, wide awake. I know Tom is, too. I can feel his eyelashes flutter on my hair. Neither of us says a word. We just breathe, frozen, as if turned to stone by Medusa's glare. I have an itch on my nose but I don't dare scratch it. The slightest move might be enough to break the spell, to bring Tom back to his senses with a tidy and formal "Okay, then, you'd better get back to your recliner."

Finally, I hear Tom doze into sleep. I close my eyes, too, and drift off, for the first time in nearly five months, in the embrace of my husband's arms.

|||

As I'm getting ready to leave the next morning to drive back home, I learn that Tom plans to stay another week, to see his father through a string of follow-up visits, physical therapy, and a meeting with the nutritionist. When I ask Tom why he needs to stay so long, why Patrick can't do what Tom's planning to do, he shrugs, and I realize that he doesn't really have an answer other than not wanting to come home.

He walks me to the car.

"Do you have any stuff?" he asks.

"Just my purse," I say. "I kind of left right away when your mom called."

"Give the kids a kiss for me," he says.

"I can't wait to see them. It feels like it's been a lifetime."

"Two and a half days with my father can do that."

I smile, slip into the driver's seat, start the car. Tom pats my forearm resting on the window, a slight rub. "Okay, then," he says. "See you when I see you."

The old Tom would have given me a list of safety precautions, would have reminded me to fill up the tank before I hit the highway, would have made sure that my cell phone was charged and the spare tire was in good shape. The old Tom would have programmed the GPS, warned me against creeps at the rest stops, would have made me promise to call the second I got home. The old Tom would have kissed me good-bye.

I'm only a block away when I start to bawl: fat, giant, soaking tears that make my chest heave and leave me fighting for breath. I rub at my face, smearing mascara. Blow my nose and cry some more. The old Tom would have cautioned me against driving while having a nervous breakdown, but the new Tom is rationing his compassion and affection, doling it out in scant pieces, storing up the rest in case there's another war.

When I enter our home, the kids are schizophrenic. At first they tackle me—literally *tackle* me—with hugs and kisses until I'm splayed on the floor with four suckerfish feeding on me.

"Mommy, *Mommy*!" Danny pleads. "It's *you*!"

"You've been gone *forever*!" Dom cries.

Sally cups my face with her hands and turns it in her direction, so that she has my full attention. "Mom, I read a 527-page book in two days!"

Emily weaves her head under her sister's arm until her mouth is an inch from mine. "Mommy, oh, Mommy, you are a *beautiful* sight!"

This devotion, this uninhibited gush of pure love, this dam breaking is followed almost as vehemently by a chorus of "We don't want Nana and Pop to leave! Can they stay? Do you have another trip to go on? Pop was just going to play a game of checkers with us. Nana was going to make snickerdoodles."

That night I let my parents take care of me along with the kids. Mom cuts me a gigantic wedge of lasagna and I eat it in a matter of minutes. I wash it down with a glass of pinot and then use my leftover bread to sop up any sauce left on my plate. Other than a little Chinese food last night, I realize I've barely eaten in two days. My full stomach pushes against the buttons on my pants. I slouch into my chair with another glass of wine. I tell Mom and Dad the whole story, about Sean and the heart attack, about how Colleen broke down when he wasn't looking, how Tom flew to Ireland and back in a matter of seventy-two hours.

Mom fills me in on the kids.

Later, after the kids are in their rooms and on their way to a good night's sleep, I settle in next to Mom and she asks me how it really went. I tell her about Tom, how he's still mad but how he and I shared the sofa last night. A smile pours across her face like sunshine and her eyes glisten. "See!" she says. "He's coming around."

CHAPTER THIRTY-TWO
Humble

TOM RETURNS HOME FROM VIRGINIA Beach with his shoulders relaxed and his fists unclenched. I take that as a good sign. It seems that our relationship is *veering* in the right direction, a few degrees of leaning, a *tilt*. It certainly hasn't yet turned a corner; we're still degrees and degrees away from forming a U-turn back to our old life, but the blinker is on. That first night we settle into bed, the gap that usually occupies the space between us is smaller, more a backyard than a football field.

The next night, I take a chance and place my hand on top of his as we watch a *Seinfeld* rerun in bed. A few nights later, I pull his head onto my lap and rake my fingers through his hair. The following night, we make love for the first time since last summer.

"I'm sorry," I cry afterward. "I'm so sorry for all of this hurt you've been put through. I'm so sorry for everything. I'm mostly sorry about the lie, how I carried it all of these years. How I didn't trust that our relationship was strong enough to survive it. I just want to be sure that you know that I am sorry to my bones."

"I know you are," Tom says. "And I know that marriages have recovered from worse. We're still a family. We can rebuild."

"I know we can," I agree, so thrilled to hear those exact words.

"We stand a chance," Tom says. "But Mary, I'm different now. I'm changed."

"Changed how?"

"What we went through," he says. "What it meant to our family. There's no turning back. It's part of us now. We can't pretend that it's not. We can move forward," he says, "but there's no going back."

We hold each other throughout the night, but once again I feel anxious. What I want more than anything *is* to go back to exactly how things were, our state of being, our familyhood, our constancy. But I know Tom is right. Whether I accept it or not, our world has been bombed. We've been through a war, and now we're battered veterans, covered in scars, traumatized, but also maybe stronger. This thought bubbles inside me: the irrevocability of it all, my wish for things to stay the same, the knowledge that it is no longer an option. By three in the morning, I drift off to sleep. I dream of bombs and ashes and every bit of life turning to dust, and when I wake up with a start, I wonder if I will ever feel peace again. With my heart thumping in my chest, I place my hand over it and stare at the ceiling. For the briefest moment, I gain the sense that there is life sprouting from this death, buds peeking through the soil of our ruin. The road back has been destroyed, and the road forward is riddled with land mines. But the truth has laid a new path, cobblestones spaced in leap lengths apart. *Maybe,* I think.

As affirmation, and confirmation, and validation of life, the morning sun sneaks through the blinds and I hear the birds chirping. When the children-grenades bomb on our bed, there is an explosion of love and bonding that we haven't shared in months. There is no separation between Tom and me. We are a pile of people, crisscrossed kindling, indomitable. A pile of sticks that together cannot be broken. *We'll make it,* I think.

The following Sunday we're seated in the pews of St. Andrew's. We're a few minutes early, so I crane my neck around to check out the line for confession. Only one lady. I ask Tom if it's okay if I slide out for a second.

When the light turns green I slip into the box. "Hello, Father," I say, making the sign of the cross. "Bless me, Father, for I have sinned."

"What are your sins, my child?"

"I've housed a lie that has hurt my husband, but he and I have worked through the deception. Now I wonder about my daughter. She, too, was part of the lie. What responsibility to the truth do I have to her?"

"Your responsibility is to be her mother. A child should not be concerned with adult matters."

"What about when she's older?" I ask.

"When she's older, you'll make decisions based on who she is then."

| | |

The days that follow are anything but normal. Tom and I attempt to get back our normal footing, but our house—our life—is booby-trapped at every turn, land mines buried just below the surface. On a Saturday morning the girls are playing Monopoly and Emily storms away in a huff.

"She's a cheater!" Emily yells, accusing Sally of stealing money from the bank. "A cheater!"

"Am not!" Sally counters. "You're a liar!"

Tom and I issue uneasy chuckles, try to settle the girls down, but the words *cheater* and *liar* are now loaded, as inflammatory as racial epithets. They're hard to ignore. They hover, and make Tom and me even more sensitive to each other. I want Tom to act like old Tom, mussing my hair, coiling his arm around me, snapping a towel at me, but the new Tom is polite, says, "Excuse me," asks for items to be passed, misses jokes.

And I'm the same. Tom and I are a pair of damaged goods that have been repaired, but we're far from whole. Look close and see the cracks in our foundation. We've been glued back together, but we're not strong.

At night we flip on the television to watch a show. Every channel is a drama or comedy about a cheating husband, a wife stepping out, a ludicrous string of lies knotted with betrayals and deceits.

Then the news: photos of Landon, the upcoming election. Coverage is thick.

By the time our heads hit the pillow each night, we're exhausted. Exhausted from trying so hard.

CHAPTER THIRTY-THREE
Make Amends

ON JUNE 15 SCHOOL LETS out. A day later, with our minivan crammed with suitcases, coolers, and boogie boards, and with Tom's and my hopes for a healing and restorative vacation, we head south to Hatteras Island, the serene coastline that washes up the edges of North Carolina.

After renting for years, we finally wrote the check for the down payment and bought a small house only about a hundred yards from the beach. Tom found the place one morning while he was out jogging and drove me and the girls by it later that day.

"Where?" I asked back then, my eyes darting in every direction. "Where's the house?"

Tom pointed it out. Shrouded in overgrown bushes and sea grasses, the house sat pitifully. Its windows were covered with plywood, and its roof sagged, as if tired of providing shelter.

"Seriously, Tom?"

"Can't you see the potential, Mare? A little work, and it'll be great."

"Maybe they'll pay us to take it," I said, but Tom just slung his arm around me and squeezed me tight. "You'll see."

That first year Tom made four trips down, twice with his brother and twice with my father. Collectively they repaired the roof, painted it, mowed down the jungle of bushes and grasses. By the time we arrived as a family the following June, the dilapidated shack we'd seen the summer before had emerged as a cozy cottage. Not quite a swan, but certainly no longer the ugly duckling.

That was a nice summer. The girls were four and five years old and Patrick was better than ever. He had been sober for nearly two years, had met Kathy, his soon-to-be wife, and was employed as a project manager for a thriving housing company at the peak of the real estate market. It was a happy time for Tom, having his brother strong and healthy, working on the house side by side with him.

Patrick and I even became close that summer, as I welcomed Kathy into our lives, became her friend, and helped her plan their wedding. Patrick appreciated my gestures, and he and I entered a period of truce, a détente that lasted until a few years later, when the bottom fell out of the housing market, and he lost his job and went on a bender, ending up on our doorstep—belligerent and cursing like a mean drunk in front of our two young daughters.

Each night at the cottage we rolled out and opened sleeping bags, Tom and I lying on our sides, Sally and Emily wedged firmly in the cave of our curves. We'd tell stories of the nights when they were born, how the moon was bright, or the sky was a magical shade of blue, or how there were oodles of fireflies. "More," the girls would beg, and Tom wouldn't disappoint, embellishing the embellished stories even more until he'd spun a blanket out of chocolate and pillows stuffed with marshmallow, all because our darling daughters had entered the world, deserving no less. They'd fall asleep with smiles on their faces and I'd think about what it would be like to be carefree, truly free from my cares, and I would fall into slumber, too, pretending it were so.

Today we make it to the house by one o'clock in the afternoon. The kids are ready to get out. Before the girls' feet even hit the driveway, they're already begging for the beach.

"We'll go," I say. "I promise! Just give me a few minutes to get situated."

"I have to pee," Dom says, holding his crotch, doing the pee dance.

"Follow me," I say, grabbing the plastic shopping bag that holds the extra roll of toilet paper, just in case. I sit on the edge of the tub while Dom cheers on his wee-wee—"Come on, potty! You can do it!" I can hear the girls storming through the house, remembering, reacquainting themselves.

"Look at all of the board games!" Emily exclaims, as if she's just been given front-row tickets to *The Phantom of the Opera*. Board games! At home the girls scowl at me when I suggest a board game. At the beach it's like tasting soda for the first time.

I hear Tom humming, pulling the blinds, and adjusting the thermostat. Even before our crisis, At the Beach Tom was an infinitely more relaxed version of Everyday Tom. I'm praying that this trip has powers, a touch of ambrosia that bestows permanence to our marriage.

Dom finishes, washes, and then heads to his bedroom with his brother. The room is nearly the size of a walk-in closet, but it holds a bunk bed, which in the boys' estimation is the equivalent of a roller coaster. Both climb the ladder and lie on their bellies, arranging their dinosaurs on the top rim like protectors of a fortress.

Once the girls have made their rounds, they're back at my feet begging for the beach. And while the mom in me would rather tinker about the house, unpacking and cleaning, getting the kitchen organized and planning dinner, I know it's not fair to make the kids wait. The first trip to the beach is akin to Christmas morning. The anticipation is electric, and nothing will ground them until their toes are wet.

Tom sees me scrambling to get the cold food in the refrigerator. "I'll take them," he says. "If you want to hang back."

My heart constricts. Post-crisis Tom is too polite, too helpful. He gives me a wide berth and I despise it. I want old Tom, my husband who would holler at me to hurry up, who would tell me that the beach was waiting, that I could organize the fridge later. I want old Tom, my husband who took liberties with me because he had the confidence to do so, a confidence that came from the propriety of knowing I was his alone.

"No way!" I say in a voice that's meant to sound perky but just sounds false, like I'm trying too hard. "I want to go, too."

So we pack up our totes and head down to the footpath that leads to the beach. The distance to the sand is just tolerable. Any farther and the kids would complain. Any closer and we wouldn't have been able to afford the house, shack or not.

Once we crest the grassy dune, Sally takes off running, plowing straight into the waves, as grateful to feel the water on her skin as a dolphin that had been drying up on the shore. It seems like it was only a few years ago when she was still holding tight to Tom, lifting her legs, clinging to his body, adhered to his chest like cellophane. Now she enters the water alone, full of too much confidence and too little fear. I have just recently read an article about the development of children's brains: how their propensity for risk grows faster than the reasoned logic to temper it. That's where we are with Sally: the invincible stage.

Emily's eager to get into the water, too, but she needs to do it in stages, holding her arms up high, standing on tippy-toes, and squealing each time a wave breaks on her back. She swivels around every few seconds or so, checking in with me, the exaggerated emotion on her face relaying her every feeling.

"Just come in!" Sally urges her sister, so sure of the superiority of her method of getting wet all at once.

"It's *cold*!" Emily screams, and then takes another step toward Sally.

Meanwhile, the boys dash back and forth, just barely getting their feet wet. It'll take them a few days to get used to the water, but by the time we're ready to go home, they'll be begging Tom to take them in again. I'm thankful the boys aren't overzealous, that they somehow sense the danger of the water. My nerves are tested enough as I keep a watchful eye on the girls.

I remember last year, watching Tom hold the boys, one on each biceps, like Poseidon emerging from a great storm, plowing through the water with the strength of a horse. And I remember how Danny got scared, and how Tom cradled him against his chest, as tender and loving as a person can be. I remember sitting on the beach watching, my toes pressing into the sand, thinking it through. How a guy, so big and strong, the product of a nearly alcoholic father and a sometimes distant mother, could yield the perfect blend of strength and compassion.

|||

An hour later, the girls are tuckered out. Emily's lips have turned blue and she's shivering atop my lap. I'm rubbing the towel and shimmying my arms tighter around her, kissing the top of her head. Tomorrow we'll come for the entire morning.

Tom grills hot dogs and hamburgers for dinner, and we eat on the deck while we watch the sun set over the sound. Afterward I mash fresh peaches from the farmers' market into vanilla ice cream and brew a pot of decaf for Tom and me. I pour a shot of Baileys into our mugs, a treat we have only at the beach. A shot of whiskey would make it even better, but I wouldn't dare.

By the time we're finished with dessert, it's nearly dark. I ask the girls to ready themselves for bedtime and they head to their room without a fuss. It's different from home, which makes it an adventure. My kids are easy at the beach.

The boys choose their jammies. Dom's in Spider-Man and Danny's in dinosaurs. We brush teeth, dab a warm washcloth across their faces, clap when they pee. Then we flip a coin to see who has first dibs on the top bunk. Technically the boys aren't old enough to sleep in a top bunk, but this bunk bed is unusually small, not very high, and the boys sleep like rocks. So with extra pillows lining the floor in case of a fall, Tom and I feel they're okay.

"Can we *both* sleep on the top bunk?" Dom asks before I've even flipped.

"It's fine with me," I say, looking at Danny. Danny nods wildly in agreement and I tuck them in tightly next to each other, with their dinosaurs scattered around them. The boys are as different as can be, in their personalities, in their temperaments. Two batches of cookies baked with the same exact ingredients, yet with completely different results. But the twin bond is undeniable. They're magnets pulled toward each other.

"I love you, Dom. I love you, Dan."

"We love Mommy!" they cheer, and I kiss them again before easing out of their room, wondering if that will ever get old: mommy adoration.

Sally's in bed reading Percy Jackson and Emily is beside her, listening to her iPod. Some moms would fret over her daughter listening to Lady Gaga, but I don't have to worry about Emily, whose tastes run more toward Andrew Lloyd Webber and Leonard Bernstein.

After the kids are down, Tom and I return to the deck. I refill our coffee. We sit on the patio chairs with our feet up.

"My brother," Tom says. "Patrick."

"What about him?"

"After high school, you know, he was offered baseball scholarships from a lot of colleges."

"I know."

"And he was also drafted by a big-league team."

"Yeah," I say, wondering why Tom is telling me all this history I already know.

"Everyone—me included—told him, 'Take the scholarships and go to college.'"

"I know, but he didn't listen to you."

"That's because I pulled him aside one day, away from Mom and Dad. I told him that he could go to college anytime. That he should try for his big shot. I convinced him to sign with the Diamondbacks, shoot for the big leagues. He listened to me because he always listened to me."

"I never knew," I say.

"He should have gone to college. His whole life would have been different . . . better, if he'd gone to college."

"You feel that now, because you have the benefit of hindsight, but you didn't know what was going to happen. He was an amazing ballplayer. None of us can see the future."

"My best mind knew," Tom says. "But my best mind was lured into the promise of something else."

"You feel responsible for his drinking because you urged him to follow his dream?" I ask. "That's not fair to you, Tom. There's a good chance that he would have fallen no matter what direction he went. It's not like a college campus would have been such a good place for a guy with alcoholic tendencies."

"Maybe," Tom says. "But I led him in the wrong direction. There wouldn't have been the devastation if he hadn't tried. The rise and the fall is what killed him. I've always regretted my advice."

"It's better that he tried," I say. "None of us can avoid devastation from time to time, right?"

"We haven't," Tom says.

"I'm glad you told me, Tom. Really, I'm glad you told me."

"It's nice to talk," he says. "I've missed it."

"I'm sorry," I say. "For everything."

"Let's be done with apologies, okay?" he says, and then slides his legs along the length of the couch, pulling me onto him. We kiss like we did when we first met, back when kissing was an activity in itself, not a prelude to sex. Back when our ears weren't pricked for the sounds of wandering children. We kiss, we stare into each other's eyes, and we kiss more. Then Tom eases himself off the sofa, lifts me, and carries me to our bedroom. We make love, slowly and tenderly, and when it's over I turn my head away from Tom and for the first time ever—since the day I married Tom—I'm not burdened. Our life—our bond—is for once in the open light. Our truth is known. We know who we are. We've taken our first step in

our recovery. The relief in not carrying the load any longer is feath-
erlight. For the first time in recent memory, I fall asleep peacefully.

|||

On Sunday morning I wake up with Dom and Danny burrowed
into my sides. Tom's gone, out for a jog, I'm guessing. I finger the
black hair that spikes across Dom's forehead and drape my arm
around Danny's bony frame. My precious twins—a single egg,
split.

A half hour later Emily snuggles into bed with me, position-
ing the length of her soft body along my side, her knee resting
over my thigh. "You're smiley this morning," Emily says, and I
squeeze her tight because that's exactly how I'm feeling. Sally,
the bedheaded preteen, ambles her way in soon after.

We nuzzle and cuddle and snuggle and watch an episode of
Happy Days. It's a frozen moment where arms and legs are crisscrossed and entwined and I wish I had a special mechanism that
would store it and keep it forever. A jar with a lid that could hold
memories, recall scents, feelings, flutters of the heart. It seems
unfathomable that time will someday fade—if not erase—this
memory from me, but I know that it will. Memories are fleeting,
and even a mother's heart isn't keen enough to recall indefinitely
the silky texture of a nine-year-old's hair or the earnest gaze from
a ten-year-old who is on the brink of growing into her own person yet still trusts her mother implicitly.

"Mass is at ten o'clock," I say, checking the time.

"I *love* the beach church," Emily sings. "Last year they played
guitar! Up on the altar!" She says it as though it's a scandal, to
think the Catholic Church would allow guitar.

"And there were doughnuts in the lobby after Mass!" Sally joins in. The girls have sat in the pews of our church, St. Andrew's, their entire lives, following the strict convention of Mass, the sidelong glances of the stuffy elderly ladies, the stern homily. The beachside church is like a party and concert in comparison.

Just as I'm sliding pancakes onto the children's plates, my phone rings. Figuring it's Angie, I answer it with a cheery "Good morning!"

"Well, good morning to you, too," Landon James says.

I duck out onto the deck, close the sliding glass door, and look left, look right, look for Tom in every direction. "Why are you calling?"

"I won the primary," Landon says like a little boy who wants attention for getting an A on his math test.

"I know, Landon. Obviously, I know. Congratulations."

"So, that's good."

"You don't sound particularly happy," I say, my eyes still darting.

"I'm exactly where I want to be," he says. "Yet I feel like crawling into bed for a month."

"Well, good luck with that, Landon. We can't be having this conversation," I say. "I'm hanging up."

"I'm surrounded by people," he says. "But I've never been so lonely."

The self-pity in his voice takes me right back. I never wished for Landon to fail, but in his times of defeat, he wanted me more. His loss was my gain, but only temporarily, no different from getting high. "There has to be someone you can talk to," I say, doing all I can to send the message that that someone is not me.

"They all want something from me: a job, a recommendation, a relationship. No one knew me back when I was just a law student and some nobody idealist with big dreams. Except you."

"Landon, come on."

"I'm sorry. It's not really why I'm depressed, anyway."

"I'm hanging up," I say, and pull the phone from my ear.

"Sally," I hear him say, and when he does, a shiver snakes down my back. I return the phone to my ear.

"What?"

"Goddamn, MM. I can't get her out of my head! I open and close my desk drawer eighty times a day just to look at this grainy newspaper photo I have of her."

"Landon . . ."

"I just want to *know* her. I want to know what she's like, what she likes. What's her favorite food, color? Is she athletic or artsy? Is she competitive or laid-back?"

"Landon . . ."

"I lie in bed at night and make up conversations, pretend that she and I are sitting on the steps of the Capitol, looking out at the Washington Monument."

"Landon!" I hiss into the phone. "Knock it off."

"You have no idea what's it's like," Landon says. "Now that I've seen her, I want to know her."

"What can you possibly think you can do about it?" I ask through clenched teeth, cutting right to the chase, because all of a sudden I feel the gun at my head.

"I don't know!"

"You've got to know."

"I'm not going to do anything about it. I'm just going to suffer, that's all."

The self-pity again. "Do you promise you'll let it go?"

"All along I thought that I was the smart one, avoiding risk at all costs. But you, Mary, were the tactical genius. You knew that fortifying a life with love was the surest way to stay strong. Me? I've been starving myself of it forever."

"Are you going to stay away?" I ask again.

But he doesn't answer me. Instead he sighs, and when he speaks it's in little more than a whisper. "There are days, Mary," he says, "that I look around me in whatever meeting I'm in— and I'm *always* in a meeting; that's my *life* now—and I think, *What is your* deal, *James? You've made it—not all the way there, but damn close. The Republican candidate for Senate, with more than a fighting chance to win the seat, if the pollsters know anything.* But all I'm thinking about is . . . spending a day with Sally."

I hit end before responding to this, without saying good-bye, because jogging up the road is my husband.

| | |

After showers, the girls and I dress casually in sundresses and sandals. Tom and the boys wear shorts. Together we walk down the beach road about half a mile to the Catholic Church that looks more like a revamped convenience store. This morning's Mass doesn't disappoint. There is a group of beachy musicians at the altar, shaking tambourines, cowbells, and maracas while singing folksy church songs. The readings and homily fly by without notice. Before we know it, the kids are chomping on doughnuts in the lobby. When Tom brings me a peanut dough-nut, I tell him I'm not hungry.

"Too many pancakes," he says, and I nod in agreement, though I haven't eaten a bite all morning. A phone call from Landon, his threat to my life, his desperation to know Sally, is enough to steal much more than my appetite.

The next morning I wake up early and stand under the heat of the shower for longer than usual, trying to convince myself to calm down. The fog is thick, and though I can't see an inch in front of my face, I have to believe that the road is there. I have to have faith. I know Landon, probably better than anyone, and though yesterday his desperation bordered on crazy, I've got to believe that he wouldn't dare risk his career for Sally. For the decade I knew him, the smart money was on Landon's selfishness. I bet against it and lost. Now I've got to believe that Landon's regard for only himself will prevail again. There's no way he'd follow through with his "I'd give it all up for a day with Sally," would he?

After breakfast we make our annual pilgrimage to Ocracoke Island, driving our car onto the ferry and disembarking a half hour later, our heads dizzy from the boat fumes and happy to be breathing fresh air. We walk around the island, ducking into souvenir shops. We watch a guy cast a fishnet into the water. He offers to let the boys try, and they clamor at the opportunity. Tom shadows Danny's body first so that he doesn't hurl himself into the water. Danny swings the net, but it lands in a clump; the graceful fan the fisherman was able to achieve seems to require practice. Dom tries next, having the same result as his brother. They're excited anyway, to have thrown a real net.

Sally pulls out her art pad and sits on a bench, sketching the marina in front of her. Her golden hair shimmers in the sun like a halo. She's staring at the horizon, thinking. Intense concentration forms a hood of her eyebrows. Her defiant chin juts forward. Her cheekbones seem more angular than normal. The resemblance kills me. I wanted her to look like Tom and so she did, in my mind. But now I see her through new eyes. And all I can see is Landon.

Emily's atop a concrete divider, lifting her knees and kicking her feet in an Irish jig. Her upper body is as straight and still as a statue, her arms anchored to her sides, but her legs flail and flip. There's a family with two daughters sitting on a bench one down from us, watching Emily, the little girls pointing with admiration. Emily's oblivious. Dance springs from her as easily as walking. It doesn't occur to her that she's talented.

We eat dinner at a nice waterfront restaurant before heading back onto the ferry. The boys fall asleep in the car, Sally stares out the window, Emily sings from *Evita*.

I look over at Tom. He's calm and relaxed and in him I see the man I was married to a mere eight months ago, the one who found goodness in every human being, the one who hadn't yet been robbed blind. When he catches me looking at him, he turns, meets my eyes. "What?"

"Nothing, hon," I say. "I love you." I reach over and rub his arm because he believes we're over the hump, though after the call from Landon, guilt sits in my stomach like a bag of coins, heavy and indigestible. I know I should tell Tom about the call, but I can't. Not after last night.

The days fall into a steady rhythm: dodging waves, searching for shells, and making sand castles in the morning. Back to the beach house for lunch, picnicking on the deck, already reminiscing about the morning at the beach as if an hour ago were five years ago, setting the memories in concrete so that we'll never forget the sting of the cold waves hitting our backs or the salt of the water sneaking into our mouths or the caress of our feet kneading the sand.

After lunch we pack into the car for a field trip. We see the Wright Brothers National Memorial one day, watch the hang gliders at Jockey's Ridge another, swim on the sound side another, digging for hermit crabs and admiring the kite surfers. Most afternoons we park at the marina, stand on the wooden docks, and watch the fishing boats come in, waiting in anticipation as the captain tosses the prized catches of the day: yellowfin tuna, dolphin. The boys are hoping to see a blue marlin like the one hanging in the restaurant the other night. Tonight we're headed to play miniature golf at Jurassic Putt in Nags Head. The boys are giddy with excitement. They can't wait to see the gigantic dinosaurs. Dom's hoping to see a T. rex.

CHAPTER THIRTY-FOUR
Working the Steps

SEPTEMBER ROLLS IN AND THE kids head back to school. Sally enters the fifth grade and Emily enters the fourth. The boys stride confidently into kindergarten. It's October before we know it. Leaves turn, Halloween comes, and the children sprint from door to door, collecting their bounty of candy.

Soon it's November and the coverage of the election has reached monumental proportions. Talk of Landon is everywhere. On Sunday morning he appears on *Meet the Press*. An hour later he's on *Face the Nation*. He and the Democrat are neck and neck. Both are giving it all they've got, slinging mud, impugning each other's credibility. The Democrat's commercials accuse Landon of hating women, of wanting them dead, because he is against federal money going to support Planned Parenthood. Landon's campaign is just as skewed, slandering his opponent for sending our troops into harm's way ill-prepared. It's hard to watch. The media feigns disgust but offers more coverage than ever. The dirtier the better. The only saving grace:

there's no mention of my photo, my name; no reference to me is ever made again. Housewife and mother Mary Morrissey means nothing to anyone. And I no longer worry about Landon wanting Sally. The passion behind his plea was fleeting. I should've known better than to expect constancy from Landon James, and for once I couldn't be happier to be denied it.

On Election Day—November 6—I go to cast my vote. I vote for Landon not because I believe he'll be an effective senator—though that's true—but because his success is my salvation. A US Senate term means a solid six years in which he'll be in the public eye and thus out of my life. Any thoughts stirring in his mind about Sally will be put to rest. I hold no animosity for this man who was ill-equipped to love me in the way I needed to be loved. I gave and he took a decade of my life because I was hopeful that he would come around. With various degrees of effort and success, he tried. He swam upstream against the current of his past.

Yet all these years with Sally, he stayed away. He kept his promise to stay out of my life. So yes, I voted for Landon, gave him one more vote in the direction of his dream, one step farther away from me and Sally.

By design I steer clear of all news channels, leaving the boys' Nick Jr. on until bedtime. If Tom guesses my motives, he doesn't say anything. By ten o'clock that night, I go into the bathroom and check my phone for the results. Landon has won, made his victory speech with aplomb, and accepted a congratulatory phone call from his opponent. I mute the sound on my phone and press play, watching him work the crowd. Part of me can almost feel the elation I'm sure he is experiencing. Despite myself, I'm proud of him.

When Tom and I crawl into bed, I'm surprised when he turns on the news. There's Landon grinning, pumping hands, waving to his supporters.

"*Seinfeld*'s on channel forty-two," I say.

"Your boy won," Tom says. The hair on my neck tingles.

"Come on, Tom," I say.

"To think, Mare, you gave up all that for all this."

"I didn't give anything up," I say, snuggling into him. "It was a pure gain on my part. Zero sum."

"But you loved him," Tom says.

I roll away. Here we go. These last few months have been good. We're almost back to normal, so I'm a little surprised that Tom's picking a fight. But then I think: a man, his ego, watching his rival win a US Senate seat.

"Don't do this," I say. "Please."

"We're just talking," Tom says. "Openly. No secrets, right?"

"It's not necessary."

"You had to love him," Tom says. "Or you wouldn't have stuck around for so long, right?"

"People stay at jobs they hate for twenty years because they think it might get better. Or they think there is nothing better out there. It was like that," I say, taking an enormous breath.

"Did you love him?"

"Not like I love you," I say.

Tom smirks. "What does that mean? You loved him more?"

"I loved him less," I say, rolling back into Tom. "I loved him much less," I repeat, rubbing his arm, coaxing him down from the ledge of his jealousy. "He was a boyfriend, but you're a husband. Do you know how much more significant that is?" I kiss his arm. "You're a *man*. He was just a *boy*. You were able to do what he couldn't. You were able to step up and make a commitment. You're a *man*, Tom. The difference is huge."

I lied to my husband, I'll say next time I'm at confession, because lying is the only way out of this conversation. There is no way in hell I will ever tell Tom how much I loved Landon James. Some secrets should never be told.

|||

Thanksgiving knocks on our door like a lost child looking for shelter. *Is it safe to come in?* it seems to ask. *Are the Morrisseys celebrating Thanksgiving this year?* My sisters come, Mom and Dad, and we go through the motions: I brine the bird, roll out dough for the pies, roast red peppers for the soup. Sally and Emily set the table, pull out the craft projects from school years past, attempt to make origami cranes out of the stiff fabric napkins. The smells of rosemary and garlic infuse the house, logs kindle in the fireplace, the Macy's parade marches across our television screen.

Tom is truly relaxed, hanging out with his brothers-in-law. I watch, and think that I see that my brothers-in-law, as well as my sisters, are hovering around Tom more than normal. Doting on him. Plying him with cold beers, hors d'oeuvres, laughing eagerly at his every joke. While my family is my greatest support, they also adore Tom, and out of some brother-in-law deference, they've circled around him, to tend to the wound that I've inflicted. It seems that my brother-in-law Kevin is avoiding eye contact with me. Teresa's husband, Paul, pours wine for Angie and Teresa but not me, though my glass is half empty. Maybe I'm making too much of it. For Tom's sake, I appreciate the care they're taking with him, love that their loyalty wraps around him, but part of me feels slighted, like the shunned kid at school whom everyone has decided to avoid just because she tripped and fell on her face.

An hour into it, the attention no longer seems so contrived. The men are in the backyard playing bocce ball, cold beers in hand. Then they're in the front yard shooting hoops. Later they're in the basement watching games on the big screen. The little guys—Dom, Danny, and their cousins Matthew and Luke— follow after their dads, imitating their caveman behavior.

Normal. Finally, it all feels normal.

I dash downstairs to the basement refrigerator to get some of the food and overhear Sally and Emily, Shannon and Kelly, huddled in the corner, talking about God knows what, admitting to what they know, what they've heard, giggling over whether the scandalous gossip is true. When I head back up with an armful of food, I hear Kelly say something about "the sperm being in the testicles" and I nearly choke, trip, and drop the food. But then I relax and think that learning the birds and the bees from their older cousins might relieve me of some of the pressure. Later I'll serve as fact-checker, vetting the information they've received.

Meanwhile, I sit with my sisters. We've never had an actual conversation about The Truth. But I know Mom and Dad have told them about Landon being Sally's biological father. I'm feeling relaxed, for the first time in so long. We're laughing and reminiscing about old times, telling stories, calling up memories. Angie is sitting next to me with her arm slung around my shoulder. A warmth runs through my heart and I have to swallow back the pride. I'm glad to know that my heart still works, that heat can still radiate from it when it's happy. There were months when I figured it had retired, had switched onto auto-pilot. *I'll pump your blood but nothing else.*

Just at the peak of my happiness, Teresa pushes a wrong button in me when she leans over and places a condescending hand on my lap and announces in her cloying voice that she's "praying for me." Like I'm a reprobate who needs extra prayers. Like I'm the bad kid who has gone astray. Like God forbid, if Teresa weren't praying for me, I'd be sure to land in hell the first chance I got.

At first I don't say anything, tell myself to let it go, that it's just Teresa and her too-pious attitude. But then I start to boil and I have to fight to keep from spewing fire.

"You don't have to pray for me," I tell her. My voice is terse, razor sharp. "I'm good."

"What's that supposed to mean?" she asks. "Are you asking me *not* to pray for you?"

"You're free to pray for whomever you want," I say.

Angie weasels her way out of this tiff, slipping out the back door to check on the boys.

Teresa looks at me squarely. "Mary, I didn't *mean* anything by it. I just want you to know that I'm thinking about you. That you're in my prayers, that's all."

"Fine," I say, turning away, gritting my teeth.

"I know you think I'm little Miss Goody Two-shoes, that I've never done anything wrong."

"And you're not?"

"I have no intention of betraying my secrets to you," Teresa says. "But the answer to your question is a resounding no. I'm not perfect. I've done plenty of things to be ashamed of."

"Yeah, right."

"It's true. There are things that you don't know about. When I was away at school. Did you ever think that maybe that's why

I'm so faithful now? Maybe I'm trying to make up for some in-discretions, too."

"No," I say honestly. "Not once. Truly, I've never once had that thought."

"Everyone falls, Mare," Teresa says. "I didn't switch colleges just for the heck of it."

I blink at her. "What does *that* mean?"

Teresa gives me only a single sharp shake of her head, then lets me sit there for a long moment trying to imagine what my pious sister could possibly have done.

"Sometimes we swerve in the wrong direction," Teresa says at last. "And then sometimes we overcorrect to try to make up for it. So there. A little bit of dirt on St. Teresa."

"I'm sorry," I say, looking at Teresa through eyes I've never used on her before. "Thanks for telling me. Whatever you didn't just tell me." I hug her and she looks at me with her x-ray eyes, and I'm left wondering—will probably be wondering for the rest of my life—what my naughty sister Teresa did while she was away at college. Even as deeply in the dark as she leaves me, I feel better.

|||

A few days later, I'm at the mall Christmas shopping when my phone rings. I now recognize the cryptic line of numbers and know it's Landon. I shouldn't answer, but I fear he might be up to something regarding Sally and so I need to keep my finger on the pulse.

"I can't talk to you," I say as forcefully as I can.

"You don't need to say a word," Landon says. "Just *please*, give me two minutes, then I promise I won't call again."

"Has it occurred to you that you might need psychological help?"

"Mary," Landon says. "Two minutes."

I duck into one of the mall's long hallways that lead to the restrooms. "What?"

"I just wanted to tell you . . . that you did things right, Mary. Exceptionally right. You have a family. Your daughters, they're *beautiful*. I just . . . I just wanted to say that, that's all."

"Thanks, Landon," I say, trying to brush it away, but a tear springs from my eyes because they *are* beautiful, truly beautiful.

"And I *know* I'll never be Sally's dad. Hell, I'll probably never even know her. But Mary, I have to tell you that I still can't get her out of my head."

I feel the blood heat in my cheeks; I pound my fist against the cement wall.

"And I just wanted you to know that I'm not such a driven, egotistical maniac that I haven't been touched by this." He pauses, clears his throat, and says in a tender voice, "I need you to know that . . . I love her from afar."

The tears rise, but I swallow them down.

"Yes, Landon," I say. "From afar. That's right." My words are taking the hard line I want them to, but he's getting to me. It's obvious he's hurting, and in a new, deeper way than he's ever hurt before. Or maybe in an old, all-too-familiar way he thought he'd tamped down for good. The boy whose father deserted him, whose mother gave up caring for him, is aching for a family he's always been denied.

A mother pushing a stroller walks by, looking straight ahead, as though she doesn't see my face drained of blood.

"I just . . . ," Landon murmurs.

"Just what?"

"I don't know . . . wish I could know her."

"Listen, Landon," I say, wiping the tears from my eyes, "get your head on straight. You *just* won a senate seat. That's your victory. That's what you *got*. Enjoy it. And stop wondering about the one thing in the world you don't have."

"I know, Mary," Landon says. "I'm not planning on causing any trouble, if that's what you're thinking. She's just on my mind."

I turn my head from the phone, look up at the ceiling, wonder if there are cameras taping this conversation. I decide I should stop talking about his senate seat. "You're already causing trouble, Landon. With this call."

"Will you tell me just one thing? About her. About Sally?"

I shake my head because that information belongs to me and Tom, not him.

"Just one thing," he presses.

I look down at the bag I'm holding, an assortment of books for Sally. I decide to give him a gift, a tidbit about Sally. "She won't dog-ear a book."

"What?"

"Her books. They're her treasures," I say. "She's a voracious reader and goes through a book a night, but she only uses bookmarks. She won't flip the corners down. She won't dog-ear her books."

Landon laughs. I imagine him slumped down in his thousand-dollar Armani suit, comfortable in his executive leather chair, his shiny wing tips resting on his desk. "What does she read?"

I've already given Landon what doesn't belong to him. "I'm hanging up," I say.

"Mary—"

"Don't call back."

After Landon and I broke up for the first time, he crawled back with promises of trying harder. We went on to date for two more years, which meant he had been on my mind—one way or another—for seven years. I was a month away from graduating from law school and the feeling bubbling inside me, a fountain of optimism rising, nudged me in the direction of starting anew. I was ready to get on with my life, my life without Landon. I'd had *enough*. After dinner one Saturday night, I told Landon I was finished. This time for good.

"You've been honest with me before," I said, a new confidence radiating in me, imagining my new life as a lawyer just around the corner. "You were honest when you told me we both wanted different things. I don't think anything has changed. I'm looking for more, Landon, and I know now you're not the guy to give it to me. I had hoped you would change, but here we are, in the same position as we were years ago. I'm ready to move on." I felt tough, like a callus had grown over my heart. Landon James couldn't hurt me anymore.

Landon looked at me across the table like he was conducting a negotiation. "I see your point, Mary, and I respect it."

I remember how his formality turned up the edges of my mouth; how it was just the affirmation I needed to feel certain that I was making the right decision. *Mr. Emphatically Not. Mr. I Respect Your Point. Ha!*

We made it through dessert with an exceptional level of civility. Then Landon ordered a shot of whiskey or bourbon—something sticky and brown, anyway—that he swirled around in the low, wide glass. The more he drank the more hangdog he became. "Come on, MM," he said, placing his hands over mine. "We've got a good thing going here."

"We've got nothing going here," I said, pushing his hands away from me.

When he dropped me off at the door to my apartment, he leaned over to kiss me good night. I let him because what the hell did it matter at that point? He pulled me close and the steely resolve in me started to soften. I had begun the night with a full battery of courage, but now it was running down and I knew that I needed to get away from him before it was depleted altogether. I pulled away and said to him what he was never able to say to me. "I love you, Landon," I said in a matter-of-fact voice. "Always have."

"I'm lucky for that," he replied.

I smiled and felt my battery charge a bit. More confirmation that I needed to get out of this relationship for good. *I'm not an emotional person. Emphatically not. I respect your point. I'm lucky for that.* All these years later, still unable to say he loved me.

"Do me a favor?" I asked. "Stay away, okay? No matter what. I'm ready to move on. I really don't need you showing up here and there, okay?"

"I get it," he said. "I'll give you space."

And he did. He gave me plenty of it. I heard through the grapevine he had taken up quickly with a secretary at his firm. Though it hurt that I was so easily replaceable, I was also glad. I needed to heal. And though I secretly hoped to see him at my law school graduation, at one of the local bars during summer happy hours, or at a legal function, I never once saw Landon. Six months followed, and the next fall I started my job as a first-year law associate at Penn & Hancock. I was working sixty hours a week, starved for sleep, and praying that I would make it to Sunday, the one night of the week when I would collapse at my parents' door for a good meal and some TLC. Mom would pack me a week's worth of meals in Tupperware. "Just zap them in the microwave," she'd tell me. "You've got to eat."

At the time my sister Angie was a new mother, juggling Kelly and Shannon. She and Kevin and the kids would come over on Sunday night, too, and I'd sit on the floor with the girls, stacking blocks and playing Barbies. My breathing would slow and I'd think, *When is this going to be mine?* Even though I was enjoying being a lawyer and the partners were expressing interest in my future—and I could still imagine myself sitting in that corner office with the view of the monuments—I really wanted to be right here, on my parents' floor, playing with my nieces, whom I secretly wanted to be my daughters.

A month later, just as I had stopped looking over my shoulder, hoping to run into Landon at the store or on the street, he showed up at my door. His arms were filled with bags of takeout, a dozen roses, and a box wrapped in shiny gold paper.

"May I come in?" he asked.

I paused, exhaled, and looked him in the eye. He seemed different. He was thinner. His eyes were bloodshot. His cheek-bones seemed more angular.

"You don't look very good," I said. "Been sleeping?"

"Are you going to let me in?" he asked, nearly dropping the bags of takeout.

I stepped aside and he strode in, placing the bags on the table.

"Have you eaten?" he said, looking around.

"What are you doing here?"

"These are for you." He handed me the pink roses and I set them on the table.

"Seriously, Landon. What are you doing here?"

"I've stayed away," he said. "I kept my promise, but I just needed to see you. Have I stayed away long enough? Is it okay that I'm here now? This is for you, too." He handed me the gold box. I held it awkwardly. "Open it."

"Landon, you shouldn't be here."

"Come on, MM, just open it."

I slid my finger under the tape on both sides, unraveled the paper and opened the box, revealing a little porcelain statue of St. Francis of Assisi. I had seen it once in a store window and commented on it to Landon.

"Thank you," I said uneasily.

"Do you remember that day? We were out taking a walk and you saw it in the store window."

"Yes, Landon. I remember."

"Do you remember what I said?"

I thought back but didn't remember him saying anything. "No," I said. "I don't."

"I didn't say *anything*," he said. "That's why you don't remember. I *never* said anything that mattered. I wanted to. I wanted to tell you that he was my favorite saint. That when I was a kid I prayed to St. Francis every night because my grandmother told me to. *Lord, make me an instrument of your peace. Where there is doubt, faith.* 'He's your namesake,' my grandmother would say. You know, Landon Francis. She said he'd look after me. But you didn't know that because I didn't tell you. Because I was afraid to tell you. There were all sorts of things I wanted to say to you, but I was afraid."

"Of what?"

"Of you knowing me too well—*anyone* knowing me too well. My mom was a wreck. She was chronically depressed because my dad left her—left *us*—when I was a kid. Abandoned his wife and three boys to fend for themselves. My mother did her best, but the depression would overtake her sometimes. And there would be my grandmother. Always a smile on her face. Always a meal on the table. I've told you my father left. That you knew. But did you know that I tracked him down a couple of years ago? Flew all the way to Tucson. Found his address and knocked on his door. Thought maybe he'd want to see his big-shot son: lawyer, politician. Know what he said to me? 'All politicians are crooks. All lawyers are phonies.' Then he asked if I could spare a few bucks for the old man. That was my male role model. That's the DNA pulsing through me. I didn't want you to know all that. That's why I never said anything. Because the past is bullshit. The future is the only thing that matters. What I can make of myself despite the old man's blood running through me."

By then I had sat down. "I can't believe you went to see your dad and never mentioned it to me."

"I know, and I'm sorry. I know you want more from me. At least you *wanted* more from me. Maybe you've already moved on. But I had to come over and beg you for one more shot. I can do better, Mary. I can be the guy you want me to be."

"You're asking to come back?" I wiped my sweaty palms down the length of my pants.

"I've got something else to show you," Landon said. He pulled an envelope from his jacket pocket. I saw my loopy nineteen-year-old cursive scrolled across the middle. "You sent me this letter, after the first time we met. Do you remember?"

I smiled. God, that seemed like a lifetime ago. I was growing old in this relationship. "I remember," I said. "And I've always been hugely embarrassed by it."

"Why would you be embarrassed by it?"

"Because I was just a kid and you were in law school. And mostly because you never wrote me back. Talk about humiliation."

"I never wrote you back, but MM, my God, I've kept the letter for all these years."

"Maybe we can burn it."

Landon smiled. "I'm keeping it forever."

Our eyes locked on the word *forever,* a promise we'd never before shared.

"Can we eat?" Landon asked. "Do you have plans that I'm interrupting?"

"I just walked in from work," I said, pointing to my briefcase and purse, which were still unpacked by the door. "My only plans were to change out of this suit and forage for food in my empty refrigerator."

"Go change," Landon said. "I'll get plates and drinks."

A few minutes later, Landon and I sat around the kitchen table, eating takeout from the Italian deli.

"How's work?" Landon asked.

"Great!" I said, and then, "I hate it. Kind of. Well, it's okay. But I don't love it. We'll see."

"Being a first-year associate is kind of rough."

I thought of Angela, little Shannon and Kelly, their silky waves of hair, their tiny Chiclets teeth, their helium-balloon laughs. I was a twenty-six-year-old woman fighting addiction—not to drugs, not to alcohol, but to peachy little girl skin and kisses as sweet as watermelon. And here I was working sixty hours a week drafting briefs and sharing dinner with my self-admitted commitment-phobic ex-boyfriend.

"You'd better get going," I said after dinner, before Landon tried to stay for too long and before I let him.

"I'm going," Landon said, "but Mary, I have one more thing to say and then I'll put the ball in your court. Let you decide whether you want to see me again."

My body stiffened as I prepared myself for Landon's final entreaty. This is when he'll argue the merits of his case: that there is value in being together *just for the sake of it.* That not everything needs to lead to something different, bigger. That it's not always better once you get there. I steeled myself to hear his famous refrain: Can't we just enjoy each other? Can't that be enough?

But Landon didn't make that argument. Instead he cupped my face with his palms, looked me straight in the eyes, swallowed hard, and said, "I love you, Mary Margaret Russo. I really love you. Always have. Always will. I'm scared because of my father, how he was. But I'm ready to dive in. I'm ready to go for the whole thing: marriage, kids. You know, the things you want. I want them, too." Then he kissed me and walked out the door. Hollywood style. Leaving me standing there to consider the terms of his deal, an offer so appealing I wouldn't need to counter.

CHAPTER THIRTY-FIVE
The Big Book

JANUARY, FEBRUARY, AND NOW IT'S March. I'm teaching religious education on Sundays, volunteering at Dom and Danny's school once a week, and helping out at the girls' school for various functions: the charity auction, Emily's next play, Sally's read-a-thon. I'm also considering taking in some legal work. Basic stuff: wills and trusts, settlements. I've talked to Tom about it and he's already started to help me design a Web site for Mary Morrissey, Attorney at Law. A photo of me in my Trust Me, I'm a Lawyer blue suit, looking stately and serious, like I've spent the past decade committing legal precedence to memory, rather than recalling every type of dinosaur and the mnemonic for the order of the planets as well as relearning how to find the least common denominator.

Just as my life is starting to rebuild, Landon—with his impeccable timing—calls.

"Mary, hi," he says, like he's just a guy, not a US senator. "How are you?"

I told Tom when Landon called me after the election because I never wanted to lie to him again. Tom nodded, and when he finally spoke, he said, "You told him not to call you, right? He can't call you again, Mary. You know that, right?" I told him I did, and now here I was, on the phone again with Landon.

"Mary?" Landon says. "Are you there?"

"Listen, Landon, you can't be calling me. When you call me, it hurts my family."

"I'll let you go," he says. "But I have a request."

"You're a senator," I say. "Don't you have an entire staff of people to fulfill your requests?"

"I was hoping you could send me a photo of Sally. Maybe her school photo? Maybe you could send me one every year?"

My heart thumps heavily because it's been almost a year and Landon is still on this. "No way. Forget it."

"I just want to see her," he says. "I just want to be able to look at a photo of her every now and then."

"Aren't you happy?" I say. "Aren't you where you want to be?"

"What's happiness, really?" he asks.

"Landon, I can only imagine all the beautiful, brilliant women fawning all over you. Why don't you choose one, get married, and have some kids?"

"Yeah," Landon says with a small laugh.

"I'm serious, Landon. I'm not being smart. I mean it. Why don't you?"

"Probably because I'm just as incapable of committing now as when we were together. I'm my father's son in many regards," Landon says sadly.

"Maybe so," I say, because after ten years of telling him that he's not, maybe it's time to believe that he is.

"Seriously, MM. What do you say? Just one photo?"

"I don't think it's a good idea," I say. "We need to think of Sally. What's best for her. What if a nosy intern finds the photo in your desk drawer? What if we're all found out?"

"I'll keep it at home," he says. "Will you just think about it?"

"I'll talk to Tom," I say. "I've got to go, okay?"

|||

The final time I broke up with Landon was the tenth year of our relationship. We had been dating for six years; had known each other four more. The first time I met Landon I was nineteen years old. On that last night, I had just turned twenty-nine. I had done four tours with him, if you counted the times I had fallen off the wagon and climbed back on. I had the battle scars to prove it. I had given my blood and was walking away with a wounded heart.

"This is good-bye," I said to him on that last Saturday night.

"I don't blame you," he said. "I know you deserve more. I know you're wasting your time with me when I'm not what you want. I'm *sorry* I'm not what you want." He hung his head low, like his inability to love me as I loved him was a defect he wished he could fix but couldn't.

"You tried," I said. Following his plaintive, desperate plea two years earlier—when he'd looked me in the eye and said, "I love you, Mary Margaret Russo. I really love you. Always have. Always will"—his ability to express himself had sprung back to its original elasticity, tight and unyielding. There were times, moments here and there, when Landon would fall hard and dive in with everything he had. "I love you so much," he'd claim in those moments, but weeks, sometimes months, later he'd pull back again, and I'd be able to detect by the pull of his mouth and the clench of his jaw how hard it was for him. Opening up to me and staying open only caused him more anxiety, made him feel more exposed, and instead of making him more comfortable in my company, it made him less so. I was patient, thought that maybe his emotional growth would shoot up in fits and starts, but the engine that propelled the original spurt stalled along the way and I was left with a car idling. It was on but going nowhere.

|||

It's the next week. As the girls sit at the counter with their home-work and the boys with their coloring, I cook corned beef with cabbage, a giant pot of mashed potatoes, and a crusty loaf of Irish soda bread. When it's time for dinner, I call the kids and Tom to the table. I serve Tom a heaping helping, fill his wineglass with a deep cabernet.

"What a dinner," Tom says. "I love St. Patrick's Day."

"I know you do," I say, bending down to kiss the top of his head. "I just thought it would be nice."

After dinner I clean the kitchen while Tom helps the boys get ready for bed. I hear him chasing them with their toothbrushes, stomping his monster feet and roaring, "'Fee-fi-fo-fum, I smell the blood of an Englishman!'" The boys squeal and run for cover under blankets and pillows.

I turn on the dishwasher, start a load of laundry, and fold what's in the dryer while Sally and Emily finish up their math and spelling homework. One of Emily's vocabulary words is *quandary,* which means "a perplexing situation or position; a di-lemma." She needs to use the word in a sentence but is having a hard time. Each of her attempts has to do with being in a quandary and trying to get out. I want to tell her the best quandary to be in is no quandary at all. Jump, kick, swerve, I want to say, but get out of the way of a situation that will roll you into a knot that cannot be undone. Trust me, I want to tell her, I'm the expert when it comes to quandaries.

By ten o'clock the house is quiet, and Tom and I are sitting on the sofa, sharing a bowl of buttered popcorn.

"You know how it's not fair to 'shoot the messenger'?" I ask.

Tom chews the popcorn in his mouth, takes a sip of soda, looks at me squarely. "In this scenario, are you the messenger?"

"In the spirit of being one hundred percent honest and truthful and living in the light and not keeping secrets . . ."

"Mare," Tom says, "what's going on?"

"Landon James called today."

"And what? You hung up on him, right?"

"I didn't," I say. "Because, as I've explained before, I'm wary of his motives with Sally and wanted to see what he was up to. Ever since he saw Sally at the Christmas parade nearly two years ago, he's had a seed of curiosity planted in his twisted little brain."

"He can't see her again," Tom says strongly.

"He knows that," I say. "And lucky for us, he's too selfish to jeopardize his career in order to take that risk."

"So why was he calling?"

"He wants a photo of her."

"He can go to hell."

"I told him that, basically."

"What else?"

"I told him to get a life of his own."

"Do you think he'll back off?"

"I think Landon has always wanted whatever was out of his reach. The more unattainable, the more desirable. I think now that he has his senate seat—the thing that he wanted more than anything in the world—he has nothing to chase. And his curiosity has turned to Sally. He doesn't really want her. He doesn't know that," I say. "He *thinks* he does, but the second he actually spent some time with her, it would just be a letdown to him, like everything else he's built up in his mind."

Tom smiles, shakes his head. "Sally could never be a letdown to anyone," he says. "She'd blow his mind with how smart she is. She'd leave him feeling like a dope."

"True," I say, and smile at the pride I see in Tom's face. "But he'll never have that chance."

"I think it's time for the three of us to have a meeting," Tom says.

I nod my agreement, but between my ears the sirens are blaring because I'm a lawyer, not a mediator, and in my court of law there are two parties, not three. In the decade that I've kept my secret, my terms have been absolute: *Tom, you belong here. Landon, you belong there.* In my quest to keep my worlds separate, I've erected a border and made certain the two sides did not share common ground. That perhaps Tom would claim a piece of Landon's territory shook my every molecule. Even more disturbing was the thought that Landon might stake a flag in my and Tom's territory.

Even so, I know that it's time to come to the table.

A week later, I call Landon, tell him Tom wants to meet, and ask him if we could get together. "Somewhere private," I say.

PART FIVE

CHAPTER THIRTY-SIX

Lent

WE DECIDE TO MEET IN a shaded picnic area at Rock Creek Park. I looked on a map and found a secluded location, but now—as Tom and I traverse a rickety rope bridge and walk along a burbling creek—I wonder whether Landon will be able to find us. We locate the picnic area, a set of tables covered by a rain shelter. I lean against the columned structure and wait, try to modulate my breath, steady my speech so that my voice doesn't sound false; so that Tom doesn't accuse me later of acting different in front of Landon. A few minutes pass, and then I see Landon coming from the opposite direction. I'm glad to know there is more than one way out.

"There he is," I say to Tom, squeezing his hand. We watch Landon walk toward us, pressing his silky red tie to his chest. His wavy hair flops on his forehead. Makes me think of Sally.

"Landon," I say. "Tom, Landon. Landon, Tom." My voice is elevated, my speech quickened. There's no way of acting normal in this situation.

Tom and Landon hold out their hands, shake.

"Did you find this place okay?" I ask. I detect a note of breathlessness to my voice, like I can't pull in enough air. There's not enough air in this park.

"No problem," Landon says. "It's nice to be out of the fishbowl for a few minutes."

"I'm sure," I say, a nervous laugh trickling out of my mouth. I force myself to stand still, to make sure I'm not shifting my hips, as Tom once accused me of doing. Tom and Landon stare at each other, both sizing the other up like dogs in an alley. I feel like I'm interrupting something private.

"I never meant your family any harm," Landon blurts, as if he has been holding his breath and can't take it another second.

Tom nods. "I believe that," he says. "Other than the fact that you slept with my wife only weeks before we were married . . ."

A miserable laugh tumbles out of me.

"Other than that," Tom continues, "I'm quite grateful to you. You made a promise to Mary—to stay out of her life—and you did for a number of years. You gave us Sally's childhood, and for that I'm thankful. I'm sure that arrangement suited your lifestyle best, but I also believe that there must have been times when you doubted what you had done. I acknowledge that you must have struggled."

I stare at Tom, have the urge to reach out and touch him, to test that he is real, because how could he—how could *anyone*—be so calm at this moment?

"I did," Landon agrees, offering Tom a grateful smile, as if finally being validated. "I do."

"But now you're having a difficult time staying out of our lives." Tom's face remains unreadable, but his fists clench and open, clench and open. I imagine the unflappable look on his face now is exactly the look he had in the boxing ring.

"I know I should stay the hell out of your lives," Landon says. "But as I'm sure Mary's told you, I just can't. . . . Sally's in my head. I can't get around it. I wish I could."

Tom looks at him, long and hard, as though gauging the threat posed by this man's admitted obsession with our daughter. And then he comes to a decision. "I think the point of today's meeting," Tom says, "is to establish some ground rules we can all live with."

God, Tom is *good* at this: holding a meeting, setting an agenda. No wonder he manages a team of twenty engineers.

"I agree," Landon says.

We all sit down at the picnic table. Tom and me on one side. Landon on the other. My handbag is sitting heavy and open at Landon's end of the table. I watch him twiddle with the strap like he's nervous.

"The first ground rule is for us to always put Sally first," Tom says. "No matter what selfish motive we might have for something, we all need to agree that the only person who matters is the child. Agreed?"

"Of course," Landon says.

"Definitely," I agree.

"The second ground rule is that we must never threaten each other. Arguably, we all have something to lose here. We of course don't want Sally learning the truth at a time other than our decided timetable. You, Landon, of course have your career to lose. The last thing a new senator would want is to be revealed as a man who fathered a child and then never saw her, correct?"

"Undeniably," Landon says, his mouth moving in tiny, nervous twitches.

"And you wouldn't want too much exposed about your father in Tucson," Tom says. "About his finances . . . how he spends his money."

My eyes widen as I stare at Tom, because whatever he's alluding to is news to me.

Landon has paled. His mouth still twitching, he nods. It's clear he understands Tom's information. "I thought ground-rule number two was we don't threaten each other," he says.

Tom nods. "It's important for us to understand one another from the start, I think. For us to agree that we all have skin in the game. None of us wants to live with a gun to the head, correct?"

"Yes," Landon says.

"The third ground rule," Tom says, "is that you—Landon—must not call Mary. When you call her, it disrespects our marriage and makes me angry."

Landon's face pulls tight. He diverts his eyes, fiddles with his tie.

"Okay, Tom," Landon says.

"Let me just say it again: You calling Mary is bullshit. Don't call her, Landon. Ever."

"I won't." Landon's eyes widen, like he knows the knockout punch is coming.

"Okay," Tom says, something settling in him. When he speaks again, he does so almost gently. "All that said, Landon, I believe you when you say Sally is in your thoughts. I can see how she would be."

Landon looks up at him, still shaking off the last series of punches. He seems confused by this detour in the conversation. "It's . . . been hard," he stammers. "Ever since I saw her at the Christmas parade. I . . . yes. I think about her a lot."

"And yet you're not ready to know her?" Tom says. "You're curious, but you're not ready to reveal yourself as her biological father. Is that correct?"

"I wouldn't in any case without your and Mary's permission, but even if I had it, I couldn't," Landon says. "Not now. Not in my position."

Tom nods. "The way I see it, we have six years. You have a job to do as a United States senator during those six years and we have a family to raise—Sally especially, as she's on the brink of being a teenager. I'm sure we have some challenging years ahead of us."

"Okay," Landon says. "So what are you suggesting?"

"I'm suggesting that we table this discussion until then. Clearly, with this being a new situation for all of us, none of us can claim to have the answers right now. As time goes on, each of us will probably waver in our positions. Six years from now, Sally will be seventeen, on her way to college. Then we'll gauge her emotional maturity, see if it seems to be a good time. It might be. It might never be."

"And now?" Landon wants to know.

"And now," Tom says, "we're willing to post photos of Sally on Facebook for you to see. A number of times a year, so that you can see what she's up to. So that you can follow her growth."

Landon sits back as though stunned. "You would do that?" he asks, and when his voice cracks and his eyes well with tears, I look away because seeing him cry is going to make me cry, too.

"Yes, Landon," Tom says. "We're willing to do that. I would suggest—from a security standpoint, seeing that it's my line of work—that you not comment on the photos. That might pique a curious hacker's interest."

"I won't," Landon says. "I'll just look."

Tom stands up, pulls out his business card, and hands it to Landon. "Send an e-mail to me at the address on this card, and

I'll let you know which Facebook page to submit your friend request to. And if you need to get ahold of us, call me, not Mary. She's no longer your friend, Landon. She's my wife. I need for you to respect that. If you do, I'll be more than fair. We'll work through this together."

Landon stands, wipes his eyes, and holds out his hand for Tom to shake. "I'm grateful, Tom. I'm truly grateful."

"Okay," Tom says. "Let's all get on with our lives now."

We watch Landon walk away. When he's gone, I turn to Tom, fall into his arms, and kiss him on the mouth. "I love you," I say. "I love that you are calm and even and reasonable and capable of making anyone—even Landon James—feel better for knowing you. I love the way you handled that. I love that you made it a win-win for everyone. I love . . . I just love you, Tom."

He nods but takes me by the arms and moves me away from him. "I love you, too, Mare," he says, his eyes drilled into mine, "but this isn't a done deal. I am now complicit in this deception, and whether I wanted that burden or not, I now carry this truth—this truth that Sally doesn't know—along with you and Landon. I don't like it. I don't like that she believes one thing but the truth is something else."

"But *you* are her truth," I say. "A father is the person who raised her. How would it be different if she were adopted? What does the DNA have to do with it?"

"Nothing," Tom says. "All I'm saying is that we're not finished with this business. At some point we will need to make the decision to either tell Sally who her biological father is or make the decision to keep it from her."

As we stand and prepare to leave, we see Landon walking back in our direction. Tom and I look at each other questioningly, then back to Landon as he reaches us.

"I slipped a bookmark into your purse," Landon says. "For Sally, because she likes to read."

I open my handbag and dig around until I feel something thin and stiff. I reach for it, peer into my bag. Laminated in plastic, it's a picture of the Library of Congress. Down the length of it is a list of great American authors: Faulkner, Fitzgerald, Frost, Hawthorne, Hemingway. A tassel in blue and red springs from the top like a firecracker. I exhale slowly, rub my thumb smoothly across it.

"I'm grateful for our deal," Landon says. "I don't want to start out on the wrong foot. I don't want to sneak anything, even a bookmark in Mary's purse." The entire time Landon is looking at Tom, not me. Landon admires Tom's strength, I know from experience, because the times when I was strong were the times when Landon wanted me the most.

"We're square," Tom says, and in unison they nod at each other, until Landon finally turns and walks away.

Tom reaches for the bookmark and we start down the path. When we pass by a trash can, he tosses it in.

CHAPTER THIRTY-SEVEN

Grace

ON PALM SUNDAY WE SIT for one of the longest masses of the year as the priest and congregation work their way through the Passion of Christ. Ironically, it's Emily's favorite. She sees it as a script, a play with parts, and is thrilled when the crowd gets to pipe in with its condemning voice: "Crucify him!" Sally's fooling with the strip of palm she was given as we came in. Each year she tries to remember how to fold it into a cross, some origami procedure I vaguely remember from my childhood. I watch her brows knit together, her chin jut defiantly, and now that the truth is out, it almost seems unreal that I kept the secret for as long as I did; that Tom never looked at his oldest child and saw the resemblance to the man I'd known for a decade. But why would he? Why would any of us see something we weren't looking for? Why wouldn't we see only the things we wanted to see: her amber hair, her athleticism, her stubbornness—all just like Tom's.

I look over at Tom, send him a look I imagine I'll be giving him for the rest of my life, something that blends together sorrow and grief and love and gratitude, something that conveys that his brokenness is my doing and I know it.

I know now that God provided me with everything I needed, if only I had seen: clues manifest in Patrick—the addict; Tom—the savior; Teresa—the faithful; even Landon—my temptation. Had I allowed myself to work the twelve steps—to admit my powerlessness, to find hope, and to surrender—things might have been different. I clung to Landon when I should have let go, should have known I could jump from the cliff when the water was out with the blind faith that it would rush back in time, should have believed that something better was waiting for me. I lied to Tom because I didn't trust he would love me through my failings. And I continued to lie because each time I took inventory of the store, it was so full I couldn't stand the thought of going under. But I should have. I should have trusted.

|||

On Good Friday I spend a couple of hours in the pews of St. Andrew's working through my tangle of thoughts. Notions that once seemed unbearable, forbidden, strictly prohibited, settle in my brain with a soft *maybe*. Now that Tom knows about Sally, now that Landon has a sliver of a presence in our lives, now that everything is out in the open with the adults, I begin to ponder, consider, the possibility that Sally might someday know the truth.

All those months, I prayed for it to get easier, for our life—Tom's and mine—to revert to normalcy, for my life to be exactly as it was. But that life was a lie and in my selfish quest to maintain it, I failed to open myself up to the possibility of change. *Different* might be uncomfortable, unknown—but perhaps better. And maybe from our destruction, we could be remade. As if Sally, with her Greek myths and Bible stories, was trying to warn me all along: All life comes from death.

The truth is, these children aren't really ours anyway. If I'm lucky, I'll have Sally for another decade before she launches herself into her future of many decades without me. Someday something in her might alert me that she would be open to hearing the truth. Someday she might hate me for the truth. And then there might be another day, months or maybe years later, when she might forgive me for the truth. I know now that I'm not the custodian of it. Tom has taught me that. It is its own entity, a beast full of steam and vigor of its own that I—a mere mortal—cannot house. We can move forward, but we can never go back.

|||

Easter morning the kids are pumped with excitement over their baskets spilling with candy and with the electric rush of the egg hunt. Tom has hidden a hundred eggs around our house and in the yard. The four children rush around in a frenzy, searching behind sofa cushions inside the house, deep into the bushes outside. I instruct the girls to overlook the obvious ones, to let their brothers find those. By the time the four of them have collectively found about ninety of the eggs, they're stalled. Tom has hidden some in tricky places and Sally, the competitive one, is getting mad. She insists on a hint and grumbles when Tom shakes his head no. Emily couldn't care less about finding all one hundred eggs. She's tired of looking and wants breakfast.

By the time we're finished, we're running late. Mass starts at ten thirty and it's nearly nine forty-five, and the kids are still in their pajamas. Tom's rushing the boys onto the toilet, and then I'm dressing them in their Sunday clothes and sticking a toothbrush in each of their mouths. For the girls, we zip and tie and help buckle stiff sandals, order them to scrub their teeth, and slap brushes in their hands to bring in the car. By the time we're headed in the direction of St. Andrew's, I'm sweating through my silk camisole, too hot to apply makeup to my perspiring face. We rush into the church and find that it's packed. The twice-a-year folks have crammed the pews and we're lucky when we're able to find a small stretch of wall to lean against.

A cool current of air breezes by me, snaking up my blouse, reaching the back of my neck. Slowly, my breath moderates. The choir starts in on the Gloria and my breathing slows even more. I look across to Tom, the kids, and my shoulders drop. The readings, the response, the Gospel, and all of a sudden I'm lifted to stand straighter, to leave the support of the wall behind me. A shiver or a shudder slithers through me and ends with a teardrop free-falling onto the strap covering my leather sandal.

All those years I believed that I was living with my back up against the wall, that the truth was holding me down, but that was never the case. The truth wasn't pinning me down, I was pinning *it* down, pushing it mercilessly against the wall with my hand over its mouth. For ten, twenty years I've been making deals, bargaining, negotiating. If Landon loves me, I'll give him another year. If I'm allowed to keep my secret, I'll be the best wife and mother ever. If Tom forgives me, everything will be all right. But I could no more wrestle the truth than I could tame the seas. I know that now. I accept that I am powerless. And for the first time in decades, I feel strong.

I won't be entirely free until Sally knows the truth, and that is years away, if ever. For now, I'll use these years to get ready—to prepare myself for that conversation and its consequences, to lean on God with childlike faith, and to make amends to all in my family, who have forgiven my trespasses.

READERS' GUIDE

Q. *What was the genesis of this novel? Did a particular character or situation come to mind first?*

A. My favorite books are those written by writers who love the "ordinary," Anne Tyler, Sue Miller. I'm the same way. I'm most interested in characters who are not spectacular in any manner, other than the remarkable ways in which they reveal themselves. I had been thinking about my Mary character, kind of seeing her in my mind: a woman steadfast in her longing for marriage and children, someone who valued a traditional, moral life. But, of course, what does that mean? No one is without fault, so the idea of placing good Mary in a life built on a lie was intriguing to me.

Q. *At the heart of this book is the moral dilemma of telling the truth versus burying it deep within a marriage.*

A. When husband Tom learns of Mary's infidelity, he asserts that he has never once lied to her. Mary counters, "That's only because you've never had anything worth lying about." Thus the philosophical question: Does everyone have a breaking point? For Mary, offering the truth for its own sake wasn't enough to risk what she held most dear: her husband, her family, her happiness.

Q. *You named the book* Acts of Contrition, *and certainly there is reason for Mary to feel contrite. How did the title come to you?*

A. The title came easily. If Mary were sorry—for the sake of it, because she did wrong and was regretful for it—then her contrition might have been "perfect." But Mary was seduced by the good life: her husband, her children, and the life she built with them. In a sense, she made a deal with the devil. So she was contrite, yes, but the reader wonders about her contrition. Certainly it was imperfect. She was more concerned about getting caught, about losing what she had, than about coming clean for the sake of it. Is this to say she was a bad person? Absolutely not. It's to say that she was human.

Q. *Why do readers connect with Mary's dilemma?*

A. I think *Acts* appeals to women who love reading about marriage and motherhood, and the undercurrents of domestic life that are often messy and rife with secrets. And certainly the juxtaposition of the tumultuous love affair that consumed Mary in her twenties against the reliable, steady ship of a marriage that occupied her in her thirties is something with which women can relate.

Q. *Mary is one of four daughters. Catholic, Italian, connected closely to her siblings and parents. How did you imagine those characters?*

A. When I was little I had a great friend, and she was Catholic, Italian, the youngest of four girls. I used to love going to her house, seeing her mother at the stove cooking sauce, her father pushed back in the recliner after work, and the drama of four girls filling the entire house. In my mind, it was a happy house built on strong foundations. I thought it would be the perfect life for Mary.

Q. *You use Tom's brother, Patrick, as Mary's mirror, in a sense—and Teresa, her sister, as Mary's foil. And there is a definite theme of addiction that pours through the text.*

A. Mary struggles with Tom's brother, Patrick, because she recognizes how much alike they are. Patrick is addicted to alcohol, but Mary is no less afflicted; she's addicted to people. And both rationalize their way out of their addictions. There is a big reliance on bargaining and negotiating one's actions. I was also drawn to the AA 12-Step program and the similarities it bears to the Act of Contrition prayer. Both require that we take a certain inventory of our lives, admit to our wrongs, and "cash in" the chips we rely on to justify our behavior.

Q. *Tom questions Mary's "order" for dealing with the lie, specifically that she told Landon first, rather than him. Later Tom wonders if her reason for doing so was because she was hoping Landon would woo her away. Did Mary hope for that?*

A. I really don't think so. Mary felt that her order was to tell Landon, get his word he would stay out of her life, and then go to Tom. I don't believe she was hoping to be swept away. I do believe she was possibly more comfortable with Landon than with Tom, seeing that she had known Landon for so long and relatively speaking, had known Tom for only a short while. But ultimately, I don't think Mary had a keen understanding about her reasons for doing things. Like most of us, sometimes we just act, without full consciousness of our motives. That's the muddy gray area that is so fun to write about.

Q. *Do you think readers will criticize Mary for steadfastly stating that her life's ambition was to be a wife and mother?*

A. Perhaps some, but I know what I'm made of, and though I've wanted to be many things in this life, there hasn't been anything more compelling than being a wife and mother.

Q. *Many writers of literary fiction claim they know their novel has come to an end when their protagonist "lands" on safe ground, when she has found herself enough to come to terms with her crisis. Does Mary get there?*

A. Mary cherished the safety of "the devil she knew," so for her, in order to "land," she needed to see that she could let go, that she could embrace a future in which things might be unpredictable, a future she might not be able to contrive through negotiation and bargaining. Once she reaches that spot, where she has opened up to the possibility that Sally might know the truth, that Landon might someday be a part of Sally's life, that the marriage she and Tom share might be made of something other than the stuff of their first decade together, she's able to grow.

ACKNOWLEDGMENTS

I AM DEEPLY GRATEFUL TO Amazon Publishing, and senior editor Terry Goodman, in particular. Amazon Publishing has been my constant champion, promoting my debut novel, *Daughters for a Time*, and because of their efforts, an unimaginable number of readers have had the opportunity to spend time with my book. Without hesitation, I was delighted to turn over *Acts of Contrition* to Amazon Publishing as well.

I am mostly thankful to my husband, Kevin. When I first started writing, I had the feeling that I should be doing it in my spare time—after *everything else* was taken care of. I viewed writing as a luxury. Kevin never looked at it that way. He is of the opinion that I am a writer. He believes I should be writing—every day—no questions asked. His support and enthusiasm for my career is a measure of his love for me. I hope he knows that I think he is awesome, too.

ABOUT THE AUTHOR

MARTY SHOUP, 2012

A NATIVE OF PHOENIX, ARIZONA, Jennifer Handford now lives in the Washington, DC, area with her husband and three children. One of three first-place finalists in the Amazon Breakthrough Novel Award contest in 2010, she published her first novel, *Daughters for a Time,* in 2012. *People* magazine hailed it as "a wrenching, resonant debut about infertility, cancer and adoption. Grab your hankies."

Jennifer is a professor of writing at American University.